by
Brian Parker

This is a work of fiction. Names, characters, places and incidents are the product of the author's imagination and are used fictitiously. Any resemblance to actual events, locales, or persons, living or dead, is purely coincidental.

Notice: The views expressed herein are NOT endorsed by the United States Government, Department of Defense or Department of the Army.

GRUDGE

Copyright © 2017 by Brian Parker
All rights reserved. Published by Phalanx Press.
www.PhalanxPress.com
Edited by Aurora Dewater
Cover art designed by Bukovero

This book is protected under the copyright laws of the United States of America. Any reproduction or other unauthorized use of the material or artwork herein is prohibited without the express written permission of the author.

Works available by Brian Parker

Grudge

Easytown Novels
The Immorality Clause
Tears of a Clone

The Path of Ashes
A Path of Ashes
Fireside
Dark Embers

Washington, Dead City
GNASH
REND
SEVER

Stand Alone Works
Enduring Armageddon
Origins of the Outbreak
The Collective Protocol
Battle Damage Assessment
Zombie in the Basement
Self-Publishing the Hard Way

Anthology Contributions
Bite-Sized Offerings: Tales and Legends of the Zombie Apocalypse
Only the Light We Make: Tales From the World of Adrian's Undead Diary

PART 1:
THE PAST

ONE

30 April 1945
Berlin, Germany

Gunfire echoed across the night as the two soldiers dug frantically with the small folding shovels they'd taken from dead men. The Ivans were so close that they could hear the reports of individual weapons. It wouldn't be long before they arrived at the Chancellery itself and they'd give their lives to defend the Führer.

The soil was harder to dig through than either of them had anticipated, but they'd finally managed to excavate the shallow pit in the garden. Then, the whistling sound of incoming Soviet projectiles drowned out the shooting, forcing the men to dive for cover. The ground shook beneath the prostrate soldiers' bodies as artillery shells slammed into the city around them

When the shelling ended, the sergeant ordered the other man to bring the body while he prepared wood for the fire. They moved quickly about their tasks, the private unceremoniously dumping the body of a woman from a wheelbarrow onto a shallow layer of split wood in the pit.

The men built a small pyre on top of her body before pouring ten liters of the Wehrmacht's precious petrol on her broken, nude body. The heavy bruising across her body told Oberjäger Mueller that she'd likely been pulled from a collapsed building for this purpose. *Everything would be examined, so she needed to seem as whole as possible,* he mused, eying the private deviously.

2 | Grudge

Neither of them knew who the woman was, or whether her family even knew that her body had been removed from the wreckage. They knew they were to burn the woman beyond recognition and that there were to be no witnesses, which was easy enough since most of the soldiers were forward, in defensive positions around the Chancellery.

Mueller bent down and crammed two cyanide capsules into the woman's throat and then used the spout from the petrol can to force them as far down her throat as possible. If they performed an in-depth investigation they may find that she died of other causes, but he'd seen firsthand how barbaric the Slavs were. They likely didn't understand forensic toxicology, so he felt it was an unnecessary step.

However, Oberjäger Mueller was loyal to the Party. He would do as directed. "Hurry!" he ordered.

"I'm trying. The damned matches won't light," the soldier replied, his fingers shaking in fear from the knowledge of his impending death.

"Imbecile. Give them to me. We must get this going before Bormann has us skinned alive."

"What do you want me to do? I can't make them dry out."

"Watch your tone, Soldat, or I will file a report on your insubordination if you continue."

That caused the man to laugh heartily. Easily twenty years older than the oberjäger, Soldat Ulrich was conscripted from his small farm only four months prior.

He'd been given rudimentary classes on the Gewehr rifle slung crosswise across his back and sent to guard the Chancellery and protect the heart of the Fatherland. *It has all been a pile of horse manure, a poisoned dream*, Ulrich thought. *I will die here and never see my beloved Gertie again.*

"Yes, Oberjäger Mueller. I wouldn't want to end up in one of your *reports*."

"Shut up and give me the matches."

Mueller snatched the box away from the private in anticipation. He'd been given a second directive, directly from Bormann himself. "We need more petrol, Ulrich. Pour the last can on her body."

"*Another* can, Oberjäger? We will run out of fuel for the generators soon enough. Is it wise to use so much?"

"Yes. Just do as I say."

Mueller watched the grumbling private as he knelt beside the pit and began to pour more fuel into the grave. In a smooth motion, he drew the Walther P38 from its holster on his belt and fired into the side of Ulrich's head, just behind the eyes, level with his ears.

The body slumped forward, splashing into the puddle of petrol. The wool of his field grey uniform quickly soaked up fuel and Mueller had to use his knife to cut the private's rifle strap and pull the weapon from the pit. *If the ruse is to work, the rifle would be a dead giveaway.*

He pushed the bodies around with the end of the Gewehr until he was satisfied and tossed the useless matches on top of the bodies. He chuckled quietly to himself when the box broke open and matches stuck to the Jew's hair. *Extra flame for the fire*, Mueller thought.

A new box of matches emerged from his pocket and he pulled one out. With a practiced strike, the match erupted into flame and he dropped it on the private's coat. The fire spread quickly, causing him to step back away from the pit.

He tossed the remaining few logs onto the fire and retreated toward the entrance of the Führerbunker, where the most important man in Germany sat, ready to depart for the port at Kristiansand, Norway.

First, they had to get him safely to the airfield and pray that the Luftwaffe's new Nightshade technology would keep the plane hidden from the Allies long enough to make it to the waiting U-boat.

*****

19 March 2020
Fort Lauderdale, Florida

The sky erupted in a flurry of explosions, bright red, green and blue sparks streaking out over the ocean.

Everyone cheered and then the music began as the concert headliner came out onto the stage. The crush of bodies jumping up and down in the sand made Gabe feel claustriphobic. Guys in board shorts spilled beer on each other and laughed while women in skimpy bikinis screamed their adulation of the artist. He was miserable.

Gabriel Murdock wondered for the hundredth time how he'd let his friends talk him into coming to the concert. They'd promised him free beer and loose women. So far, he'd seen neither. It was a bunch of dudes looking for the same thing. They charged fifteen bucks for a beer and every girl that he *did* see was with her boyfriend.

Talk about a waste of time. He could have been at the bar, paying only six dollars for a beer, or even better, back at their hotel room where they had three cases of beer that they'd already paid for.

He was a senior at Missouri State University, majoring in Military History, so money was tight. Gabe was in the ROTC program there and would commission as a second lieutenant in the US Army in two months. He'd assessed into the Infantry, so he'd report to Fort Benning, Georgia immediately after graduation. As an infantryman, he had about eight months of training between the Infantry Officer Basic Course and Ranger School before he made it to his first unit and got the opportunity to lead soldiers. It seemed like a lifetime away from where he stood, digging his toes into the sand.

"Hey, Kilgore!" Gabe shouted to be heard over the music.

"I know, man! Isn't this great?" his best friend, Todd Kilgore, yelled.

"What?" he replied. "No! This sucks. Let's go back."

"Huh? No way. This is awesome. Look at these women! And the music... What's wrong? Are you drunk already?"

6 | Grudge

Gabe thought about the question. If he said yes, would they leave? Probably not. "No, I'm just not feeling it."

"Are you kidding me? This is our last spring break before we have to become adults, man. I'm not leaving this concert—unless some chick wants me to take her back to the hotel."

"Come on, Kilgore. We've got beer back at our room."

"Nah. I'm gonna stay here. You can go."

"That's it? You're not gonna watch out for your battle buddy?"

"I can't believe you're gonna pull this crap, Gabe," Kilgore said in disgust. "I'll meet up with you later."

He turned back to the stage and Gabe threw up his hands—or at least he tried to. There were too many people around to accomplish the gesture, so he began the arduous task of pushing his way through the press of bodies toward the back of the crowd.

After several minutes of slipping between people, stepping awkwardly around groups, and generally feeling like a jerk, he made it out to the back where people stood in their own little groups, not part of the larger crowd. This was more his style, not being in the thick of that undulating, drunken mob.

With the closeness of the crowd behind him, Gabe was able to breathe a sigh of relief. He wasn't claustrophobic in the classic sense, but large crowds of people had made him nervous ever since the marathon bombing in Boston. He'd been there as a spectator, missing the qualifying time by a full twenty minutes. The smoke and explosion was horrendous. People screaming. Blood everywhere. Disorientation. Sirens…

He stopped next to a concrete barrier and bent over, placing his hands on it to take a deep breath. His heart was racing, like it did every time he thought about that day. He was fortunate that he hadn't been injured, but his proximity to the attack had left him scarred nonetheless.

"Hey, are you okay?" a girl with a southern accent asked as a pair of boots came into his line of sight.

"Huh? Yeah, I, uh…" he looked up. She was pretty, not drop-dead gorgeous like a lot of the coeds down here in Fort Lauderdale seemed to be, but in a girl next door sort of way instead. The blonde wore a pair of cutoff jeans with cowboy boots, and a modest tan tank top that reminded him of a hundred girls he'd met over the course of the week.

"Sorry, yeah. I just didn't like the crowd," Gabe finished.

"That's why we're back here," she indicated a few people, both men and women, a few feet from where he'd chosen to have a panic attack. Gabe tried to do a quick count of the male-to-female ratio, but didn't succeed before the girl continued, "I'm Olivia."

"Gabe," he replied, shaking her hand lightly.

"Do you like the band?"

"They're okay. Not my usual type of music, but it seems to be what everyone listens to down here."

"You don't like rap?" she asked.

"No, it's not that. I just—"

"Me either. I just want some old school country music now and then."

Gabe smiled. "That's my favorite too."

She pursed her lips and squinted her eyes. "Are you just telling me what you think I want to hear?"

"No, really. I like country music. Promise." He made a stupid crossing of his heart gesture that he regretted immediately. "So, where do you go to school?"

"Mississippi State. You?"

They spent the next several minutes in conversation, ignoring the concert, Olivia's friends, and everything but themselves. It turned out that they had much more in common than Gabe would have ever thought imaginable. He really liked her, cursing his luck that she lived in Mississippi and he was in Missouri.

"Hey, do you want to go to a bar I know over on Seabreeze?" He pointed to her empty plastic cup. "It's just about a block off the beach."

Olivia glanced at her friends and then back at Gabe. "No funny business, right?"

"Scouts honor."

"Are you a Boy Scout?" she asked.

"No… It just seemed like something appropriate to say."

She laughed and leaned into him. "I'm not going to sleep with you, if that's what you're after."

"What?" he squeaked. "No, of course not. I—"

Strange lights out over the ocean above the girl's shoulder caught his eye.

"You can't even think of a good lie to tell me?" Oliva teased.

The first few larger lights he'd noticed separated into hundreds of individual lights. They looked like they were streaking toward the beach.

"I… I think we need to get to cover, Olivia."

"Huh?"

He pointed and grabbed her wrist with his other hand. The lights were *much* closer than they'd been just seconds earlier.

"Hey, let me go!"

"We need to get out of here!"

She let herself be pulled along, feigning reluctance. "It's probably another light show. Quit freaking out."

"No, those are… I don't know what those are, but I know we—"

Multiple explosions nearby threw him sideways and he lost his grip on Olivia. Gabe flew through the air, hitting his head on one of the concrete barriers he'd rested against earlier and darkness took him.

TWO

06 July 1945
Davis Sea, Antarctica

The sailor took a deep drag from the cigarette, relishing the heat in his frozen lungs. After a full month underwater, Oberleutnant Otto Wermuth's boat had reached their objective and he'd ordered the signal sent to the waiting troops. Below decks, resting in the cabin that had once been his, the Führer continued to plan the war with his closest advisors—even though everyone knew the Fatherland was lost.

In addition to the Führer, *U-530* carried the sum total of Nazi scientific experimentation for the past two decades. Hundreds of boxes filled with blueprints, plans and in some cases, prototypes of equipment filled the holds where the torpedoes would normally have been. His boat carried the future of the Nazi party.

They were still two miles from the beginning of the ice, but if the Führer's plan was to be believed, *U-530* could show no signs of run-ins with the floating ice. So now they waited; for what, Otto had no clue.

He'd been shocked by the order to throw all but four of their torpedoes into the harbor at Kristiansand, more so when they were ordered to dismantle the deck gun and shove it over the side as well. Shortly after those tasks were completed, the documents began to appear. A large contingent of Waffen-SS men worked tirelessly to load case after case of paperwork and materiel.

Once everything was loaded, the crew was ordered to the dock. Otto watched in mute anger as eighty percent of his men and all the officers were sent off in trucks, replaced by SS men who reportedly knew how to sail. The original crewmen who remained held specialized positions that weren't easily replaced. All were directed to surrender their soldbüchers, which contained information on their identity, a photograph and pay information. It was very strange, indeed.

Before he departed, the SS-standartenführer pulled Otto aside. He ordered Otto to sail exactly twenty-four miles southwest into the North Sea and surface for an exchange at midnight. The final thing he said before leaving was that the crew of *U-530* was not to record a ship's log for the upcoming patrol.

The plane that landed effortlessly on the water beside *U-530* had been something that he'd never imagined possible. It was hard to see against the dark ocean, even with the half-moon above, but what he could see was a marvel of engineering. The plane resembled a kite, similar to what he'd flown as a child in Württemberg. It seemed impossible that something like that could fly under its own power, let alone operate as soundlessly as it had when he first spotted it in the sky above.

He'd almost ordered the men to open fire on it, but held the order as a light began flashing from the foundering plane. This was the rendezvous contact they'd been waiting on. It floated close enough to see several men standing on the top of it, although he hadn't been able to see how they got there. Otto ordered the gangplank lowered and four men came aboard his boat—correction, *three* men and one woman.

If he'd been shocked about the disposal of the torpedoes, he was completely dumbfounded to see the face of the Führer, his hair soaked from the sea spray and his jacket crumpled from the trip. The man had returned his salute crossly and staggered toward the hatch which took him below decks. Rounding out the party was a dark haired woman named Eva, the Führer's secretary, Martin Bormann and a mountain infantry sergeant named Mueller.

The plane sank into the sea and *U-530* followed suit, sailing around the British islands and commencing a few torpedo attacks off the coast of New York as a ruse before making way toward Antarctica. Now they were here, waiting on their next contact.

Two lights appeared on the horizon and he brought the binoculars to his eyes. They were still too far to see what type of boats the soldiers from Argus Base sent. He called below to tell the men that their mission was ending and they'd need to transfer the boxes to the boats. The order was repeated below and soon, the Führer's head appeared at the hatch.

"They are here?" he asked.

"Yes, Mein Führer," Otto replied nervously. "Those lights are the boats coming from Neuschwabenland."

"Good." The Führer slapped him affectionately on the back. "You must carry out the rest of your mission, Oberleutnant."

"I will, Mein Führer."

The shorter man squinted at Otto. "You do know why you were chosen for this mission, don't you?"

"To be honest, no, Mein Führer."

Hitler waved his hand to encompass the boat. "This boat has had limited success in the war. Did you know that it has only sunk two ships?"

Otto nodded. "Yes, I did. She's been plagued by misfortune."

"Bah!" the Führer chopped the air. "That misfortune as you call it will be the crew's safety net. They haven't taken part in the sinking of many ships, so they will not be punished upon your surrender."

The young captain nodded once again, hiding his displeasure at the order to surrender. "You are correct, Mein Führer."

"Of course I am. *You* were also chosen specially for this mission. You've been in the U-boat force for how long?"

"Six years, Mein Führer."

"Yes, that's right. In six years, you've never sunk a boat while in a leadership position. That will serve you well when they try you in court. You can claim innocence, ignorant of the war's ending, and you will be released shortly. Take a woman and remain faithful to our cause."

"Yes, Mein Führer."

"The key to making this believable is that every member of your original crew pleads ignorance and remains silent about the nature of this patrol."

14 | Grudge

The task is much easier since only eight of my original men remain, he thought wryly. "I will ensure that it is done, Mein Führer."

"Good. I knew you were the right man for this mission. I just wish that Skorzeny could have joined me. He is too highly placed and well-known to escape as easily as you. The Reich is a lesser place without his exploits of loyalty and daring. I have instructed him to make his way to Argentina after the war in Europe concludes, if at all possible."

Oberleutnant Wermuth turned his face away from the Führer and frowned. He'd heard of the so-called 'Most Dangerous Man in Europe'. SS-Obersturmbannführer Otto Skorzeny had been the darling of the Reich for the entire war, most notably for leading the mission to rescue that fool, Mussolini, a couple of years ago. Then, the next year, Skorzeny had somehow managed to take control of the Wehrmacht during the tumultuous days after several high-ranking Wehrmacht officers attempt to assassinate the man standing beside him at the U-boat's railing. The most influential—and disastrous as far as Wermuth was concerned—was Skorzeny's plan to use English-speaking soldiers to infiltrate American lines during Operation Watch on the Rhine, what the Americans called The Battle of the Bulge. The Wehrmacht lost many good men that could have continued to defend the Fatherland during that operation.

Good riddance," Otto thought. Out loud, he said, "The loss of his expertise will be sorely missed."

The lights had gotten much closer and Wermuth could make out two large, flat-bottomed craft that had giant fans in the rear to propel them. They didn't appear to be touching the water underneath; it was almost as if they rode on a cushion of air instead of their rubber hulls. *What an odd contraption*, he thought.

Once the boats were beside the U-boat, they settled down onto the surface of the water and the sound of hidden fans underneath the skirting ceased. Men from the craft scurried across to secure lines and used their own gangplank instead of the U-boat's to begin offloading the boxes.

"Remember, Oberleutnant, you chose to ignore the order of surrender from Dönitz. You and your men continued the fight. It is of utmost importance that you not mention the Antarctic expedition—ever."

"Yes, Mein Führer."

Hitler clapped him on the back once again and then followed a man in a snow-white uniform wearing the rank of an SS-standartenführer. It was an odd sight compared to the normal, deep black fabric of the SS uniforms he was accustomed to.

The Führer and the other three special passengers disembarked to one of the boats and the strange whirring noise resumed, raising the boat about a meter off the surface of the water. The large fan in back engaged and the hovering craft shot off across the sea toward the ice shelf.

Unloading took the rest of the night and *U-530* had to sacrifice one of her lifeboats because the remaining craft was full and could hold no more.

By morning, *U-530* was alone in the sea. Otto ordered her to slip back under the waters and she began the slow trip to South America. He'd been told to surrender in Uruguay, but he knew that if they did that they'd be executed in the public square immediately.

Leutnant Otto Wermuth exercised his first and only act of rebellion against the Nazi party and the Führer's orders. He directed his remaining crew to sail to Argentina instead of Uruguay. If everyone kept their mouths shut, the port of surrender wouldn't matter.

*****

19 March 2020
Fort Lauderdale, Florida

Gabe woke to a cacophony of noise and for a moment he wondered whether it was the sound of the Heavenly Host welcoming him home, or the spawn of Hell delighting in the damnation of another soul.

He thought he was dead, but realized he wasn't as his mind focused and pain flooded through his body. Everything hurt, especially his head. He couldn't open his eyes. *I'm blind!* he thought. *No, that isn't right, there's something...*

He slapped weakly at his face. It was covered with some type of sticky, gritty substance that he wiped away and had to use his fingers to pry open his eyelids. Olivia lay a couple of feet from him, her red tank top lifted up high enough to be practically indecent.

Hadn't she been wearing a light-colored top? he wondered. The details were hard to remember and everything was still fuzzy.

His vision swam in and out of focus as he tried to process what was happening. What he saw—or imagined he saw—was impossible. Small circular objects, each with a light on the top and bottom, zipped this way and that in the sky, firing rockets into the large beachfront hotels and using what sounded like machine guns to mow down fleeing people.

"This can't be happening," he moaned, trying to sit up.

"No! Stay down," Olivia whispered hoarsely.

He looked up at her face. Her eyes were wide in fear and the blonde hair was plastered wetly against her forehead. "They're shooting…everyone who moves."

"Who?" he asked. He couldn't remember much beyond seeing the stage explode and bodies flying through the air like rag dolls.

Several single gunshots rang out nearby, then a string of automatic weapons fire answered farther away.

"The grey men," Olivia mumbled in response to his question.

Gabe's eyes focused on hers. They were glassy and she didn't seem to be looking at him. "Are you okay?"

She didn't answer. He reached out to her and felt the wet sand between them. *Blood.* The sand had sucked most of it away, but there was still enough of it to make his hand red as he pulled it away.

"Olivia… Are you okay?" he whispered once more.

Harsh laghter and some type of gutteral, foreign language interrupted his attempts to check on her. Someone screamed and a gunshot rang out. It was close. Gabe was disoriented, but if he had to guess, the shooter was less than fifty yards away.

The sound of approaching feet on sand confirmed his belief that they were close. He lay still and closed his his eyes, trying to appear dead. Through tiny slits in his eyelids, he saw a line of men. It was difficult to tell for certain, but he believed they were advancing *from* the ocean.

He could see them plainly in the light of the burning stage. They wore an older style of dark grey or possibly black military uniform and carried a mix of weaponry. Some of it looked like old World War Two rifles, while others seemed more exotic, much like an AK-47, but different somehow. The soldiers fired into the backs of anyone moving amongst the wreckage, making sport of their victims.

In addition to the assortment of weapons, the invaders wore a mixture of modern and antique helmets. The older style kevlar helmet that the US Army had replaced with the narrower, lighter MICH during the war in Iraq was prevalent amongst the men. Sprinkled here and there were the coalscuttle steel helmets of the German Army in WWII.

Gabe watched in horror as they stabbed bayonets into people nonchalantly, laughing and joking amongst themselves. A harsh voice cut through the air, coming from a speaker system somewhere overhead. The men quit joking and turned back toward the surf.

In minutes, the grey men were gone and the flying machines above had disappeared. The sounds of the one-sided battle were replaced by moans of the dying and the cries of those unfortunate enough to be alive.

He crawled over to where Olivia lay. Two fingers against her carotid artery told him what he already knew. She was gone, like so many others.

Gabe thought about Kilgore and sat up cautiously. He was rewarded with a new stream of blood dripping from cuts somewhere above his hairline and tilted his head to the side to avoid getting it in his eyes again.

He stared in shock and disbelief at the horror around him. Hundreds, maybe even thousands of bodies littered the beach where the main concert venue had been. Off to the west, the city burned. The beachfront hotels and few high-rise buildings that Fort Lauderdale possessed were engulfed in flames. Every one of them.

How is that possible? The precision targeting by the grey men was unheard of on such a massive scale. Even the US Air Force wouldn't have been able to do so much damage in such a short amount of time.

He began to get dizzy, the wound to his head forcing him to lay back down. He'd have to wait to see if Kilgore was alright or else risk further injury to himself.

In the distance, he heard sirens as the city's first responders finally began to respond. It was only a matter of time before help came. They would be able to find his friend and treat Gabe's injuries.

Everything will be okay in just a little while, he told himself, avoiding Olivia's blank stare. *We'll figure out who did this and make them pay.*

THREE

17 October 1946
Argus Base, East Antarctica

Adolf Hitler limped beside Generalmajor Griese, Argus Base Chief Breeder, for an inspection of his army. It had been three and a half months since he'd last been in the nurseries, spending most of his time in recovery at Neuschwabenland Base. The Führer had suffered from a wicked attack of gout which started in the toes on his right foot and within weeks had spread almost to his knee.

His doctors tried to tell him too much acid in his blood from the high concentration of meat in his diet caused the gout; he blamed the constant cold in the facility, their incompetence, and of course, the Americans. They were the reason that Deutschland had to be abandoned and a new army created.

The new Deutsch Army would know from birth that the Americans were the reason they lived underground. The Americans were why their diets were so strict. The Americans were the reason they would be beaten and molded into the finest soldiers the world will ever know.

He would have his revenge upon the Americans.

"Tell me, Generalmajor, how is the program?" Hitler asked.

"It goes better than expected, Mein Führer. Ninety-two percent of the stock has survived their first year of life and will be weaned by November. Of the bitches, a further fifty-seven percent are already pregnant with their second soldier and we anticipate the remainder will take once their offspring no longer suckle at their tits."

Hitler wiped the sweat of exhaustion from his brow with a handkerchief. He tried unsuccessfully to remember the amount of breeding stock he'd shipped to Argus over the years. The records at the camps were meticulously altered to record the death of thousands of women, most of them non-Slavic Poles and Scandinavians. They were transported in secret from Europe to their final destination in Argus Base to reconstitute the Wehrmacht.

"Good. What are the numbers?"

If Chief Breeder Griese was surprised that the Führer didn't know what number ninety-two percent of the stock correlated to, then he didn't let it show. "We have 81,305 remaining breeding stock—after the culling you ordered, Mein Führer."

They'd started with several thousand more women whose lineage was called into question. Those who had any hint of being Jewish, Roma or Slavic were killed and their bodies processed for meat to feed the remaining bitches. Generalmajor Griese had overseen the culling personally.

There were 8,212 adult male soldiers, medical personnel and party members in Argus and the majority had fathered multiple children on the stock. Griese's technicians kept track of all successful fertilizations and the parentage was meticulously recorded to avoid errors in the breeding program in successive generations.

"The first year group of the New Reich contains 74,581 boys and girls—40,108 of those being male. We can reasonably expect between four and six year groups from the current stock before we are forced to reduce production for approximately ten years, fourteen being the optimal age to begin breeding the current generation."

The Führer was a man of concepts, not individual numbers. He had other men for that, men like the traitor, Hermann Goering. Goering had overseen the final planning and completion of Argus Base during his expedition to Antarctica in 1938 and later supervised the transport of the breeding stock and some of Europe's greatest scientific minds to the base after they'd taken Poland.

The war against the French and British—and later the Americans—never allowed Goering to return to Antarctica to observe what he'd created and the man served Germany with honor, even though the Luftwaffe wasn't able to stop the Allied invasion. Only days before the Exodus from Europe, Goering had sent a telegram to Hitler asking permission to assume leadership of the Reich. It was treason and he'd stripped Goering of all titles, ordering his death and excluding him from the Exodus plan.

Hitler learned through radio intercept that his onetime friend and confidant was condemned to hanging at the trials and had chosen an honorable death by committing suicide at Nuremberg just two days ago.

"How long until my new army is ready, Generalmajor?" he asked, his head swimming with the numbers that the doctor had given him.

"Given your directive that both males and females of the will be included in the army, we believe it will be ready in thirty-three decimal four years, with a strength of approximately 890,000."

Hitler stopped and stared daggers into Griese. "Thirty-three years? I'll be…ninety years old before we are ready to strike. The Americans had eight *million* men in uniform by the end of the war!"

Griese blubbered something about the human womb and the inability to speed up the growth process, but the Führer didn't hear him. Instead, he saw his dreams of glorious conquest slip through his grasp once again. With less than a million soldiers, the New Deutsch Army would be annihilated in a matter of months.

The realization that they hadn't ordered the abduction and transport of more breeding stock hit him hard and he began screaming obscenities at the Chief Breeder. Hitler was not at fault for the shortcomings, it was that imbecile Griese.

"Shoot him! Shoot him now!" he screamed to his guards, gesturing wildly toward the incompetent Generalmajor. He wouldn't live to see the final retribution against the Americans because of an error in recordkeeping.

The Führer's protests stopped suddenly and he clutched his chest. *What is happening?* he thought, staring down at the pristine Nazi uniform he wore.

"No. Not now," he pleaded with his body. The scientists were *years* away from replicating the regeneration serum that the Aryan used. *If only Dr. Morell had made the journey, he could help me.*

Hitler knew that he needed to calm down. He needed to get away from that moron who'd ruined his plans for revenge. His hand grasped at the railing in an attempt to stay upright, but the pain—the pain was too intense. A range of emotions passed through him as he sank slowly to his knees, chief among them was embarrassment; the men shouldn't see him like this. Next was a sense of loss. He knew that he wouldn't see the German Army march forth and destroy America, using the newly-designed flying discs to reduce their cities to ashes.

Adolf Hitler's chapter in this world was ending. He had come so close to accomplishing a feat that no one had ever done before. His dream of the Third German Reich, stretching from the Atlantic Ocean to the Ural Mountains had been within his grasp—until the Americans entered the fray. *They* supplied the Soviets so they could fight a delaying battle until winter set in. *They* rallied in support of the British, sending fighter planes and pilots to thwart the Luftwaffe. *They* bolstered the British in Africa and took away his ability to use the Suez Canal. *They* stole Italy from him and broke through the Atlantic Wall to steal France as well.

Hitler gasped, unable to speak as his mouth clamped tightly on his tongue. Warm, coppery fluid filled his mouth and even he could appreciate the irony that he'd bitten off the end of his tongue, much like many of the Jews did when they were gassed.

The great Führer was reduced to nothing but a man in his final moments, pleading with the gods of science to allow his doctors to arrive in time. Unfortunately, no one came to his assistance and the world went dark.

The men who'd risked everything to follow Hitler to the end of the Earth watched in horror as the man died in the breeding facility. Only a year had passed since they'd staged an elaborate hoax to rescue him from the closing pinchers of the Soviet and American armies, traversing first Europe and then the entire Atlantic Ocean to the secret facility buried in the ice and rock of Antarctica.

Now what were they supposed to do?

*****

20 March 2020
Pentagon, Washington, DC

Two stories underground, the Joint Operations Center, known in the Pentagon as the JOC, could withstand direct hits from even the largest conventional bombs. Service members from every branch and career civilians, most of whom were former military, manned it twenty-four hours a day, seven days a week, keeping a watchful eye on US military operations around the world.

Normally, at this time of night, the JOC was abuzz with activity as the CENTCOM Desk managed ongoing operations in Iraq eight hours ahead of Washington, or in Afghanistan, which was nine hours and thirty minutes ahead. The Pacific Desk got a little play each time the North Koreans wanted attention and even the African and European Desks had enough going on to occupy their time, especially with the recent Russian activity in the Crimea.

James Branson, the Department of Defense civilian who'd been lucky enough to score a full time position as a GS-12 working the North American desk overnight, stared at his terminal in shock. In three years, he'd never really had any emergencies. Sure, he'd had to keep a finger on the pulse of a few riots here and there and collect data on National Guard humanitarian relief missions, but military operations didn't take place within the continental United States.

The reports coming in from Florida were alarming. It had to be a hoax of some kind, not a real report. He glanced furtively toward his friend, Aletia, who managed the South American desk. She was just as lucky as he was to have a high-paying job with very little work.

"Hey, are you seeing anything strange coming out of South America—or even Central America?" James asked. Central America, while firmly in his portfolio, was one of those blurry areas where information could flow up different reporting chains to either desk.

"Hmm," she replied, tapping a few keys to refresh her screen. "No. I don't see anything. Why?"

"I don't know. I just got a report from the Fort Lauderdale Police Department. Something about multiple explosions. They're reporting hundreds of people dead. That can't be right though."

Aletia tapped a few more keys before answering. "It *is* spring break. If there was a major terrorist attack at a venue, then it's possible. I think you should report it."

His heart skipped a beat. "Are you... Are you sure? Colonel Carpenter is an ass. Do you remember when he ridiculed John for weeks after the Canberra incident?"

The JOC watch commander, Colonel Mark Carpenter was a notorious hothead who rode his subordinates hard, took credit for their successes and abandoned them when they failed. He was the epitome of what the DoD called a toxic leader, but hid it well enough throughout his career to get promoted and assigned to increasingly rewarding positions.

The incident in question had been an unannounced fireworks display in the Australian capital city of Canberra. The supporters of one of the city's rugby teams had financed and purchased the pyrotechnics themselves in celebration of their team winning the Canberra Raiders Cup. John Weeks, one of the Pacific Desk analysts, made the announcement that the Australians were under attack. Carpenter mocked him for weeks afterwards.

James wasn't sure if he was prepared for that kind of scrutiny—or bullying.

"Yes, I'm sure, Jimmy," she responded, seemingly ignoring his mention of the JOC watch commander. "It's our job to bring up credible threats to national security and let the brass make the decision about what to do."

"You're right," he said, pushing his glasses up his nose. Aletia was always right. She'd been in the JOC for six years—almost *double* the time James had worked there.

He took a deep breath and raised his hand. "Excuse me, sir?"

FOUR

21 March 2020
Fort Lauderdale, Florida

Gabriel Murdock stared in disbelief at the small television screen mounted on the wall of the bus station. Several terrorist organizations had claimed responsibility for the attack on the city two nights ago, but according to both the Department of Defense and the FBI none of the claims had panned out as credible.

The pundits were discussing whether aliens had attacked the United States. They weren't simply entertaining an errant crackpot with wild hair, they were legitimately discussing the merits of whether an alien race had invaded the globe.

Grainy camera footage from the concert showed the lights appearing over the ocean and flying rapidly toward the beach, where they opened fire, killing thousands across the city. The footage was raw and uncut, reminding him of a shitty horror movie where the director uses the technique to disorient the viewer and cause fear.

While smoke and mirrors of the movies didn't bother him, the video footage did. He had to look away or risk becoming violently ill, like he did when he thought about the details of Boston.

Gabe spent Thursday night and half of yesterday at Holy Cross Hospital before being subjected to eight hours of questioning by federal agents about what he'd seen at the beach. There had been few survivors and any information he could provide was carefully recorded, cross-referenced and fact-checked.

In truth, he had little to give them. He hit his head after the first explosions and then woke up to Olivia telling him that the "grey men" were killing survivors. The investigators—who never bothered to tell him which agency they were from—played the sounds of people talking in German and asked if that's what he'd heard. It sent chills down his spine. He hadn't put the two together at the time, but the grey men were speaking German. He also told them about the uniforms and the occasional coalscuttle helmet that he'd seen the soldiers wearing.

Whoever—or whatever—attacked the Florida coast had certainly gone through a lot of effort to disguise their identity. Everything pointed to an excellent duplication of the German army from the 1940s, which was ludicrous in its own right since the Allies had kicked the Nazis' ass all the way across Europe and then hung the worst of them after the Nuremberg trials.

Gabe grinned as he thought of his grandfather, a tough old WWII veteran who volunteered at the 45th Infantry Division Museum in Oklahoma City until the day he died of a heart attack on the job. He gave hourly tours and a question that always seemed to come up was if he had any regrets. His grandfather, true to form, would answer, "My only regret is that they made me stop killing goddamned Germans once the war was over."

He wondered what the old man would say about these invaders. His smile faded.

In all his studies and the military training he'd gotten, he hadn't heard of anything like what he saw on that beach. Those flying machines looked an awful lot like every UFO drawn in those bad science fiction pulp magazines from when his dad was a kid. And their accuracy…that was insane. They hit *every* high rise building in the city, and a lot of other infrastructure like police and fire stations, the airport, even the grocery stores and gas stations.

Gabe wondered why they left the bus station intact, but as he thought about it, leaving it operational was probably part of their plot to spread terror. They'd planned their attack perfectly, coinciding with the annual spring break pilgrimage of college students to maximize the damage. It was both sick and brilliant. Fort Lauderdale attracted students from all over the continental United States, virtually ensuring that people everywhere were affected and not just a small region. Those who weren't killed would be shipped out on buses and tell others what they'd seen.

The speaker overhead chimed, causing him to glance at the arrivals and departure board. His bus to Atlanta was here, so it was time to go. He picked up the nylon bag of spare clothes the Red Cross gave him when he left the hospital and walked over to the group of disheveled passengers queueing for their buses. Most of them seemed to be survivors, like him, headed off to tell their friends and families about the terror from the sea.

He took his seat on the bus and stared vacantly at the empty seat beside him until another college-aged person sat down. Todd Kilgore should have been sitting beside him. They should both be returning to Missouri State with their batteries recharged, full of stories of debauchery that they could recall together over beers years from now.

Instead, Gabe was returning alone, without knowing whether Todd was truly dead or alive. He was up near the stage the last time Gabe saw him, so the overwhelming odds were that he was dead, if not from the initial attack, then from the subsequent ground assault where the grey men murdered anyone left alive after the explosions.

Their hotel had burnt to the ground and his friend's cell phone no longer rang, it just went straight to voicemail. Until the government could sort through the tens of thousands of bodies in Fort Lauderdale, there was no trace of Kilgore.

The bus merged onto the Florida Turnpike and Gabe sighed heavily before resting his head against the oversized window. He had to get his head straight. In two months he'd be an infantry officer in the US Army and then he'd get the opportunity to get his revenge on *whoever* did this.

*****

21 March 2020
Pentagon, Washington, DC

James Branson stretched at his workstation. They were nearing the end of the night shift and his daytime counterpart should arrive any minute. Major Johansen was notorious for not showing up until the last minute before anyone would notice. He'd stroll in like he'd been in the office for fifteen minutes, listen to the JOC shift changeover brief and then get the North America-specific brief from James.

Johansen's nonchalant attitude combined with James' timidity created poor products from the North American desk at a time when they needed to be expressive and provide helpful information. And Colonel Carpenter had noticed.

"Barnes! Where's Major Johansen? Shift change is in ten minutes."

"I—I don't know, sir," James replied. "He's normally here."

"Bullshit. Stop covering for him," Carpenter growled. "This is one of the most important events to ever happen on US soil, if not *the* most important. I can't have a North American desk lead that doesn't give a shit about anything except their paycheck."

The colonel's eyes roved across the room. He was visibly agitated and looking for a target to lash out at. "Hollinsworth!"

"Yes, sir?" a Navy commander said.

Grudge | 35

"Get your ass over to the North American desk. You're now the daytime desk officer."

"Sir, I'm attached from the CNO's office for the express purpose of—"

"Drop it, son," the colonel cut him off. "This is the number one thing on our plate. The Pacific can wait."

James cringed in anticipation of Hollinsworth pushing back against Colonel Carpenter. The JOC watch commander was notorious for the public dressing downs he gave subordinates who screwed up, and Hollinsworth was definitely on the verge of screwing up.

The Navy man seemed to consider his options for a moment and then picked up his notebook. He skirted behind the chairs in the stadium-style JOC until he made it to the aisle and then walked quickly to where James sat at the North American desk.

"Bryan Hollinsworth," he said with an easy smile and outstretched hand.

"James Branson, sir."

"You don't need to call me sir, James. I'm doing the same job as you. Please, call me Bryan."

He ducked his head. James already liked him better than Johansen, who'd insisted on being addressed as either sir or Major Johansen. *Small dick complex*, James thought with an internal guffaw.

"So, what have we got, James?" Commander Hollinsworth asked. "The attack down in Florida has got everyone scrambling for answers. What have you found out?"

James swallowed hard before replying. "We put out feelers to all the normal agencies, FBI, NSA, DHS, State, CIA… We got nothing. Nobody knows where these people came from."

He paused as Bryan frowned. "So we don't have any leads? No satellite imagery of where they came from? Airport radar? Sea floor sonar stations? Shell casing analysis from the expended ammo on the beach? Anything at all?"

"No. They attacked when there wasn't a satellite overhead, the airport radar didn't pick them up until they were ten miles away, so we know they came from the ocean side. The sonar didn't pick up anything more dangerous than a large pod of whales." James typed into his email's search box. "And the shell casings came back as two types: either vintage World War Two zinc-coated mild steel, or as a square casing that nobody's ever seen it before."

"WWII?" Bryan asked, pronouncing the "W's" individually. "Who'd be crazy enough to use that old stuff? I can't believe it still worked."

James shrugged. He didn't know if ammunition had a shelf life—another question to ask his contacts at the Florida State Police. "I *did* get an odd email from a military historian at the US Army Center for Military History. She said she may have an answer as to who attacked us."

"What would a historian know about events four days ago?" Bryan scoffed.

"Not sure. I was going to run it by Major Johansen when he finally got in this morning."

"Well, he's out of a job and I'm it. What does this guy want?"

"Girl."

"What?"

"The historian is a female." He scanned his email inbox for a moment until he found her note.

"See, here it is," James said, tapping his screen. "Major Gloria Adams. She says that after the war, we were convinced that the Nazis were hiding in Antarctica and launched an expedition to root them out, even nuked the continent. Whole thing was covered up as an experiment to test cold weather gear."

"Pretty thin cover up," Bryan replied. "How did they justify launching nukes?"

"I don't know," James admitted. "She doesn't go into that kind of detail in her email and says that things quickly get into the classified realm that she can't discuss in an unclassified email."

"Any port in a storm, eh?" Bryan mumbled. "Okay, let's call her up. Did she give you her SIPR email?"

James searched the historian's signature block. There wasn't an email address for the secret SIPR network, but there was a phone number for her.

He pointed at the number and Bryan picked up the green-stickered, unclassified phone. After a few minutes of talking to someone on the other end he hung up the phone and frowned.

"What is it?"

"The info can't be passed over unclassified phones and it won't even meet the criteria for the red box," Bryan stated, using the JOC slang for the secret computer network.

They had three different classifications of systems in the JOC: the green unclassified network, the red secret network and the purple coalition network. There were other systems that required higher classifications, but James hadn't seen any of them in use outside of the National Security Agency and the Defense Intelligence Agency.

"So, what's that mean?"

"She's going to come over here from Fort McNair to discuss it with us," Commander Hollinsworth replied. "In the meantime, she told us to read up on Operation Highjump."

"Highjump?"

"Yeah," he answered, the frown deepening into a scowl. "More specifically, she said to read the conspiracy theories behind the operation, not the official histories."

"Conspiracy theories?" James asked skeptically. "Like the tinfoil hat-wearing, 9/11 was an inside job, kind of conspiracy theories?"

"I guess so. Do a search for it real quick before the shift changeover brief."

James did as he was asked and the two of them read the first website that came up as a hit.

"Whoa…" Bryan muttered.

"Hey, James," Major Johansen stated, ambling up to the North American desk. "Ready for the brief?" He paused, then looked at his desk area where Bryan sat. "What's up, buddy? You're in my seat."

"Uh, sir?" James looked to the commander for guidance.

Bryan nodded and stood up, saying, "Major, I've got some bad news for you."

"Johansen!" Colonel Carpenter shouted upon seeing the major. "You're fired. Get out of my operations center."

FIVE

24 December 1946
Dronning Maud Land, East Antarctica

"Sir, the Western Task Force reports that they've reached the Amundsen Sea and are preparing their landing craft to put soldiers onto the ice."

"Thank you, Commander," Rear Admiral Cruzen replied and took another sip of coffee from the mug on the table in front of him. Perry Como's record *Merry Christmas Music*, released just before the task force embarked, played softly in the background of his cabin. It helped to lighten the admiral's mood, pretending the permeating cold was part of the holiday ambience and not an environmental factor that the diesel heaters couldn't overcome.

"What's the latest report from Dufek?" he asked his intelligence officer.

"The Eastern Task Force checked in this morning, bouncing their radio signal off the *Mount Olympus*. They are three hundred and fifty nautical miles from their initial staging point off Prydz Bay."

"Are they still making thirty knots?"

The commander checked his notes. "Yes, sir. They anticipate making the bay by this evening, tomorrow morning at the latest."

Cruzen did the math in his head and turned to his operations officer. "If they're three hundred and fifty miles out, they should be ten hours from their destination. I want Captain Dufek scouting that ice shelf first thing in the morning."

Commander Jenkins cleared his throat. "Sir, tomorrow is Christmas. Do you want the men to launch the operation?"

"Did I stutter, Chris? As long as the weather holds, I want operations to commence in the east no later than tomorrow morning. Do you understand?"

"Yes, sir. I'll send the order immediately."

"Good." The admiral's face softened and he gestured toward the record player. "Look, I understand that it's Christmas. The sooner we get this mission over, the sooner everyone can go back to their families."

Jenkins nodded, but remained silent.

"The War Department has multiple reports of Nazi activity down here," Cruzen continued. "We know the Germans sent at least three documented expeditions to the continent, but the belief that *anyone* could survive on the Antarctic continent—even those crafty bastards—is ludicrous. We need to find evidence of their abandoned attempts to establish a base and then get the hell out of here."

Richard Cruzen had made no effort to hide his skepticism that the expedition would find anything of value. Temperatures routinely dipped into the negative fifties and sixties along the coast, reportedly much lower in the interior, closer to the South Pole. Long-term occupation by the Nazis was impossible. Admiral Byrd, the officer in charge of Task Force 68 and famed Antarctic explorer, shared his reservations. Both were experienced Antarctic sailors and professional Navy men.

Regardless of their personal feelings on the subject, they'd do as ordered.

Task Force 68 was charged with carrying out Operation Highjump to find evidence of German bases in the Antarctic. *If* they found anything, they were to either subdue or defeat all Nazi elements. Publicly, their mission objectives were to extend US sovereignty over the continent and train the soldiers they carried in conditions that were colder than any ever experienced by conventional forces. The public ate it up hook, line and sinker as new fears of conflict with the Commies took hold of the American psyche. Task Force 68 would accomplish their mission and be home by Saint Patrick's Day before the Antarctic winter began in earnest. *Then* the men could celebrate Christmas.

"Yes, sir," Commander Jenkins answered. "We'll have the troops on the ice first thing tomorrow morning."

"Thanks, Chris." Cruzen finished his coffee and waved off the steward who appeared with a steaming carafe. "I want this operation to go safely and smoothly. Ensure the men follow all cold weather protocols and keep an eye on each other. The war's over, I don't want any more deaths on my watch."

*****

21 March 2020
Pentagon, Washington, DC

James was tired. After the shift change brief, he'd gone to the food court to get some decent coffee, not the acid water they served in the JOC. He eyed the cup in front of him on the table dubiously and pushed the hard butter croissant away. His appetite had disappeared.

Normally, he'd already be on the Metro, almost to his apartment near the Dupont Circle Station. This time of morning, the bakery on the first floor of his building put out fresh, flaky, buttery croissants that were excellent, and their coffee was heavenly. Maybe the atmosphere of the café made everywhere else pale in comparison, he wasn't sure. But, he *did* know that he wasn't happy with his decision to stay in The Building to talk with the Army historian today.

Across the food court, he saw Commander Hollinsworth walking beside a tall blond woman in a dark blue military dress uniform. The stupid, light blue pants with a yellow stripe sewn on them told him that she was in the Army. *That must be Major Adams*, he thought.

As they got closer, he waved his hand to catch Bryan's attention and the two of them altered course, heading toward his table.

He stood. "Good morning, ma'am."

She switched the handle of her briefcase from her right to left hand, then reached out with her right hand, offering it to him. "Please, call me Gloria."

He shook her hand. "James. We spoke via email."

The major was about his height, five nine, maybe a little taller, but the heels she wore could have added a couple of inches. She was pretty without any makeup, thin in the form-fitting uniform and had a chest full of ribbons that James had no clue what they meant. He glanced at her left hand out of habit. No ring.

"Yes, of course. Thank you for responding," she said. "When I read about the reports coming out of Fort Lauderdale, I had an idea about what it could be."

Gloria stopped and looked around the cafeteria. "You'll have to forgive me, but I can't discuss my theory here. We need a secure area, preferably a SCIF."

James wondered what information she had that would require the sensitive compartmentalized information facility, or SCIF for short. The Joint Operations Center had one, but he'd have to get Sergeant Jacobs, the intelligence sergeant, to allow them access.

"I can get us into a SCIF," Hollinsworth stated. "But it may take a few hours if there's anything else going on in there."

She considered his words for a moment before answering. "I don't need the SCIF. I can get you enough information without going Top Secret that it'll whet your appetite and get you thinking. Hopefully, you'll agree with my assessment and get me in front of your boss."

"So, secret is fine?" Bryan confirmed.

"Yes, sir. There's really only a few things that are classified TS."

"That's easy then," he said. "James and I can talk to you in the small conference room in the JOC."

"Thank you. That'll be great."

"Coffee?" James offered, pointing at the coffee shop.

"Sure," she grinned. "After that harrowing fifteen minute commute from Fort McNair, I could use something to calm my nerves."

James walked through the line with Bryan and Gloria as they got their drinks and then escorted them through the labyrinth of hallways, elevators and locked doors to return to the JOC. As they went they made small talk about the DC traffic, the process for becoming an Army Historian and the odds of the Capitals making the Stanley Cup finals this year.

Luckily, the conference room in the JOC was empty and the schedule posted outside the door said they had three hours before the next meeting. They went in and shut the door.

"Thank you for the tour. It was very informative," Gloria complimented James, making him blush. "Now, let's get down to business."

She opened her briefcase and pulled out a manila envelope, then used a pen to break the seal. Inside was a locked document bag that she used a key to open. Gloria laid out several pieces of photocopied paper. The modern copier had picked up the colors of the originals, resulting in photocopies that looked yellowed with age.

Most of the papers were maps, but there were two copies of a packet containing about a hundred pages each. James skipped the maps, sure that Major Adams would discuss those. He focused on the top page of the packet. It looked like the beginning of a standard military operations order. In the upper right corner was a purple stamp of a penguin on top of an iceberg, trying to pull out the anchor of a naval vessel in the sea below. The stamp was labeled '**OPERATION HIGHJUMP: Antarctic Expedition 1946 and 1947**' and below the picture was the name '**TASK FORCE 68**'.

"Is this the OPORDER for Operation Highjump?" Bryan asked.

"Yes, sir. All three pages of it. If there were additional instructions, they were verbal—or destroyed. Behind that is the after action report, heavily redacted."

"We read the conspiracy theories, like you asked," James stated.

"Well, what did you think?"

"I think there are people out there with *way* too much time on their hands."

She laughed and James noticed that her teeth were perfectly straight and white, not a single one out of place or oddly spaced from the one next to it.

"Normally, I'd agree," she said once she'd stopped laughing. "However, after working at the Center for Military History for three years, with a focus on the European Theater of Operations in World War Two, I'm not so sure that this one is entirely off the mark."

"You mean to tell me that the US military went to Antarctica after the war was over to fight snow-Nazis?" Bryan scoffed.

"What I mean is that you can read Task Force 68's mission statement, it's plain as day what they were doing down there, regardless of what they told the public. As to what they found, we have to read between the lines. Whatever they found warranted the detonation of three nuclear warheads a decade later."

"Wait," Hollinsworth held up his hand. "Your email said as much, but did we really use nukes in Antarctica?"

"Yes. That information has been declassified for decades. Officially, it was a test of the effects of high-altitude explosions on electronics—"

"You mean an EMP?" James asked, referring to the acronym for an electromagnetic pulse.

She nodded. "The detonations occurred in August and September, 1958."

"Okay…" James said as he did the math in his head. "So, twelve years after this expedition, we tested some nukes in the same area. Seems like a big coincidence."

"Don't be so naïve, James. You work for the US Government. Are you willing to bet our future on a coincidence?"

"I don't know," he admitted.

"We brought her over here to hear what she has to say," Bryan stated. "Let's give her a chance to explain her theory without shooting her down just yet."

"Thank you," Gloria replied. "I'm getting ahead of myself and when we're talking about the detonations, we risk crossing over into the TS portion, which we can't do without the SCIF."

48 | Grudge

She paused for a moment, glancing between the two of them. "I can see that you're skeptical—so was I when my predecessor gave the WWII histories to me right before he retired. Why don't you guys read the Operations Order, which gave Task Force 68 their mission parameters and then I'll show you a few pages in the report. Of course, I'll leave the entire packet here for you to read through when you get time."

James reached across the table and slid one of the packets in front of himself. The order was written in military teletype, all capital letters, making it hard to read. The first paragraph had a thick black line through everything, redacting the Friendly and Enemy Situation. However, the next two paragraphs laid out Task Force 68's mission plainly:

```
2. MISSION. O/A 02 DECEMBER
1946, TF 68 DEPLOYS TO DETERMINE
THE FEASIBILITY OF ESTABLISHING
AND MAINTAINING BASES IN THE
ANTARCTIC, WHILE SIMULTANEOUSLY
INVESTIGATING EVIDENCE OF GERMAN
//NAZI// ACTIVITY NEAR DRONNING
MAUD LAND TO ENSURE THE ENEMY IS
NOT RECONSTITUTING COMBAT POWER
WITHIN STRIKING DISTANCE OF U.S.
SOIL.
3. EXECUTION.
```

> A. CONCEPT OF THE OPERATION. TF
> 68, COMPRISED OF 13 US NAVY
> VESSELS AND 3 US ARMY INFANTRY
> BATTALIONS, IS SUBDIVIDED INTO 5
> GROUPS: EAST GROUP, WEST GROUP,
> CENTRAL GROUP, CARRIER GROUP,
> AND BASE GROUP.
> 1) SCHEME OF MANEUVER.

James stopped reading. He didn't need to know what formation Task Force 68 sailed to Antarctica in; that might be something his Navy companion wanted to know, not him. He'd seen enough. He put aside his reservations about the average conspiracy theory and asked Gloria about the results of the expedition.

"Did you read the websites?" she asked.

"Yeah," he replied. "One guy went on for thirty pages. Crazy stuff like the commander of the operation, Admiral Byrd, was murdered a few years after giving an interview that said his men fought UFOs in Antarctica. Then, he said the Secretary of the Navy at the time of Operation Highjump, who later became the Secretary of Defense, was institutionalized and then committed suicide by jumping from a window at Bethesda Naval Hospital."

She tapped the documents. "That's in here, but the official record is that both instances were unrelated. James Forrestal was admitted to the psychiatric ward at Bethesda for depression after he resigned his post as the Secretary of Defense and committed suicide there two months later.

Likewise, in 1947, Admiral Byrd gave an interview to a newspaper in Chile about fighting a war against flying objects in Antarctica. He went on to call for military bases at both the North and South Pole to defend against the threat. He was hospitalized and not allowed to give any more interviews."

"No shit?" Bryan muttered.

"No shit, sir," she replied with a wry smile. "Those are facts. Now, whether they were murdered or not, I have no idea." She glanced back at James. "I'm pretty sure I know which webpage you're referring to. There's a lot of garbage in there, but he's got a lot of truth as well—whether that's from research, or purely accidental remains to be seen. He's right about the massive number of missing Nazi troops and scientists as well."

"The article said 250,000 troops were unaccounted for. Is that right?" James asked.

"Yes," she acknowledged. "Although, it's highly unlikely they all went to Antarctica. A lot of them died in Russia and their deaths were never recorded."

"Okay, so we sent troops to the South Pole after the war. Big deal," Hollinsworth groaned. "The official purposes of testing cold weather gear and learning techniques about how to launch planes from icefields make sense. We were convinced by the late 1940's that we would go to war with Russia. What can you tell us that will make me believe we found evidence of Nazi activity there? Even more important, what the hell does this have to do with the incident in Florida?"

"It's… It's complicated," she replied. "James, can you please see if that SCIF is available? It would make everything easier."

James nodded and left the room. Sergeant Jacobs was available according to the magnet placed in the "**IN**" column drawn onto a whiteboard outside the entrance to the SCIF. He pounded on the door, hopefully hard enough to be heard through the heavy muffling layers around the door.

A small door opened up at head height and a pair of brown eyes appeared. "Can I help you, sir?"

"Good morning, Sergeant Jacobs. I'm James Branson, I work the North American desk. I don't think we've met formally."

"No, sir. We haven't. Can I help you?"

"I have a visitor from the Center for Military History and she needs to be able to talk TS. Is the SCIF available?"

"It is. But since she doesn't work in the JOC, she's not on the SCAR."

"SCAR?"

"The secure access roster," he sighed. "Before somebody is allowed in the SCIF, they have to be authorized to come in here."

"Oh. Am I on it?" James wondered.

"Yes, sir. You work in the JOC. You're authorized. I'll need to get her JPAS information." Sergeant Jacobs must have seen the confused look on James' face. "It's a system that checks security clearances. Do you have her social or DoD ID number?"

"Hold on, she's right up there in the conference room. If she passes your check, we can use the SCIF right now?"

The eyes disappeared and then returned. "For about forty-five minutes. Then I've got a meeting in here."

"Perfect. I'll be right back."

James went and told his two companions that the SCIF was available, they just needed to get Gloria cleared to enter.

SIX

25 December 1946
6 miles off the coast of Prydz Bay, East Antarctica

Lieutenant Craig Albany pushed the throttle on the *Galloping Ghost* to full and lifted away from the water. He'd flown fifteen combat missions in the PBM-3D Mariner seaplane and it appeared that the Navy thought he might get into another scrap with the *Nazis* of all things.

"Most ridiculous thing I've ever heard."

"What was that, Craig?" the navigator, a new officer to the crew named Bales, from Birmingham, asked.

"Ah, nothing, Bales. I'm just wondering what we're gonna see over there."

Craig banked the *Ghost* toward the coastline and away from the *USS Pine Island* to coincide with his statement.

"Looks like somebody wants us to fight, sir!" Waxler, a waist-gunner laughed into the radio.

"You just keep that fifty secured inside, Waxler," the crew chief barked. "If we don't expose 'em to the sea spray or the cold, we'll have a hell of a lot easier recovery."

Craig listened idly for a moment as the enlisted men chattered over the crew's internal frequency and then tuned them out. His primary mission was to map the coastline on the eastern side of the continent. The mission's secondary objective was to find evidence of a Nazi base.

The *Ghost* would accomplish her primary objective, he was certain of it. The second objective... Craig really didn't know what to think about that one.

Intel said that the whole operation was predicated on two U-boats turning up in Argentina several months after the war in Europe was over and reports from ships traveling around Cape Horn off of South America of flying disks that made strange light patterns in the sky at night over the continent. Argentina was the typical resupply point for ships exploring Antarctica, so the presence of the U-boats was circumstantial at best, although there shouldn't have been *any* lights over the uninhabited Southern Continent.

But come on. Nazis? That's stretching the paranoia a little too far, Craig thought as he stared at the endless expanse of ice and snow below the seaplane. He settled in for a long, and boring patrol. *Actually, if it weren't so cold, this might be pleasant.*

*****

23 August 1950
Kobe, Japan

"Are we certain that they can be trusted?"

"As certain as anyone can be," Hauptmann Mueller replied. "The Japanese hate the Americans as much as we do. They fought a noble, if bloody, war with them and the Americans changed the game by using atomic weapons. The emperor was forced to surrender or else face the total annihilation of his people."

"Yes, but the war is over," Oberleutnant Hamm pressed. "It ended four years ago. The Americans—" He stopped and looked around at the faces in the market stalls. When he was satisfied, he began speaking again in a lower tone. "The SCAP manages almost every aspect of Japanese government and economy. How are we supposed to make contact without alerting them?"

"The SCAP? Bah," the captain scoffed at his mention of the Supreme Commander of Allied Powers—the man in charge of the military occupation of Japan. "MacArthur has run this country's economy into the ground. There is a severe recession occurring in Japan as we speak. Their economy is in a shambles. They have too many people and not enough resources—or employment opportunities.

"Did you know, Herr Hamm, that there is a legitimate concern amongst the Japanese people that the country will become communist after the Americans leave?"

"No, I didn't, sir."

"They see how the Soviets have prospered from communism, feeding the masses who live in the snowbound wastelands—not unlike the hell that we are forced to endure in Neuschwabenland. The writing is on the wall in China as well. The communists won their civil war earlier this year and are implementing their ideologies nationwide. Even the conflict that's enveloped the Korean Peninsula for the past two months is a fight between the communist North and the capitalist South. Do you think the communist model would work for Japan, which faces a lot of the same economic problems as the Soviet Union and China?"

"I don't—"

"It won't. Communism itself is flawed. There can be no true egalitarian society. There will always be the haves and the have nots; those who govern and those who are governed. It is the way of mankind."

"I—"

"But, I digress, Sabastian. I did not mean to discuss my personal beliefs on the theory of communism or the Soviet dogs who practice it, in name. What I meant to say before I departed on that tangent is that the Japanese government—or at least some in the government—are ripe for the picking. This is our opportunity to re-forge a partnership with them in secret."

"I understand, sir, but I go back to my original question. Can they be trusted? Or are they too far down the road of dependence upon the American occupational army for their livelihood? Our entire existence on the Southern Continent is dependent upon remaining secret until the time to strike is at hand."

"That remains to be seen, doesn't it?" Hauptmann Mueller answered. "The reports that we've seen say that a complete economic collapse is imminent. That fool MacArthur has made it his mission to break up and destroy large Japanese companies. Those companies stand to lose millions of yen—the Japanese currency—annually. You don't think those business owners have an axe to grind with the Americans?

"We can promise them retribution, both for the war and for what is currently happening to their nation under the occupation. We have foodstuffs from Argentina and

Brazil, and oil from Venezuela and Egypt. We need Japan's steel to produce more düsenjägers and panzers."

They quieted their conversation as they left the crowded ethnic market and made their way across a small open area. There was a new steel company formed earlier in the month that German operatives had assessed may be willing to work with the Reich since its original corporation had been dismantled by the SCAP.

The *Fourth* Reich's supply of steel had diminished rapidly after building their first ninety-three flying discs, known to the Luftwaffe as düsenjägers. They lost several of them in training and a few more engaging the Americans in ill-advised aerial combat. Mueller thought they should have stayed hidden, but the commander of the Neuschwabenland Base disagreed, choosing to attack the observation planes instead of letting them pass unmolested as the Argus Base commander allowed them to do. In addition to the düsenjägers, the Heer was clamoring for armored weapons and transports if they were to fight a ground war with the Americans any time soon.

Mueller scratched his beard that he'd allowed to grow for the trip to Japan. All the steel in the world wouldn't be enough if the scientists couldn't figure out how to manufacture the Aryan's regeneration serum. Already, as evidenced by his recent promotion, the older leaders in the Wehrmacht were beginning to die off. They needed a medical breakthrough if they were to carry out the Führer's plan for retribution.

But, for the moment, Hauptmann Mueller would affect what he could. That meant negotiating a beneficial contract with several companies in Japan that might be sympathetic to the Reich's cause.

Two armed Americans guarded the entrance to the small company front that was the Germans' destination. It was a common, if annoying, occurrence in occupied Japan. The Americans were everywhere.

Mueller glanced at the sign over the door before they went inside. Written in both English and Japanese was the name '**Kawasaki Steel Corporation**'.

*****

25 December 1946
Princess Elizabeth Land, East Antarctica

"Contact!"

Craig shook his head to clear the fuzz that had built up after hours of flying over snow, rock and ice. "What was that?" he asked into the intercom.

"I saw something," Waxler replied. "Off the port side, sir."

Craig looked out his window to port. He couldn't see anything except a few puffy white clouds above the landscape.

"Are you sure it wasn't a mountain, Waxler?"

"I... I don't know, sir. It looked like an upside down cake pan."

"A cake pan?" Private Henderson cut in. "Waxler, we haven't been out here nearly long enough for you to be missing your momma's cooking."

Craig smiled at the starboard waist gunner's comment. "Okay, Henderson, that's enough. If he thought he saw something, he's doing the right thing by reporting it. We'll take note and— *Holy Jesus!*"

A large, circular object flew directly in front of the *Ghost*, coming from the clouds below. Craig pulled the yoke quickly, sending the seaplane jerking hard to port as the object disappeared into the clouds once again.

A chorus of questions berated him over the crew frequency as his men were likely thrown around by his sudden maneuver. He pulled his headset off and slapped his hand against Freddy, the co-pilot. "Did you see that too?"

The man was white as a ghost. He'd seen it.

"Fred, I don't need you losing it. Are you okay?"

Fred slowly nodded his head. "What was that, Craig?"

"I don't know, but I'm thinking we've gone about as far as we're gonna go today."

"Sounds good. I don't think we should push our luck."

Craig gritted his teeth and steered the seaplane in a wide 180-degree turn and added a little throttle once they were pointed back toward the *Pine Island*.

What the hell was that thing?

*****

21 March 2020
Pentagon, Washington, DC

It turned out that Gloria had a higher security clearance than Sergeant Jacobs.

"This is much better," she said, looking around the small space. It was almost exactly like the facility they had back at her headquarters on Fort McNair. They were in a room inside a room, insulated against eavesdropping and they were authorized to discuss up to Top Secret, which should be sufficient. There were still parts about the extraterrestrial threat that she wasn't authorized to discuss, even in the SCIF.

"So, we got a little ahead of ourselves out there while I was trying to get you to buy in on Operation Highjump's real objectives, but that's okay. To be able to tell you exactly what we're up against, I need to take you back to 1938."

"You mean the final known German expedition to Antarctica?" Bryan asked, clearly referencing what he'd seen on the website.

She smirked. "Yeah, that happened in 1938. It was led by Hermann Goering, the head of the German Luftwaffe and the President of the Reichstag at the time. Seems like an odd pick to lead a maritime expedition to the middle of nowhere, don't you think?"

"Hitler was known for his eccentricities and he only trusted a few people, so it's not *that* odd," Bryan remarked.

Good, he knows a little bit about the Nazis. That may work in my favor, Gloria thought.

"True. It was a very important mission—the third that we know of to Antarctica. The official story is that they were looking for new whaling grounds, but again, what was Goering doing there? We think—actually, we *know* that the Germans built a base in Antarctica, in the Dronning Maud Land. Byrd's forces fought against them there before being forced to retreat in the face of superior weaponry."

"So you're saying that Americans *did* fight Germans in Antarctica after the war was over. That's true?" James asked.

"Yes. It's one hundred percent true. There were limited ground skirmishes down there over the years, primarily the Brits during their Operation Tabarin in 1943; most of our fights were in the air against the Nazi flying discs. And we got our asses handed to us."

"Wait," Hollinsworth stopped her. "We were engaged in dogfights with the Nazis in Antarctica in 1946? How have I not heard about that?"

She shrugged again. "People get sworn to secrecy and if enough incentive is placed upon keeping that promise, then it will stay secret forever."

"You said we got our asses handed to us—how did we keep casualties out of the news?"

"People got killed all the time in the military, still do. We have an inherently dangerous job."

"So, they were just covered up?"

"Pretty much. Operation Highjump only lasted eight weeks. It was supposed to take eight months, but they were out of fighter pilots and worried about attacks against the ships, so they returned to the States."

"So we just gave up?" James asked.

"No. The Defense Department launched Operation Windmill over the Antarctic summer of 1947–1948. In addition to overflights of the continent, they also conducted 'underwater demolition surveys'."

"In other words, they were using depth charges to destroy subs."

She nodded. "They found Nazi sub pens off the coast of the Ross Ice Shelf on the opposite side of the continent. As far as we know, they destroyed the U-boats. The flying discs continued to dominate the American fighter planes, forcing another retreat.

"Then, Harry Truman won reelection in 1948 and further expeditions to Antarctica were denied as we faced the growing communist threat," Gloria continued. "We got embroiled in Korea in 1950 and didn't go back to the Antarctic continent until 1955 with Operation Deep Freeze I. We've been going back every year since then."

"When were the nukes detonated again?" James asked.

"1958," she answered. "If you know your history, we were once again heading into a war in Vietnam. We had advisors in the country as early as 1955 and the writing was on the wall that we were going to end up in full-scale combat operations. President Eisenhower couldn't afford to keep fighting a secret war down south and an open conflict in southeast Asia, so he decided to stop dicking around and nuked the Nazi base in Dronning Maud Land."

She paused, letting the information sink in. "Until four days ago, everyone thought that the Nazis in Antarctica were an interesting footnote in the secret US military history."

"But *why* is it still secret?" Bryan asked. "That's the part I don't understand. If we kicked their asses, why hasn't it been released to the public?"

"I have to apologize," Gloria said. "I'm a historian by trade and I allow myself to get distracted and go off topic. It's my biggest fault."

"You seemed to take us right down a linear path," James stated. "You started with the 1938 expedition, went through the operations in the intervening years and then the final destruction of the Nazis. I don't know what else we could have missed."

You don't know the half of it.

"Thank you. You're right, to an extent. Those are extremely important and pertinent to the discussion. But, they're not the full reason we're in the SCIF. I wanted to discuss the other major event that happened in 1938, before the expedition."

Gloria looked over to where the sergeant sat at his computer terminal, trying to appear as if he weren't listening. "Sergeant Jacobs?"

"Yes, ma'am?" he responded, spinning in his chair.

"Can you please give us ten minutes? This information is strictly need to know at this point."

Jacobs' face fell. He'd obviously been looking forward to getting the juicy details of the story. "Yes, ma'am."

She watched as he logged out of two different systems and pocketed the cards required to log in. He shut the door securely behind himself and Gloria turned back to the two men. She shuffled through her briefcase for a moment until she found the pages she wanted and pulled them out, placing them in front of James and Bryan.

"These are standard nondisclosure forms. This information does not leave this room. I'll need you to fill in the information and then you can witness the documents for each other."

She waited as they filled out the paperwork. Years ago, she would have felt like an asshole making them fill out forms that they'd already had to fill out for their regular jobs, but now she barely batted an eye. This was some terrifying stuff and if the information got out to the public, then it would be mass hysteria.

"Alright, that's done," Bryan stated. "What's this about?"

"In 1938, there was an alleged UFO crash in the Bavarian Alps. It was recovered by the Germans, we believe there was a crew of six, but we know for sure that at least one of them survived and assisted the Nazis with their engineering projects."

She'd spit the information out fast, all in one breath, to get it all on the table before the questions began.

"Uh… I don't know how to take that," Bryan mumbled.

"So aliens are real?" James asked.

She nodded. "The crew of the Bavarian crash was humanoid, possibly even human. That part is sketchy in the notes we were able to recover after the war. The survivor called himself an Aryan. Sound familiar?"

"The master race," James said.

"It's what Hitler built his whole ideal of racial purity around," Gloria continued. "We have no idea where the Aryan came from, whether he was a time traveler or from some planet in space, we just don't know. None of the German scientists we brought to America after the war had any firsthand information. They told us what they'd been told by others: the generalized details of the crash and a description of the man, but that's all they knew.

"The Germans were able to recover an intact power plant, but the airframe was damaged," Gloria pressed on. "That's why there were so many radical designs discovered in the engineering and manufacturing facilities of the German plane builders during the war. They had the propulsion, but not the design of the airframe."

She took a breath and waited a beat to allow them time for a question. It didn't come. "We, on the other hand, discovered a basically intact airframe at Roswell, but the power plant was destroyed in the crash—or sabotaged by the crew prior to being apprehended."

"Oh, Jesus Christ!" Bryan burst out. "I've been a naval aviator for nineteen years. I've never seen any little green men flying around out there."

"*You* haven't, but plenty of your fellow pilots have," Gloria countered. "And they're not green, they're grey—at least the ones we know about."

"Hold on," James said. "You mean those stories of little grey men with big eyes who have a fondness for anally probing people are true?"

She laughed. "Sort of. We've recovered two crashed UFOs since the 1947 Roswell Incident and both of them contained the bodies of the Greys, as people call them. We have no evidence of the so-called Aryans. You'll have to remember, my main area of focus is WWII, and anything outside of a five-year window on either side of the war is just a side hobby for me since I can access the information. From what I gather, we have no way of knowing if they really abduct people or if that's all made up. I've read that some of the people who claim to have been abducted have had interesting medical examinations after the fact, but that's not official.

"The Center for Military History's position is that the Nazis were working hand-in-hand with the Aryan to develop more advanced weaponry and technology. There have been multiple reports across the globe of UFOs with Nazi insignia and the occupants speaking German. Again, this could be paranoia or outright lies, but when you couple it with the reports filtering out of Fort Lauderdale that the soldiers on the ground spoke German…"

"You think we didn't kill them all when we nuked their base," James finished her thought.

"Exactly. We discovered the bodies of almost ninety thousand adults and another seventy thousand children in the base afterwards—"

"We did?" Bryan asked skeptically.

"Yes," she replied. She could tell she was losing him. "One of the benefits of high-altitude nuclear bursts is that it spreads a lethal dose of radiation below, but keeps the infrastructure intact and the radiation from that type of burst deteriorates quickly. We were able to go into the subterranean base in Dronning Maud Land and found a massive complex capable of holding hundreds of thousands of troops."

"How did we hide the fact that we killed that many people, including the children?" James asked.

"It was all ordered sealed and everyone involved ordered to secrecy. The children all appeared to be of uniform age, ten or eleven, and wore Nazi uniforms, so they were likely training them to be soldiers."

"That's disgusting."

"It is what it is. The Nazis had a long history of brainwashing young children to their cause and using them as soldiers," she said. "Inside the base we found all sorts of beneficial technology that advanced our sciences rapidly. Remember the space race? We went from flying propeller planes at the end of WWII to landing on the moon, in less than twenty-five years. All the unshielded electronics were rendered useless by the EMP, but we reverse-engineered a lot of them to figure out their purpose."

"You are so full of shit, Major, that I don't know how you can justify that paycheck Uncle Sam gives you each month."

"I used to be just like you, sir," she replied. "I didn't believe my predecessor when he trained me. But there's simply too much evidence for it not to be real. Yes, there are tons of faked stories, but we have a lot of facts and physical evidence from at least three crash sites.

"Don't you think it's strange how the Nazis—the party leadership of the Nazis at least—were so absorbed with researching the occult? They sought ways to tap into the earth for powers and some of them prayed to deities never heard of before. Not to mention, how did they convince the average soldier to gas millions of innocent people without the promise of something better if they followed through with it? They were absolutely in contact with aliens."

Gloria dug through her case again while the commander argued her points. She didn't even try to listen. They were the same points she'd argued as a new captain, designated to work as a historian for the rest of her career. The truth was simply too hard to swallow for most people without hard proof.

She tossed an original Kodak VELOX paper photograph onto the table. "That's from the 1959 Deep Freeze expedition. Yes, it's original, you can tell by the Department of the Navy stamp in the bottom corner."

The photograph showed several soldiers, bundled up against the cold wearing gas masks, clustered around a large, four-barreled weapon of some kind. It was vaguely similar to the WWII flak guns that Gloria was accustomed to, but the barrels were flat, not round, and the metal was white, not black or grey like most gun metals. Smaller hand-held weapons and rifles were lined up on the ground by type on either side of the larger weapon.

"Is that…?" Bryan trailed off and picked up the photograph to get a better look. "That looks similar to our railgun prototypes, except what we have are giant compared to that thing."

"Reverse engineering," Gloria replied. "This picture was taken at the facility in Dronning Maud Land that we destroyed with nuclear weapons. Officially, the Nazi presence in the Antarctica was eliminated and we stopped searching for them. But we never found—"

"The airfields," James interrupted. "Where are the airfields? What about the UFOs that the original expedition fought against?"

She smiled at the analyst. "Exactly. I think there was a second base, possibly even larger since we're still missing all those soldiers. Not to mention, where were the women who'd given birth to all those children? Surely they didn't think a force of a hundred and sixty thousand would be able to do much."

"And now they've come back."

"Yes, James. Now they're back. I need to speak to your boss. Will you vouch for me?"

She could see the emotions cross his face and even the commander looked as if he was starting to believe what she presented. "I don't know," James replied. "Colonel Carpenter is a hard man to convince."

"Then let me do the talking. All I need is an audience with the man."

"Alright. I guess… I guess this is a lead we can't ignore."

SEVEN

30 December 1966
Argus Base, East Antarctica

Generalfeldmarschall Claus Mueller examined the troops under his command. His soldiers stood in perfect formation, stretching as far as he could see across the Grand Cavern. He stood on a platform so they could see him as well.

At the moment, he had 263,291 troops at his disposal. That number consisted of the remaining soldiers of the Third Reich, who'd made the transatlantic crossing, and the second and third generations of the Fourth Reich, bred and born underground.

Not enough. That would never be enough. The Americans, worse, the Soviets, would smash that small number without much thought. He needed five times that many soldiers, at least, to attempt an attack. But, there were problems with amassing that number. The field marshal sneered. In reality their problems were threefold and every one of them dealt with the capacities of Argus Base.

Argus was bursting at the seams. It was originally built as the airbase and breeding facility with the capacity to hold two hundred thousand men and around a hundred thousand breeding stock, plus the nurseries and dormitories for the children. The Neuschwabenland Base was supposed to hold the bulk of the soldiers for training and weapons manufacturing.

The Americans destroyed the primary site and captured most of the advanced infantry weapons—along with all the soldiers who weren't guarding Argus or part of the Luftwaffe. Most of the experienced soldiers who'd been born in Germany and the entire first generation of the Fourth Reich, who'd moved to the facility to begin training only months before the nuclear detonations, were dead. Now, Argus Base held both the Luftwaffe and the Heer, the breeding stock, the scientists, *and* the manufacturing. His engineers had made thousands of the machines of war and there was nowhere to put them due to the overflow of people.

The next problem was food. The farms operated at maximum capacity, no longer producing enough food to sustain everyone. There was already talk of illegal trade amongst the population. Once the first generation of breeding stock began to have their own children, they would be out of options to feed his people. He would need to choose whether they fed the children or the adults, the engineers or the scientists, the breeding stock or the soldiers—none of those options were feasible as all played an important part in the building of the Fourth Reich.

Finally, the miners had filled the base with metal ores waiting to be transformed into weapons and flying discs. They'd dug deep, too deep to heat the new chambers they'd opened effectively. The newer spaces in Argus could be used for storage, but not for living quarters.

After today, that would change. The capacity problem would ease. The Reich's scientists had finally made a breakthrough and the tests were conclusive. Today was

Grudge | 73

the day that the Fourth Reich would become a reality. They just needed to wait for revenge a little while longer.

Generalfeldmarschall Mueller stepped in front of the microphone to address his men. He waited for the chants of adulation to die down, smiling. Twenty years ago, he'd been a lowly corporal, burning the bodies of a Jew and an army conscript in one of the greatest acts of subterfuge in history. They'd tricked the world into believing that Adolf Hitler and his new wife committed suicide side by side. Today, Claus was the most powerful man in the Nazi Army.

"Wehrmacht!" he shouted. "Stand at ease. There is no sense in you all remaining rigidly at attention while we talk. I have found that the soldier's mind wanders when you are forced to stand at attention for long periods of time. I am pleased with the reports from the 938th Training Brigade. Our second and third generations are now fully trained and the fourth and fifth generations are progressing splendidly. Our strength grows every day!"

The cheering erupted once more. The youth had been indoctrinated from the moment of birth that their sole purpose in life was to fight for the Reich. Mueller found it easy to manipulate their minds in the controlled environment of Argus Base without the distractions of the outside world.

"The Luftwaffe now has two thousand flying discs, fully operational, in storage, prepared to attack. The Panzer Corps has one thousand hovertanks, also in storage, and we continue to manufacture projectiles for the magnetic weapons. Our army has the supplies. We only lack the forces to use them.

"Last week, we took the first step in ensuring the longevity of the Wehrmacht. You may have noticed the feelings of power, of vitality, coursing through your veins." He laughed and continued, "I know the breeding stock noticed your manliness. You are animals! My army of magnificent animals!"

The men cheered and screamed as if they *were* animals. The regenerative serum had that effect on them. It boosted their testosterone by nearly four hundred percent. They were barely contained, only the threat of severe punishment kept them in line. He'd allowed them to rut freely amongst the stock in their off duty hours, ensuring that the next generation would be the progeny of this one.

"We prepare every day to avenge our fathers and mothers, murdered at the hands of the Americans in the Fatherland. I would bet my life on any one of you against ten American soldiers. Unfortunately, at our current strength, we face sixty-to-one odds. You're all very good, but this is too much, even for you."

The men shouted, "No!" in unison. They truly thought they could defeat the Americans, even with their small numbers.

"Yes," the field marshal shouted back. "We must make way for the next generation. You know that Argus cannot support our current strength, which is nowhere near enough. That is why we must do this today. I will go with you into that long sleep. Once the numbers are in our favor, we will reawaken and go forth!"

The cheering of the men was deafening and Mueller saluted the men before sitting in a chair. Cameramen circled him, broadcasting their images to the large projector screens around the room. The field marshal waved into the camera and smiled as medical technicians fitted a mask over his nose and mouth.

He immediately began to get lightheaded. The aerosolized drugs were already taking effect, mingling with the regeneration serum the same technicians had administered to him the day before. Mueller could feel the two interacting, one fighting to send his body into a deep sleep before being frozen, while the other worked to keep his organs working and his muscles intact.

This was the future. This was how the Fourth Reich would rise given the limited resources they possessed in the frozen land. Only the soldiers from the training brigade would remain unfrozen to train future generations of the Wehrmacht. Once those men and women were trained, they would be put into cryogenic hibernation in the lower chambers and the next generation would move up from the breeding grounds to the training grounds. It would take time, but he wouldn't know that any had passed.

Field Marshal Mueller felt his heart flutter and for a brief, panicked moment, it stopped. *Is that supposed to happen?* he asked himself in alarm. He turned wildly in his chair to see the smiling face of the Aryan, the grin he'd affected seemed more sinister than pleased. *Has that alien bastard betrayed me?*

*****

16 May 2025
Fort Stewart, Georgia

The captain examined his notes for a brief moment as he paused. He'd kept his change of command speech plain so far, but his experiences wouldn't let him leave it at that. Gabe Murdock took a deep breath before reading the paragraph that he knew would be controversial.

"Finally, to the soldiers, noncommissioned officers and officers of Bravo Company, Three-Seven Infantry, I say to you that we will train hard in preparation for the upcoming fight. It's been more than five years since the attack in Florida. I was an ROTC cadet on the beach that day. I saw the Grey Men. They showed no mercy and neither shall we."

Gabe glanced up from his speech. "Berserkers! Let's get ready to kill some Nazi assholes!"

The men cheered his statement as he marched to his position in front of the company first sergeant. The man saluted him and said, "Damn fine speech, sir. I can already tell that you're gonna be a handful."

Gabe dropped his salute and then First Sergeant Thomas dropped his before executing a right face and walking quickly around to the back of the formation. The new company commander took one step forward, and then executed a flawless about face to turn toward the small crowd.

Lieutenant Colonel Calhoun was already standing on his mark.

"Sir, this concludes today's change of command ceremony," Gabe stated as he saluted.

"Commander, take charge of your company," Colonel Calhoun replied, returning the salute.

Gabe waited until his new boss dropped the salute to drop his arm. He watched the battalion commander until he'd exited the field and then completed another about face movement.

"At ease, Berserkers," Gabe ordered. "Actually…fall out. Bring it on in, around me."

The soldiers complied, breaking ranks and forming a semi-circle around him so they could hear what he had to say.

"For those of you that I haven't met during the change of command inventories the past couple of weeks, my name if Captain Murdock. I'm from Missouri and I meant what I said about training to fight the Nazis. It's an unpopular opinion about who they were, but I was on the beach when they attacked and killed sixty-three thousand Americans. They came from the sea and I was thrown into a concrete divider in an explosion. When I woke up, they were already leaving. I *heard* them talking to each other and saw their weapons and uniforms. They were Nazis. I don't know how…"

He trailed off. *Best not to let them think you're a looney on day one, Gabe*, he told himself. "Anyways, regardless of who they were, we're going to train hard. We will be prepared to answer the call when the time comes.

"But first, we're going to eat," Gabe amended. "There's food inside the battalion classroom. I want to speak with the NCOs and officers at 1130 in the company orderly room. E-4 and below, you are released after you eat. PT is zero-six-hundred Monday morning. We're gonna go on a little run, so make sure you're hydrated."

Gabe grinned at the reactions of the enlisted men and had them reassemble in formation before calling the first sergeant up to take the company. He needed to hurry and get inside the classroom to host the reception. He was single, so Michelle, the wife of first platoon leader Jake Wilcox, had helped him set up and was acting as an interim host until he returned.

He thanked Michelle profusely for her help once he arrived. She'd been invaluable; he'd have to get the family a bottle of wine or something nice as a thank you for helping him out.

Within minutes of his arrival, the battalion commander and the battalion operations officer pulled him aside. They looked like they wanted to talk.

"Gabe, Major Hopkins tells me that you've already requested a change to the training schedule and want two rifle ranges for next week and scheduled three days of combatives in between," Lieutenant Colonel Calhoun stated. "Then the following week, you plan on taking your company out to the MOUT site for urban operations training. Is that right? I don't remember approving that training schedule when Captain Laporte submitted his six-week post-change of command order."

"Yes, sir. Those are the initial changes. I'll have more as I assess the needs of the company over the next few weeks."

"Have you talked with your first sergeant yet? He's going to be your sounding board, the man you'll lean on to get the pulse of the company. I'm not prepared to authorize a change to the training schedule that requires overnights in the field. One of our responsibilities as officers is to ensure that our soldiers have predictability in their schedules. Unless you can convince me otherwise, their families need to know at least a month out when they're going to the field. Some of them may have childcare issues or leave scheduled that they'll cancel because they want to show you they're team players. What's your reasoning behind changing the training schedule?"

"Sir, I feel like we're on the brink of an invasion. We need to be prepared to defend our shores. That's why I chose to come to the 3rd Infantry Division. Here in Savannah, we're positioned to respond to any attack in the southeast. I—"

"Wait a minute, Gabriel," the colonel stopped him. "Is this about the Florida attack a few years ago?"

"Absolutely, sir. I saw the brutality of those men firsthand. We need to prepare our soldiers to be just as violent as our enemies, on a moment's notice. We've got to be flexible and willing to think outside of the box."

"I cut my teeth in Afghanistan, Iraq *and* Mali, son. I was the operations officer for the 1st Ranger Battalion when we were sent into the heart of Africa to defeat a private army financed by a Chinese lithium mining company. Our mission was to stop human rights violations without starting an international conflict with the Chinese. Don't tell me about thinking outside the box."

"That's not what I meant, sir," Gabe protested. "The Nazis were—"

"Stop that Nazi shit, Gabriel. I let it slide in your speech, but I don't want to hear any more about it. We don't know who attacked us, but I'll tell you right now, it wasn't the Nazis. My great-grandfather was in the 101st. He drank wine at the Eagles Nest in the mountains of Bavaria. They kicked those sick bastards' asses and there's nothing left of them except a bunch of documentary footage."

The battalion commander paused for a moment to calm down and then said, "Denied. Berserker Company will follow through with the six-week training schedule established by the previous commander. That schedule allows you to properly integrate into the company and battalion battle rhythm."

He placed a hand on Gabe's shoulder. "The battalion is ready to respond to any attack, Captain Murdock. We've trained nonstop for the past five years, ready to go if whoever attacked us ever shows their face again. But, we've got to be able to wind down and take care of our people also. Enjoy yourself. Celebrate your new command, and be prepared to hit the ground running come Monday morning."

The commander walked away and Gabe watched him go.

"Well, that went about as good as can be expected," Major Hopkins stated. "I told you that he was a stickler for protecting the training schedule."

"Yeah, thank you for asking for me, sir."

"Come see me next week. I'll lay out the battalion's annual training plan and you can pick dates for the events you want to schedule. You don't have to deviate from your ideas or plans for how you want to run your company… You'll just have to delay them a bit."

"Thanks, sir," Gabe replied. He'd wanted to come in strong and get his men focused on the fight, but Laporte had been a ticket-puncher. He didn't care about getting the men prepared for war; he wanted to get his record stamped that he'd hit all the required gates for promotion. As a result, Berserker Company was conducting all of their annual administrative briefings for the next two weeks—something that the former commander had put off until after he left.

Whoo hoo, Gabe thought as he wandered over to the table to make a plate of food. *More classes about suicide prevention and privately owned vehicle maintenance.*

EIGHT

04 June 1982
Argus Base, East Antarctica

Frederick raced down the hallway toward the storage closet he and his friends had taken over as their clubhouse. Their lessons and drills were complete for the day and they had two precious hours to themselves before room checks. The Heer Henchmen used that time to gather and discuss what they'd do to the Americans once the Wehrmacht was finally released upon them.

He was bundled against the deep cold of below, but he was used to it by now. The Henchmen had been going to the storage rooms for their meetings for eight months. It was amazing what your body could become accustomed to.

The training brigade's unteroffizieres knew that the boys formed clubs like the Heer Henchmen. It was one of the few luxuries allowed to help combat the boredom of Argus Base, deep beneath the surface of the ice above. Likely, most of the men in the training brigade had been in a club of their own before being told in their last year of preparation that they would not be frozen and would instead join the ranks of the 938th. It was a crushing blow for any boy to learn that he wouldn't take part in the mission he'd trained for his entire life—and yet another reminder that the Reich owned every aspect of your life.

In just two days, on the anniversary of the American invasion of Europe, Frederick would learn of his own fate. He'd scored well enough, he hoped, to be in the top five percent of his generation who were allowed to choose whether their name went into the training brigade lottery. They wouldn't find out *that* part until tomorrow.

It was all so much to process for a seventeen year-old boy. He'd been preparing his entire life to be a Wehrmacht soldier, frozen in the ice like thirty generations before him, until the day to attack came. If he fulfilled his duty to the Reich, then he would see battle one day. If he chose to opt in to the training brigade lottery, he had a chance to stay with his beloved Greta and their three-month old son, Henrik.

Frederick didn't want to condemn Greta to life as a breeder. If he joined the training brigade, then he could marry her and continue to produce children. Otherwise, she'd be given to the next available male that the breeding program declared was a good genetic fit —something he didn't want to happen. Could he give up his opportunity to avenge his nation's betrayal?

The walls passed from the rough granite of the original base to the smooth basalt rock that the miners discovered the deeper they went. The basalt, a remnant of the lava flows that helped form the continent millions of years ago, also helped to shape the current design of Argus Base as engineers followed the grain of the rock where they could. The result was oddly-shaped rooms and corridors throughout the lower levels that one had to be careful traversing or risk injury.

He navigated down eight more levels, passing thousands upon thousands of soldiers, cryogenically frozen and stacked four high, head to foot, before a solid metal shelf separated another layer of four men stacked in the same manner. Each was dressed in the grey combat uniform of the Fourth Reich's army, minus the helmet and web gear.

Technicians worked amongst the unmoving soldiers, checking their minimal vital signs to ensure that each man survived the ordeal. Tending to the frozen soldiers had become a job unto itself in Argus as the sheer numbers became too many to simply be an additional duty shared by combat troops and medical personnel.

When he finally reached the tenth level, he bundled himself against the cold he knew would set in now that he was no longer exercising on the stairs. Ten levels belowground was the deepest that they'd gone—so far. The miners were always digging deeper, but for now, the Wehrmacht had sufficient storage space. Within two or three generations, though, they'd need to open another level since the tenth would be full.

Or would they finally break out from Argus to attack before that was required? While he hadn't seen the recent numbers, when he was the lowly Soldat Frederick Albrecht, newly elevated from his years in the farms at age fourteen, he'd been told that the Wehrmacht stood at 782,000 men. There were another two hundred thousand or so in the four-year military training cycle at the moment.

He'd seen old newsreel footage of Generalfeldmarschall Mueller speaking of the number of troops needed to attack. One million was what he stated; surely they were nearly ready?

That idea warmed him as he walked the two kilometers from the stairwell to the meeting room of the Heer Henchmen. They hadn't always been so far from the stairs, but as the storage rooms filled, necessity caused them to push further and further away.

Finally, he arrived. The lighting had recently been completed in this segment where it hadn't before. In less than a month from now, this chamber would be filled with sleeping soldiers as well. Frederick wondered if he would go into the long night as bravely as the others had.

"Gefreiter Albrecht! Why are you standing in the hallway? You'll catch your death of a chill out there."

Frederick looked up to see his friend, Obersoldat Wagner, standing in the doorway to the storage room they used as their meeting space. "Gregory," he acknowledged with a dip of his chin. "How was your obstacle course run today?"

"Six minutes and fourteen seconds!" Gregory Wagner grinned. "The best in my brigade. I am sure to be sent to fallschirmjäger candidate school with those scores."

Frederick returned the smile and congratulated his friend. "Good job. You have a month to beat the record."

"I know. I'm only eleven seconds away, so if I can just skim a few, then I will earn the record."

"You deserve it—and you'll get it, too."

"Thank you," Gregory replied, ushering Frederick into the meeting room of the Heer Henchmen.

There were ninety-nine members of the Henchmen, but tonight there were only the club's officers. They'd hold the final general meeting after the announcement of everyone's assignments on June 6th. All told, there were fourteen men present; one from each of the thirteen Army brigades in training, plus the president of the Heer Henchmen, Alfred Bormann, a direct descendant of the Führer's personal secretary, Martin Bormann.

Frederick and Gregory settled on one of the metal shelving units that awaited the next generation of soldiers to listen to their president speak.

"Welcome, Henchmen!" Bormann shouted.

They cheered in response, not caring whether anyone heard them. All across Argus Base, organizations would be holding their own meetings in preparation for the assignment lottery.

When the cheers died down, Bormann continued. "Tonight, we have a special treat before we discuss leadership options for the next generation. Christoff? Where is he?"

Everyone looked for the club's signalman. He was slippery, always disappearing when he was needed, and yet, somehow, coming through at the last minute with outstanding communications.

"Here! Here I am, Alfred!" the radioman called from the darkness. A strange squeaking sound accompanied his voice "I'm sorry that I'm late, gentlemen. I wanted to give you all an even greater surprise."

He appeared, pushing a television set on a cart. It was a newer, giant twenty-four inch model that the suppliers had purchased on their last trip to Japan. The cart was the source of the squeaking.

"I was able to get a television set!"

The men clapped approvingly. Normally, they listened to rock music on the radios that Christoff brought, but tonight, they may have the opportunity to see an uncensored television program from America.

"Are we going to watch *All in the Family*?" someone shouted.

"Even better," Christoff smirked. "Tonight, we will watch a program called MTV!"

*****

19 June 2025
Dupont Circle, Washington, DC

"*Ugh!* These are the most unflattering uniforms I've ever seen," Gloria sneered at her frumpy appearance in the body-length mirror of her apartment bedroom.

"You look great, babe," James assured her, wrapping his arm around her and rubbing her swollen belly.

"And you're a goddamned liar, James," she chastised him, causing him to retreat into the closet for safety. "Seriously, there aren't even any pockets in the stupid pants. Where am

I supposed to keep my ID card when I leave my workstation?"

Lieutenant Colonel Adams-Branson hated the US Army maternity uniform. *Hate is too mild*, she thought. She *abhorred* the US Army maternity uniform. The only pockets in the entire damn thing were the ones on the front of the blouse, so she was supposed to keep her keys, her ID tags *and* wallet in two ridiculously small pockets on the front of her uniform, where they would press against her stomach any time she stood up.

"*God*, you can tell that men designed these stupid uniforms," she grumbled as she looked at herself once again. "What a crock of shit."

She'd held off switching to the maternity uniform as long as possible, but at five months, her old uniforms were no longer a viable option. She'd gotten away with no belt at first, then one, two, three, and finally *four* unfastened buttons on her pants, but those days were past. Her protruding belly made it impossible to fit into her size four-tall trousers any longer. Today was the day that she had to make the switch.

But I am not *going to wear tennis shoes in uniform*, she promised herself, thinking of the pregnant soldiers she'd seen walking in uniform with sneakers on their feet.

"At least my hair is more full and practically shimmering."

"Just like the rest of you, dear," James called from the closet.

She bit back a question about what he meant. They'd been married for two years, so at this point he could have been complimenting her *or* making fun of her because his words could have been taken either way. She chose to think he meant them as a compliment and not a jab at her expanding waistline.

"I'm craving steak," Gloria said, changing the subject of her size. "Want to go out to dinner tonight after you get off work?"

"Uh…" James emerged from the closet wearing a tie and holding his suit jacket over his left arm. "Yeah. I won't be done until six, then Metro back to here and then—"

"Just meet me at Old Ebbitt Grill at 6:30; that way you're not fighting the crowd to get back here and then back into downtown."

He smiled, obviously relieved that he wouldn't be fighting the Thursday after work crowds coming and going. "That's a good suggestion. Thank you."

Gloria glanced at the clock. They were both going to be late if they didn't get out the door. Her boss would cut her slack and let a few minutes slide since she was pregnant; James' boss would not. The section she'd helped him create at the Pentagon was in danger of being shut down and any slip up would be another nail in the department's coffin.

Five years ago, they'd convinced then-Colonel Mark Carpenter to go before the Joint Requirements Oversight Council and argue to establish a separate section within the JOC for the coordination of the defense of North America, not just monitoring events and letting others know. The new office was to be more responsive and have greater control over active duty forces with the ability to work directly with the state National Guard and the Coast Guard instead of going through the cumbersome National Guard Bureau or the notoriously slow Homeland Defense Agency.

In the wake of the Florida attacks, in an election year, the office was created with little or no resistance and resources were shifted internally to fund the organization. James was elevated to the deputy position of the new organization and they worked tirelessly to ensure the safety of our borders.

They'd coordinated shoreline response drills, established rapid transit corridors for military units in the heart of the country to the coasts, worked with the various state highway administrations to improve evacuation routes, often securing funding to increase the width of the roads where possible, and even increased partnerships with privately-funded space-monitoring agencies. The Joint North American Defense Branch was truly value-added to the nation for the first three years.

Gloria had even briefed the president on the Operation Highjump theory and the Navy sent a task force with almost ten thousand Marines to Antarctica. Satellite imagery, ground-penetrating radar, aerial flyovers and men on the ground had been unable to discover any remaining secret base. Intelligence agencies worldwide were unable to find a credible source to take responsibility for the attack. The attacks might as well have originated from the moon—or the depths of the ocean.

Then military funding dried up with the new administration earlier this year. There had been no new, large-scale attacks on American shores, just that one isolated and unexplained incident. The American public fractured along political lines once again, moving on from the loss. The new administration took power in January, seemingly with the express desire to deplete the military and undo all the hard work that had been done over the years.

James rushed by, kissed her on the cheek and bent down to kiss her stomach. "I'll see you at dinner tonight."

"Yeah, okay. Love you!" she yelled after him.

"Love you too!" The front door slammed shut on their apartment and she was alone.

Gloria walked slowly down the hallway to the kitchen. She wasn't quite big enough to call her movements a waddle, but they sure weren't as graceful as they used to be. There was a paper bag of butter croissants from the bakery downstairs on the counter. One of those went into the toaster oven while she cracked an egg in a frying pan on the stove.

The idea of James losing his position as the deputy was depressing. He wouldn't lose his job, he'd be moved somewhere else in Crystal City or back to the Pentagon, but he'd really grown during these last five years. When she'd met him, he'd been content with his role in life, swimming along and not particularly caring about improving himself. The deputy position had helped to shape him into the man he was today and it worried her that he'd lose part of himself if they shut down that section.

What made the idea of the closure of the Joint North American Defense Branch even more depressing for Gloria was that she was sure that they hadn't seen an end of the attacks. The last one was so sudden, so random—and yet, coldly calculated, with overwhelming force—that there were going to be more of them. James had worked hard to prepare for that eventuality and it was already beginning to unravel due to political infighting.

Regardless of the current data to the contrary, her historical documents convinced her that it was the Nazis. They were coming back, she just didn't know when.

NINE

02 December 1982
Ballykelly, County Londonderry, Northern Ireland

"I don' like this one bit. Smells like a setup," Colleen muttered from the passenger seat.

"Aye, it's odd," Sean replied. "But, if what this guy knows gives us a chance against those RUC fucks, then I'm willing to risk it."

"You willin' ta sit in tha Maze for ten years if your contact turns out to be a RUC agent or some other Brit intelligence officer?"

He glanced to his left, through the window beyond the gorgeous brunette who sat beside him. They'd been together on assignment from the Irish National Liberation Army for almost six months. So far, she'd waved off every one of Sean's advances. If today's meeting went well and the techniques the German offered to teach were useful, then he'd kill scores of Paras and their collaborators, maybe some of the Peelers as well.

Colleen'd be droppin' her knickers for me then, he thought as he turned the rickety Renault food and coffee truck toward St. Finlough's Catholic Church.

As they crept down the drive, Sean examined their destination. The timeworn, grey church was large by Ballykelly standards, what with the massive height of the roof itself and the belfry atop that, plus the four drum towers on each corner. The church looked like it could have held off a siege for weeks. The rectory, much newer than St.

Finlough's, was where they were to meet with the man whom Dominic had told Sean would teach them how build bombs capable of wiping out an entire platoon of British soldiers.

He pulled the truck into the lane marked for disabled persons and shut off the engine. A priest appeared at the rectory doorway and lifted a hand to shield against the cold gusts of wind coming off Lough Foyle from the north.

"That's our man," Sean stated, jabbing a finger toward the priest.

"That's the German?"

"For fuck's sake, Colleen. No, the priest is not the German. He's our contact. He'll take us to the German."

"Well ya weren't very clear, were ya now, Sean? Ya don' need to be an arse all the time."

Sean suppressed a growl and opened the door. He looked around the premises warily, still on edge that Dominic, the current leader of INLA, had been given bad information and they were walking into a trap. The revolver's reassuring lump in his waistband gave him the confidence to carry on. He wasn't going to prison.

"Good mornin', Father," he called.

"Good mornin', my son. The sanctuary is sealed 'til Vespers. Is there something you may need assistance with?"

"Aye, there is. I'm Sean, that's Colleen," he pointed a thumb over his shoulder to where his partner stood on the opposite side of the bonnet, wisely using the lorry as a shield. "I'd like to talk to ya about preserving our Catholic heritage."

The priest beckoned him forward and he looked back at Colleen, tossing his head toward the rectory. She nodded and came around, holding a cut-down shotgun.

"Please, it's just us here, child," the priest said. "You can put that away."

"I'll be keepin' it where I can use it, thank you much," she replied and continued toward the rectory with the weapon.

The older man sighed, clearly used to stubborn republicans who refused to surrender their weapons. "Come inside then. The weather's turnin' and we'll get a blow soon—maybe even some snow. I love snow. We get a lot more here than in Derry where I lived as a lad. Well, actually, I lived in Culmore, which is part of Derry these days. I—"

"Nervous, Father?" Sean asked, chuckling at the priest's unending flow of words.

"I'm a man of God—and loyal to Ireland—but I don't like what's a brewin'," the older man replied. "I assume you're here to meet with *him*."

"Is the German here?" he asked.

"Aye. That big, scar-faced brute is inside. He's drank four cups of tea in twenty minutes and smoked at least half a pack of my cigarettes. Things must be harder to come by in East Germany than I thought."

"Let's not keep the man waitin' all day, then," Sean said. "He's through here?"

The priest nodded his head and swept his arms wide. "Please, come inside."

They filed past him and Sean heard the rectory door lock firmly behind the priest, who then shuffled past them once more and led them into the parlor where a cloud of choking grey smoke nearly obscured a large male sitting on the sofa. Even sitting down, Sean could see that the man was massive, easily two meters tall, probably more than eighteen stones. His nose was crooked, remnants of having been broken multiple times over the years, but the man's dominant feature was a large scar running from his chin to the corner of his mouth and then continuing across his face to disappear in the hairline above his ear. Sean wouldn't want to get in a scrap with that one.

"Ah! You must be the agent Dominic has sent to me to learn how to make bombs," the man stated with a thick accent that wasn't quite like what Sean had heard German tourists use in Derry before the Troubles began and drove them all away. He wondered if the big man was one of them "transported Germans" living over in South America. Didn't really matter to him, though. If Dominic trusted the man enough to have two of his deepest operatives meet with him, then he must be on the up and up about helping the republicans put an end to the British occupation.

"Aye, that'd be me." He stuck out a hand. "Sean O'Connor. This is my partner, Colleen Kavanagh."

"Women aren't good fighters," the German muttered, not bothering to introduce himself or shake Sean's hand. "What do you know about shape charges?"

"I... Uh, I know how to use Frangex and some old clock parts to make a time bomb."

"You're bomb is not good," the German declared. "Shape charge can tear through armored vehicle, the side of a building, the only thing limiting you is your imagination."

"I've heard of shaped charges—the British Army uses 'em."

The big man leaned over the arm of the sofa and picked up a canvas satchel. "This is how to make a shape charge. Very simple."

He swept his forearm across the coffee table, sending the ashtray, empty cup and saucer, and even a bible falling to the floor.

"Excuse me," the priest protested.

"Go away, little man. I wouldn't want you getting exploded." He dumped the contents of the satchel onto the wood and turned back to Sean. "Is that how you say it: exploded?"

"Close enough," he replied, eyeing the familiar parts on the table. "Father, would ya please excuse us?"

"Yes, of course. I'll be in my office with the door *closed*."

The German watched the priest leave and then nodded his head approvingly when the office door clicked shut. "I know you're planning on bombing a disco in a few days," he stated.

"How—?"

"It's my job to know. A shape charge is perfect for this. Place it near a support pillar and the roof will collapse, causing much more damage than a simple fragmentation bomb like you know how to make."

The wheels began turning in Sean's head. The Droppin Well *did* have a pillar supporting the roof in the middle of the dance floor. If he could time it to detonate when the British soldiers from Shackleton Barracks were there with their sympathizing whores…

"Does this make sense to you?" the big man asked, lighting another cigarette.

"Aye, the concept makes sense."

"Good. Let me teach you the proper way to make a shape charge. I hope you are a fast learner."

"Going somewhere?" Colleen asked.

"*Ja.* I have a plane to catch. I have a meeting with the leaders of several Mujahedeen tribes thirty-seven hours from now and then I'm going to Indonesia to a teach a few of the East Timor nationalists how to make the shape charge as well."

"Muja-what?"

"Mujahedeen. They are a collection of warrior tribes in Afghanistan. They're fighting against the occupying Soviet Army—much like you are fighting against the British occupation of Northern Ireland."

"Busy man, aye?" Sean smirked, picking up the curved piece of metal from the pile of supplies on the table.

"You don't know the half of it," the German winked. "Everything is harder these days. I've been *dead* for seven years and still people in the airport recognize me. Damn television."

Sean squinted his eyes, trying to determine who the man was. "I'm sorry, you never gave me your name," he said.

"Skorzeny," the brute replied, laughing as he said it.

*****

12 March 2020
Argus Base, East Antarctica

"In one week, we will strike! We will remind the Americans of what it means to fear," Frederick shouted to the other senior officers in the meeting room. "The camera footage will be invaluable as a motivational tool for the Wehrmacht as we begin the unthawing process next year."

"But don't you think we risk showing our hand too early?" Joseph Schwartz, the chief engineering scientist, asked. "If they track your small demonstration force back to Argus, then all is lost."

"Have you done your duty to the Reich, Herr Schwartz?" Oberst Albrecht demanded.

"Excuse me, sir?"

"Have you done your duty to the Reich?" Frederick repeated without elaborating.

"I… You know I have. I live for the glory of our Reich. Every day in this environment is a sacrifice that I willingly make, Oberst. You have been inside this base your entire life, but I have been to the outside world—and chosen to return. I have helped our teams to infiltrate military bases and steal the most heavily guarded of technologies. I have been to the corporate headquarters and marketplaces of the capitalists to purchase products that we can't manufacture ourselves. I—"

"Enough, Joseph!" the oberst cut him off. "I know the sacrifices you've made—the sacrifices that we've all made," he amended.

Frederick took a moment to suppress his feeling of loss. His beloved Greta had committed suicide in front of him two months ago. Once their sixth child was frozen, she told him that her duty to the Reich was complete. He asked her what she meant and she plastered the wall of their quarters with the insides of her skull.

That was the way of things in Argus Base. When someone's usefulness was complete, they were encouraged to end the burden upon the food supplies.

Now, the only thing Frederick Albrecht had was his command of the 938th Training Brigade and the Fourth Reich, which he'd spent his entire life establishing. The Reich was finally ready, in his opinion, to strike against the Americans. They were complacent, undisciplined, self-centered and arrogant. *He* would lead the first strike against them and then unthaw Generalfeldmarschall Mueller. Frederick believed it was his destiny to fight for the Reich, not to die without ever having taken up arms in support of it.

"What I meant," Frederick finally continued, focusing his eyes on the chief engineering scientist, "was to ask you if the stealth technology is complete."

Joseph inclined his head. "Yes, sir. With the help of the Aryan, I have been able to finalize the shrouding device. I must warn you, it draws so much power, that it can only be placed upon a large cargo ship. We're decades away from figuring out batteries that are efficient enough to generate that much energy, but small enough to be transported by a düsenjäger."

"That is of no concern," Frederick stated, slicing his hand across the air, both to dismiss the fact that the flying discs were too small for the device and to remind the scientist that he didn't want to hear anything further of the Aryan. The man was an enigma to him, refusing to divulge the truth of where he came from or how he knew so much about technologies that Frederick couldn't comprehend. The man had an agenda of some sort, but no one else could see it. He was the only one who seemed distrustful of the Aryan.

"Arriving undetected is of utmost importance," Frederick continued. "The jet fighters do not need their own shrouding device. The Americans have nothing capable of competing against them in aerial combat."

"Or so we believe, Oberst," Andreas Wolff, the oberstleutnant in charge of the Luftwaffe training battalion, interjected. "We do not truly know how the düsenjäger will perform against the F-35 or even the older F-22. Neither plane has engaged in non-simulated combat."

"You're making my point for me, Andreas. We need to engage the Americans with a small expeditionary force to determine their response capabilities. The last time our forces fought against the Americans, they were new to jet engines—using stolen plans and kidnapped German scientists, I might add. Since then, they've gone on to create different types of engines of their own and have had air superiority in every war they've fought in since the Korean War."

He took a deep breath. "They have not been tested. And neither have we."

"Treason!"

"It is not treason, Joseph," Frederick countered. "It is a fact. The Luftwaffe has not engaged in combat in more than sixty-five years. When the Americans destroyed Neuschwabenland Base, we made the decision to go completely underground and abandon combat with them, to let them believe that they'd annihilated us. So, as I said, it is a fact that the Luftwaffe has not been tested."

"We fly missions weekly, Oberst Albrecht," Andreas reminded everyone.

"Yes, to gather intelligence and make supply runs—not to engage in combat. I am confident in every generation of our pilots, frozen and unfrozen, but the truth remains that they are untested. That is why I propose a mission to attack the southern coast of the United States, during their so-called 'spring break'. We can effectively wipe out a large portion of their educated university-age youth in one small-scale attack, risking only the soldiers currently assigned to the training brigade."

Several of the men around the table argued amongst themselves, while Frederick leaned back to listen, gently steering the conversation when he needed to. He would have his way. He hadn't worked his way to the top of the Reich's High Command without knowing how to manipulate others.

"Without the full power of the Wehrmacht at our disposal, I believe we may show our hand too early," Joseph said.

He's clearly the leader of the opposition, maybe he should suffer an accident on the ice, Frederick thought.

"We will not show our hand, Herr Schwartz. I will have the Luftwaffe markings removed from the düsenjägers and I won't take the panzers. We'll have limited men on the ground, just enough to destroy any of their surface-to-air missile sites at the point of invasion."

He turned his attention back to the assembled council. "Gentlemen, this is the time to test our forces and the tactics that we've trained generations of pilots to perform. We have reached the quota of two million fighting men and will begin unthawing them soon. There is no better time to attempt this than now."

Frederick leaned forward. "The time for talk is over," he said. "I propose a vote whether we will authorize a limited, preemptive strike against the Americans utilizing the cadre of the 938th Training Brigade and Generation Fifty-Eight."

"I second the motion," the voice of Doctor Michel Kuhn, the Chief Breeder, reverberated off the walls of the small meeting chamber.

"All those in favor of attack, raise your hand," Frederick directed. His eyes roved across the men assembled before him as he counted. "I believe the number to be eight.

Including myself, it's nine. With a council of fourteen, there is no need to vote in opposition."

He stood, causing the scientists and engineers in the room to jump. "I will personally fly a düsenjäger and lead the attack. We will draw first blood in our renewed conflict with the Americans. Then, we will thaw the entire Wehrmacht and truly avenge our ancestors."

They cheered his theatrics and he smiled. The blackness that had settled over his heart since Greta's suicide would finally have an outlet. He would make the Americans suffer as he had been forced to suffer.

INTERLUDE

03 July 2025
Aokigahara, Mount Fuji, Japan

Timbak walked amongst the giant cypress and hemlock. Their branches effectively blocked the sun from penetrating to the forest floor, creating a deep gloom that made him wonder why so many of the Terrans commit suicide here at a higher rate than anywhere else on their planet. He particularly enjoyed the feeling of depression and sadness; it reminded him of home.

He'd been stuck on this miserable planet for too long and petitioned, unsuccessfully, for his retrieval. The High Council refused his request, citing his placement amongst the Reich as a perfect place to sew discontent and establish the conditions for their return.

Timbak had thought the time was ripe for the return at the conclusion of the Second World War. Most Terran nations were weakened and weary of war; the others would have easily been suppressed. Once again, the Council refused, causing him to think it was a problem with their leadership, *not* the fleet's ability to fight.

The sounds of a couple talking around the next bend made him pause in his journey. He could kill them easily if it came to it, but there was always the chance that they weren't alone and part of a larger group that would miss them, causing a search for their bodies—and potentially complicating his meeting.

It was best to let them live, he decided. They weren't worth the problems, so he continued. Rounding the bend, he saw two of the small people, the male with his hand under the female's shirt. They noticed him immediately and turned away from the path, staring into the trees as he passed, ignoring him. The sting of embarrassment was almost palpable. He wondered how the Japanese had devolved into such a shy race.

Terra had been seeded with the same stock as a hundred other planets across the solar system. The diversity that developed here was truly remarkable, not occurring anywhere else that he knew of. Not only physically, but socially and spiritually as well.

This was the only planet in the known universe where humans believed that a higher power rewarded or punished them for their actions. Throughout their history, they'd slaughtered themselves by the billions for the sake of those ideologies—surely the stock was flawed. Timbak blamed the earlier generations of scientists for involving themselves too much here, allowing themselves to be seen instead of simply observing.

A light began to blink on his retinal overlay, indicating that he was close to his destination. He turned and broke through the brush beside the path, hoping the Japanese couple were too embarrassed at having been caught fooling around to follow his trail. Another three hundred meters and he arrived at the predesignated meeting place.

"Good morning, Timbak," a fleet officer he'd never seen before stated when he emerged from the trees into the small clearing.

"I don't know what you think is so good about it," he replied.

"Is this forest not beautiful to you? Can you not feel the power?"

"I can feel it. I've been on this planet, living amongst the Terrans, for eighty-two years. I'm sick of it."

The officer glanced down at his lapel and then back at Timbak. "I wondered if my rank had fallen off, *Science Officer* Timbak. It hasn't. You've been an invaluable asset for the fleet, advancing our goals without allowing them to develop planet-killing weapons, however, don't forget your place."

The man's arrogance made the Aryan want to punch him. Maybe if he did that, he'd have a chance at leaving this planet.

"I'm sorry, *sir*," Timbak emphasized the honorific. "I meant no disrespect. I'm simply ready for the High Council to grant my appeals to return home."

"Soon, Timbak," the admiral assured him. "The experiment here is complete. We are sending forces to cleanse Terra for our use. The invasion fleet is large, but as you know, it is much easier to destroy a weakened enemy than a healthy one. The American military is formidable and focused. It has shown the capacity to garner support from other nations and provide unity of effort through leadership. Therefore, it is imperative that you convince your hosts to begin the war against them. With the Americans distracted and embroiled in a fight of their own, they will not notice problems elsewhere until it is too late."

Timbak smiled broadly. It was the first time he hadn't faked it in years, possibly decades. "The Americans are greatly diminished on the global stage from what they were when I first came to Terra," he stated. "The Reich launched their attack vessels a week ago. They are waking their troops as we speak. I gave them enough information to develop weapons and reduced-capacity aerial fighters—although they are much more capable than the jet planes of their enemies. This will be a blood-letting unlike any in Terran history."

"Good. The High Council wants this planet cleansed in a matter of weeks," the admiral replied. "And Timbak?"

"Yes, sir?"

"Your loyalty to the Council will not be forgotten."

"Thank you, sir."

PART 2: PRESENT DAY

TEN

04 July 2025
Near Malmstrom Air Force Base, Montana

"*Two minutes!*"

Oberleutnant Gregory Wagner felt the transport plane begin to slow and his stomach dropped. He and his men had rehearsed several simulated jumps from harnesses inside a hangar at Argus Base, but before today, he'd never been airborne. They'd been given drugs to combat the potential for sickness. The Luftwaffe didn't want their precious aircraft getting dirty.

"*One minute!*" the transport crew chief shouted into the headset he wore, which was transmitted into an earpiece in the leutnant's helmet. "*Opening doors now.*"

The transport slowed even more as a set of cargo doors cracked open in front of Gregory. The fallschirmjäger platoon commander ordered his men to stand up and then hook their static line to the long cable running the length of the transport's body.

"*The navigator just said the base is alerted to our presence. You must go as soon as I say.*"

"I understand, Feldwebel," Gregory replied woodenly. As far as German intelligence knew, there was a half squadron of older F-15 fighters, split between their target and a base in North Dakota. The other base was the objective of an entire company of fallschirmjägers, so they shouldn't run afoul of the American jets. The Americans below also had an advanced Phalanx system that engineers assured the pilots and paratroopers couldn't acquire them if the transport dropped the shroud directly over the base long enough to accomplish the jump.

The cargo doors continued to widen and he gripped the static line tightly in his right hand. Gregory wondered if his brother, Matthias, felt the same fear as he did now. He was going ashore somewhere on the United States' eastern shore while Gregory's platoon was tasked with securing the two nuclear launch facilities near the Air Force base.

He stared blankly through the open door of the transport at the early morning landscape below. It was a dun-colored mass of irregular shapes delineating property boundaries, spotted with the occasional patch of green. He'd studied his target along with the information provided by the intelligence section for more than a week, memorizing details in the event that he lost his map—although he wasn't quite sure what good the additional info they'd chosen would do.

The intelligence section had given him a geography lesson rolled up with economics and a brief highlight of the major events in Montana's history, including when the Luftwaffe visited the Air Force base in 1967 to test their ability to interfere with missile launch controls.

The temperatures of Montana averaged thirty degrees Celsius in July. The economy was dependent upon agriculture and tourism from the two most prominent outdoor exercise locations in the nation. Yellowstone National Park and Glacier National Park encompassed thousands of kilometers, which would make becoming stranded there a death sentence.

Interestingly, the Malmstrom Air Force Base and the Great Falls area was one of the most heavily visited sites by UFOs and led the nation in UFO sightings. However, Gregory knew from discussing with the Luftwaffe intelligence and operations personnel that Luftwaffe düsenjägers had only visited a handful of times. He wondered whether those other sightings were the legitimate sighting of another group or if they were some type of mass hysteria, passed along from generation to generation.

"Fifteen seconds!"

Gregory gripped the static line tightly and stepped forward to the line painted on the floor. It was time to accomplish his mission. There was no more time for contemplating the silly and unhelpful facts that the intelligence section gave him about the area.

"Go, fallschirmjägers. Good luck!"

Gregory stepped into oblivion.

The wind at the low altitude the transport flew buffeted him sideways the moment he exited the aircraft. There was a brief sensation of weightlessness and then he was jerked violently backward as the static line ripped the parachute from the backpack, causing him to bite his tongue. He pissed himself slightly as the harness ground into his crotch and pressed into his stomach, ejecting the fluid that had built up in his bladder during the ten hour flight from Argus Base.

He was disoriented, swinging wildly one way, then the opposite direction like a pendulum. The lessons from a few weeks ago—years ago in reality—came back to him. He needed to grip the risers on the opposite side of the direction he swung to collapse the chute slightly and control the oscillation. He'd likely need to do it a few times, switching sides to counter the direction of the swing, to get his descent under control.

Gregory's back muscles strained in protest at being used to lift his bodyweight on the riser after sitting in the cramped transport for so long. He swung toward the left, so he pulled on the right side and then reversed it as the oscillation carried him back toward the right. He only needed to correct his fall the two times before the chute filled with air completely and his body stopped the unnatural pendulum swing.

Then he was floating in the air on the surplus US Army parachute. Miles to the west, the lights of the main Air Force base illuminated the sky and tracer rounds arced skyward toward the transport as it continued its slow flight while the remainder of the paratroopers jumped.

A massive fireball above detailed the destruction of the transport. Of course they all knew that it was a possibility, but their intelligence section had told them that the anti-aircraft systems wouldn't be able to acquire, track and fire in the two or three minutes that the shroud would be down. Either the American weaponry was more advanced than the German intelligence understood or they were very lucky—neither of which bode well for the paratroopers floating down to the earth.

To the west, Gregory could barely discern the four düsenjägers that had escorted them from Argus Base disengage from their primary mission of strafing the runway and hangars. They zipped rapidly toward the anti-aircraft gun and fired their cannons into the site repeatedly. One of them exploded, hit by the Phalanx before the others destroyed the system. Then they returned to the airfield to finalize the destruction of the base's fighter capability.

You're late, Luftwaffe, Gregory thought bitterly as he looked away. Without the transport, the fallschirmjägers were stuck until they could find a different transport to return to base or somehow fight their way to the coast thousands of kilometers away. *Possibly into Canada first and then to the coast.* The idea was daunting.

Below him, he could see the searchlights on the target facility sweeping the ground rapidly. They'd been alerted to the attack, but they hadn't been told that the threat was descending from above. He pulled his riser to angle closer toward the launch control facility.

He'd established a rally point five hundred meters to the east of the facility prior to leaving Argus. In the darkness, there was no way of knowing whether his men were converging on the rally point or if they were floating off somewhere else. The dun scrub brush loomed and he pressed his feet and knees together like he'd been taught, bent his knees and stared straight ahead to avoid the human tendency to reach for the ground.

Gregory's feet slammed into the earth at different heights as his left foot landed on a rock. Pain shot through his leg, up his spine and into his brain. He collapsed to the side and clutched his knee so he could see his ankle. It throbbed in time with his heartbeat, but he couldn't see the flesh through the heavy, black boots he wore…allegedly for protection against ankle injuries.

He pulled the release on his parachute harness to avoid getting dragged by the wind and shrugged painfully out of the harness. Gregory knew his ankle was broken. Somehow, he'd landed incorrectly and had paid the price. Nearby, he saw the platoon medic touch down and execute a perfect parachute landing fall. First the balls of the medic's feet hit the ground, then he twisted to the side and let gravity take him as the side of his calf impacted against the ground, next the thigh and buttocks, finally, his back hit and he allowed his legs to lift into the air to alleviate the force of the impact. Textbook.

Oberleutnant Wagner waved at the medic, who rushed over to his lieutenant and knelt beside him. "It is broken," Gregory muttered, pointing angrily at his ankle.

"Can you put pressure on it?"

"No."

The medic unzipped his pouch and brought out a brown vial. "This is the regeneration serum," he stated. "The same that you were given a few days before being frozen."

"This will mend my ankle?"

"In time. Give me your arm."

Gregory did as directed and the medic inserted a needle into the vial, then tapped out the bubbles before plunging it into the vein in the crook of his arm. An exhilarating rush of energy hit his brain within seconds as the serum spread through his body.

"I'll tape a brace around your ankle and you'll have to endure the pain until the bones mend."

"That's fine. Just get me patched up enough to continue the mission."

The medic unfolded a U-shaped piece of rigid plastic and placed it under Gregory's foot. He winced at the pressure as the plastic was forced over his ankle.

"What is your name?" the lieutenant asked.

"Schütze Markel, Oberleutnant," he replied, producing a giant roll of two-inch wide tape, which he used to secure the plastic around Gregory's ankle. Then he proceeded to wrap multiple layers to immobilize movement in the ankle as much as possible.

"You will need a cane or a crutch for the next several hours. The serum is already working to repair the damage, but it doesn't happen instantly, Oberleutnant."

"Thank you, Markel," Gregory grimaced.

"Oberleutnant? Is that you?" a new voice called from the lightening darkness.

"Feldwebel Anders? You made it from the transport!"

"Yes, sir," the platoon feldwebel replied, materializing beside the two paratroopers. "Are you injured?"

"I will be fine," Gregory replied. "Schütze Markel has given me a treatment and wrapped my ankle."

"Can you walk?"

"I'm fine," Gregory repeated forcefully. "Bring the men to my location and we'll prepare to move into the attack position."

"Our transport was destroyed."

"That is a problem we'll address after we complete our mission, Feldwebel."

"Understood, sir. I'll gather the men that survived the jump."

He disappeared once more and harsh whispered orders drifted out of the night. They would continue their mission and then determine a course of action for their exfiltration.

*****

04 July 2025
30 miles off the coast of Delaware, United States

Oberleutnant Fischer's insides felt as if they would empty onto the deck at any moment. The Luftwaffe pilots and soldiers of the Heer were not needed for the journey from Antarctica, so they'd been shoved below decks as the Kriegsmarine sailors managed the transport ships.

The tilt and roll of the ship combined with the reverberation of the shrouding device to make him queasy. Added to that was the god-awful heat of the American coastline. Why Generalfeldmarschall Mueller chose July to attack was beyond him. The summers in North America were some of the worst in the world, the heat drove the Americans mad, inciting them to invade other countries. The desire for a more hospitable climate is partly why they destroyed the German way of life in the previous war before the relocation to Argus Base.

The young lieutenant went over the mission in his mind. From here, the Luftwaffe would divide into five battle groups to attack multiple targets. The two smaller groups with only fifty düsenjägers each would attack the airfields at Dover Air Force Base in Delaware and Andrews Air Force Base in Maryland. The large cargo planes stationed there were capable of moving thousands of troops and equipment into the fight against the Heer, so their job was to destroy them on the ground.

The next group was larger, with two hundred of the flying discs assigned to it. They were responsible for wreaking havoc amongst the American government by destroying buildings in and around Washington, DC. Cutting off the head of the snake wouldn't kill the beast, but it would cause panic and a disjointed response.

Finally, the two largest fighter groups would attack the naval bases in Virginia Beach and Norfolk. Intelligence said there were currently three aircraft carriers in port at Norfolk, so sinking them, along with their fighter planes and destroying the planes on the ground were paramount to the success of the initial invasion. His squadron, Vengeance Squadron, would participate in the Washington, DC attack ahead of the amphibious landing forces.

"You know, they say the Americans have anti-aircraft missiles that will shoot down all of your precious düsenjägers, Berndt," a familiar voice interrupted his misery.

Fischer looked up to see his friend, Matthias Wagner. "*Ugh*," he groaned. "And their panzers will litter the sand with the bodies of the Heer. You won't even make it off the landing craft before you are ground up and fed to the farms."

Matthias gripped his forearm. "Good luck today, brother."

"Thank you. Good luck to you and your men also." Fischer patted the vacant space beside him on the bunk. Once Matthias had settled beside him, he continued, "I mean that. Good luck. You have a much harder mission than I do."

Wagner shrugged. "If I'd tried harder on my aptitude tests, then maybe I could have qualified for pilot training also. But, there were so many girls who required bedding. It was my solemn duty to the Reich to be with as many of them as I could."

They shared a laugh that petered out after a moment. The Reich's young men were encouraged to copulate as often as possible with the women before they were frozen. No one, not even the Aryan, knew if the male reproductive system survived the massive testosterone flood when they were injected with the regeneration serum and then put to sleep with a cocktail of drugs.

"What do you think they'll be like, Berndt?"

"Who, the women?" Fischer asked, confused.

"No, not the women. The *men*. The people who will fight. Are they as cruel and heartless as the professors say they are?"

"Yes," Berndt replied immediately. "They destroyed Germany. Our ancestors were simply trying to secure a better way of life for themselves and the Americans partnered with the Slavs to destroy us. They bombed our cities, murdered our children, and raped our grandmothers—they even hunted the Reich to the ends of the earth and used nuclear weapons to wipe out our second base. What kind of people do that?"

Matthias nodded his head. "What is the term when one group of people tries to rid the world of another?"

"Genocide," Berndt replied coldly. "The Americans are murdering bastards that have no clue we're coming for them. They will regret their actions against the Fatherland."

"What do we do with their women and children?"

"It's—" Fischer paused. "I'm not sure, Matthias."

"I'll tell you what you do, oberleutnant," an unfamiliar voice boomed across their small space.

Neither of the men knew who the man who'd spoken was, but his braided shoulder epaulet indicated that he was a light infantry major. They stood rapidly and saluted.

"The American women and children are to be bypassed to save ammunition. Even those who wear the uniform are assigned to medical and supply roles. It is known through our research that they pose no threat to an invading army; their women are known to be weak and often do whatever their males tell them to do. However, if Generalfeldmarschall Mueller chooses to become an occupying army, then we may have more problems with them that require a permanent solution."

"Will we occupy the continent?" Matthias asked.

Fischer flexed his wrist, slapping his partner on the leg. *Why is he asking so many questions today?*

"It's fine, oberleutnant," the major said, obviously noticing Berndt's movement. "It will be decided in the future. We also have a score to settle with the Slavs, but for now, the entirety of the Wehrmacht is focused on defeating the Americans. We'll make quick work of their inferior military and be back on the boats by September."

"And from there, Major?" Matthias pressed. A small crowd had gathered around Berndt's bunk space as men pressed close to hear what the senior officer had to say.

"Once the Americans are defeated, we may attack the Russians or we may return to the Fatherland as victors. It is unknown at this time, but I assure you, Mueller is a brilliant tactician and won't overextend the Wehrmacht. He was handpicked for the rescue of the Führer in 1945 and was one of the architects of our way of life in Argus Base. We are fortunate to have such a great man as our leader."

"Yes, sir. We are very fortunate," Berndt answered woodenly. He'd never met the man or even heard him speak, but he'd heard from a few men born in earlier generations that the generalfeldmarschall was a motivating speaker. As he thought about the demons he was about to face in combat, he hoped that Mueller was more than a good public speaker. He had to be like the great Erwin Rommel—better than him in fact. Rommel had never sent his men into the heart of American the stronghold.

It would take every ounce of strength and determination to win this fight. The Reich was capable, but they had to stay focused. *He* had to stay focused and survive his first mission.

The claxon directly overhead began to blare and a red strobe light sprang to life, bathing the small crowd in garish shadows. The transport speakers crackled and then the announcement followed, "**Attention, all Luftwaffe pilots. Report to your düsenjäger for immediate launch. This is not a drill. Revenge is at hand. Report to your düsenjäger for immediate launch.**"

Berndt hugged his friend quickly, wondering if it would be the last time he saw the man, then he picked up his helmet and jogged toward the düsen bay. Men lined the corridors, cheering the pilots onward. They'd move to their landing transports soon enough, but for now, they would encourage the Luftwaffe.

In the bay, male and female technicians scrambled to make last-minute adjustments to the fighters. Row upon row of düsenjägers sat ready for their pilots. The circular craft were stored in an upright position to maximize the amount of space available on the cargo ship. Berndt's heart swelled with pride at the knowledge that he'd be one of the first Germans to attack.

He weaved between rows until he made it to the fifth row where the Vengeance Squadron's fighters were suspended. His was the eighteenth from the end. When he stepped in front of Düsenjäger 519, he pushed the helmet down over his ears and shook his head slightly to seat it firmly on the crown of his head. A technician appeared and handed him two cyanide pills and a box of ammunition for his pistol, which he dropped into the pocket on his pant leg.

A different technician held a foldable four-meter ladder for him beside his fighter, which he climbed cautiously to the cockpit. Berndt gripped the pilot-assist handle and swung down into the craft, then situated his back against the seat to secure the harness across his chest. He'd have his legs in the air above his head until he launched, but he'd spent months training in the massive underground hangers of Argus Base, so mentally, he was prepared for it.

However, as it turned out, what felt like only a couple of weeks to him had been six years. He'd been frozen for a quarter of the time his body had been on the earth. There was a slight stiffness in his joints that hadn't subsided in the week since he'd awoke aboard the cargo ship, but he was confident that it would go away with time.

He plugged a cable into his helmet that would allow him to speak to the members of his squadron and began the startup procedure. A yellowed, handwritten checklist was affixed beside the display and he smiled. He'd written those notes before he was frozen and used them during his simulator training. Somehow, one of the technicians had found it in his post-thaw folder and placed it inside his cockpit.

Berndt followed the list down to the radio check and called in, "This is Oberleutnant Fischer, call sign Vengeance Nineteen."

"Düsenjäger Command acknowledges your radio check, Vengeance Nineteen. Continue through your startup procedures. Do not activate your düsen's engines until your squadron commander orders. Understood?"

"Understood," he replied and continued following his written instructions.

He counted seventy check-ins over the radio until the commander came on and told the Vengeance Squadron to initiate engine start. He punched the button and the craft roared to life around him, vibrating slightly against the retaining clasps.

Then out of his periphery, he saw the other düsenjägers being released one by one, beginning at the fighters nearest the opening. When his turn came, the retaining clasp opened and his craft hovered midair. Using the display screen, he maneuvered away from the düsen behind him and then rotated so he was horizontal.

The cargo hold opening loomed brightly, growing larger as he eased the fighter toward the open sky. A ripple of excitement tingled his skin. Berndt had never flown outside of the hangars in Argus Base.

Once he was beyond the opening, the sun shone brightly above him and the wide expanse of the sky beckoned him to explore for the briefest of moments. Then he fell into formation and the shadows of thousands of düsenjägers blotted out the heavens above.

*****

04 July 2025
Ronald Reagan Washington National Airport, Washington, DC

"Excuse me," Gloria called to the baggage attendant, who glanced her way and then scurried behind a door as if he hadn't seen her. "*Hmpf*," she grumbled and pulled her suitcase the rest of the way to the counter.

She'd had a hell of a trip on the Metro to make it to the airport after a nasty fight with James. He was furious that she'd been told the previous evening that she'd be going to Europe today, on Independence Day, traveling over the three-day weekend for a conference with the Belgian government, which had announced their desire to permanently close the Henri-Chapelle American Cemetery on Wednesday. He was so mad that he went into the office today, a federal holiday, refusing to say much more than, "I love you," and, "See you next week."

Gloria didn't like it any better than he did. She felt like shit, already more than twenty-five pounds heavier than she was at the beginning of her pregnancy, and she had to wear a uniform top that made her look like she was auditioning for a job at the circus—as the tent. It wasn't ideal for her to travel across the Atlantic, but at the end of the day, she was a soldier, and she was currently the US Government's most experienced military historian. So, it was off to Europe for a few days.

She checked herself in at the airline kiosk and gladly handed over her suitcase to the attendant, who weighed it and then threw it onto a conveyor belt behind her. "Oh! Be careful, my uniform…"

"Ma'am, that bag is gonna go through a whole lot worse down with the baggage handlers," the attendant sighed. "Do you need me to stop the belt so you can repack your bag?"

"I—ah, no," she answered. Her uniform would get wrinkled anywhere she put it inside the suitcase, so she'd just have to do the old shower steam in the bathroom trick once she checked in to her hotel in Brussels. "Thank you, though."

"Mmm hmm, sure. Gate thirty-six," the airline attendant said, handing Gloria her boarding pass. "Security is off to my right, your left."

She took the tickets and thanked the attendant once more. She negotiated security quickly until she went through the scanner. The male TSA agent told her that she'd been selected for a random screening. She had to wait until a female screener finished with another passenger, which took much longer than anticipated.

After a few nervous remarks about the size of her stomach, Gloria got patted down and was allowed to pass through the security area to collect her purse and carryon. Then she made her way through the terminal toward her gate.

As she walked along, several large shapes darted past the windows on the runway side to her right. *What was—*

She didn't finish her thought because the two planes immediately outside the window exploded. Pieces of shrapnel shattered the glass, literally scaring the piss out of her since the baby pressed against her bladder.

Miraculously, she was uninjured by the flying debris, but people were already beginning to panic and she needed to get out of the walkway. She glanced around, assessing her options rapidly, making the decision to move to the far side of the railing, away from the windows and hopefully far enough out of the way that she wouldn't get trampled. Getting crushed under the feet of a thousand panicked travelers wasn't high on her list of priorities for the day.

She turned to move and then cried out in pain, clutching at her lower back. She'd twisted it awkwardly when she turned away from the glass. "Dammit," she cursed and hobbled to the railing to get out of the way.

Travelers streamed steadily past her location, surprisingly calm as the minutes stretched by. Gloria began to relax, stretching her back as best she could with her growing stomach. Surely her mind had played tricks on her with the objects speeding by before the explosion. It was probably birds. There were perfectly mundane explanations as to why the planes blew up, like a spark during refueling or the catastrophic failure of a part in the engine.

She even began to chuckle at her own wariness. She and James worked too much, they needed to take a break from planning for the return of whomever had attacked Florida five years ago. Someone else could manage it for a few weeks while they soaked up the sun in the Caribbean and drank piña coladas. Well, *virgin* piña coladas anyway.

The terminal was buzzing with passengers talking excitedly about the explosions and Gloria decided it was time for her to make her way to the gate. She'd take her directions from the airport personnel there.

Then the alarm bells began to blare across the terminal and red strobe lights set into the ceiling flashed in warning.

Gloria instinctively looked to the broken windows. Beyond the immediate wreckage and firefighting crews, a large, fat airliner was on final approach. Two saucer-shaped objects appeared behind it, zipping in from somewhere beyond her line of sight. They hovered perfectly still behind the jet. Small puffs of smoke came from each of the saucers and Gloria realized they were shooting.

A massive fireball engulfed the back of the plane. For one, awful second, Gloria thought they would continue their approach and land. Then the nose of the airliner pitched forward, causing the fuselage to tear apart midair. They were close enough that she could see individual people flying through the air, their bodies still traveling at the speed the plane had been going before the explosion.

They were under attack.

Screams of panic reverberated across the terminal and Gloria pressed against the railing near a small kiosk selling cell phone accessories. The crowd sped by her, crushing slower people and the elderly underfoot. Over the heads of the crowd, she saw four massive, white cargo planes lined up to land on the runway, impossibly close to one another. They hadn't been there a few seconds ago.

The cargo planes passed below her line of sight as more of them appeared on the horizon. They were far away, somewhere over the city, but long lines of parachutes appeared behind them as they disgorged their paratroopers for the rapid attack. She'd studied the airborne operations of World War Two; the key to a successful parachute drop, besides accuracy, was overwhelming numbers that could eliminate local resistance piecemeal.

The enemy certainly had the overwhelming numbers on their side.

Across the river, a large, fiery cloud rose skyward as the US Capitol building, standing above all at the highest point in the city, was incinerated. Multiple explosions followed closely on the heels of the first.

Gloria searched for a way out of the airport before the soldiers from the landing cargo planes made their way inside the building to begin their indiscriminate killings. Nothing presented itself immediately, but the stream of people fleeing had slowed down, so she pushed away from the railing painfully, ignoring the hitch in her step from her twisted back.

She pushed her way through the crowd of people trying to make it to the Metro and went down to baggage claim. It was a madhouse as well; however, most of the passengers seemed content to wait inside the building. She knew better and did her best to slip in between the press of bodies, groaning in pain as she was jostled, bumped, and prodded. At some point, her carryon fell from her shoulder. She left it.

Finally, she emerged through the doors into the passenger pick up area. There weren't any taxis waiting, they'd already left. Without thinking, she turned toward the city and started walking. She knew from her years in the city that the Mount Vernon Trail, a wide, paved jogging and bicycling trail, picked up right outside the airport.

If she was lucky, she could get a cab somewhere along the trail. If not, thank God she wore tennis shoes for traveling; it was six miles to the safety of her home in Dupont Circle.

*****

04 July 2025
Andrews Air Force Base, Maryland

"Sir, we're detecting multiple unknown entities at twelve miles out. They're moving at a sustained rate of Mach 4!"

Colonel Nguyen turned to the White House Communications liaison officer, who was already making the call to the Secret Service. He looked over to the row of radio operators and shouted, "Airman, alert the air defense batteries in Washington." He jabbed a finger at a new female airman he hadn't gotten the opportunity to talk with yet. "You. Yeah, you. Get me General Wilson, now!"

"He's at a retirement ceremony, sir," the radio tech replied.

"Then get General Beckinsworth," the colonel growled.

"Roger, sir."

"Sir! The National Guard unit in DC has been alerted," the first airman called out. "Reports of an attack at Reagan National."

"Status?" Nguyen demanded of the radar operator.

"Fast-movers are now five miles from DC."

"Too fast…" the officer muttered. "Too damn fast. Did you get General Beckinsworth?"

"No one is answering in her office, sir," the woman replied.

"Fuck it," Nguyen said. "Lieutenant Healy, scramble the Raptors."

"Yes, sir," the lieutenant replied and picked up a phone.

Nguyen leaned heavily against the desktop. He'd just given the order to launch armed fighter jets over the nation's capital. If he was wrong, then his career was over. If he wasn't, then maybe he gave people a fighting chance.

"Fast movers are one mile from the White House," the radar tech shouted.

"Satellite, what do you see?"

"Nothing, sir. They're moving too fast to register more than a streak on camera. Given the refresh rate—"

Nguyen stopped listening. He didn't care about satellite image refresh rates. The giant screens on the walls showed hundreds of illuminated blips streaking across the National Capitol Region at impossibly fast rates. They had to have been missiles; there was no way an aircraft could move that fast at low altitude.

Phones began ringing on every desk in the command center and his men did their best to answer them, but it was too much. There were too many requests for information coming in at the same time.

"Sir! Explosions reported in DC," someone shouted from several rows behind him. Nearly simultaneously, the *thumping* sound of nearby explosions echoed through the hardened walls of the command center.

"Goddammit, Satellite. Show me what you've got!" the colonel ordered.

The radar picture changed to an overhead view of Washington, DC. At the far southeast of the image, several blurred lines indicated the fast movers.

"Sir! We've lost all four of the Raptors on the ground," Lieutenant Healy stated. "They didn't even make it into the air."

The lieutenant's words reached Colonel Nguyen's brain, but he failed to comprehend what was said. Instead, he recoiled in shock at the images displayed on the wall in front of him.

The satellite's refresh rate was only ten seconds, but each subsequent refresh showed more columns of fire and plumes of smoke rising into the air above the capitol.

"The White House... It's gone," he mumbled.

Colonel Nguyen was dimly aware of a *whooshing* sound before the room around him exploded.

ELEVEN

04 July 2025
Crystal City, Arlington, Virginia

"Holy shit!" James exclaimed as he shoved his chair backward from the desk.

"What was that?" Major Leeland demanded, emerging from his office for the first time that James could remember. Since he'd been assigned to the Joint North American Defense Branch in April, the rotund officer sat in his office playing solitaire on the computer all day. The assignment of a major to head the branch, two ranks below the required colonel, had been the final nail in the coffin by the Pentagon leadership.

"There was an explosion on the other side of the river!" he shouted. "It's over near where the Independence Day concerts are set up."

"An explosion? What kind of—"

The horizon lit up with more gouts of flame as several explosions occurred simultaneously near Capitol Hill.

"That was the Capitol," James muttered. "We're under attack. We need to initiate the North American Defense action plan."

"Now hold on, James. I'm not about to lose my career by activating all of those units and starting a panic. That could have been a gas line explosion or…or anything."

The windows in their tenth floor office space rattled as the shockwaves from the blasts across the Potomac hit them. More explosions erupted across James' field of view through the windows and fat, white cargo planes appeared. They began disgorging hundreds of paratroopers, directly over the city.

Some type of jet sped along the river, faster than his eyes could make out. A few seconds later massive explosions nearby told him that the Pentagon probably got hit. He said a quick prayer for Gloria and their unborn child at the airport. James had a moment of hope that her plane had already left, but she wasn't scheduled to leave for another couple of hours.

He whirled on the piece of shit that the Pentagon assignment officers had stuck him with. "Don't you get it?" James shouted. "This branch was designed specifically for this reason. We can go around all of that bureaucracy. You won't lose your job if you're acting in response to an attack. There are Air Force units twelve minutes away that are on the tarmac, ready to go. They just need to know what's happening and they'll get airborne."

"This is... I can't make those decisions," Tom Leeland wailed. "I lied about my experience. I never left the FOB when I was in Afghanistan. I was supposed to come over here and wait it out until my mandatory retirement date. I'm not—"

James didn't wait to hear what the blubbering officer would say. He rushed into the communications room and jammed his common access card into the reader on a laptop. Two years ago, he'd had a full staff of hard-working individuals; they were all gone now. He was the last civilian, ensuring everything transitioned smoothly over to the Pentagon Joint Operations Center, as the branch shut down due to budget constraints.

He sent a rapid "all hands" message over the network detailing the devastation that he'd seen outside his window. He hadn't seen who or what attacked them, but he knew. Gloria had told him all those years ago what to expect. The Nazis were back.

The first response was from the commander of Naval Air Forces, Atlantic. It was a simple, one-word response. **"Acknowledged."**

He stared at the computer screen, trying to determine what that meant. Was the Navy going to get their planes in the air or were they dismissing his instructions like every other branch of government had dismissed the Joint North American Defense Branch after it became marginalized by the new administration?

James's body lifted into the air as the deafening sound of an explosion and waves of heat passed over him. He was thrown backward over the desk behind him into the wall. He knew instantly that something wasn't right as pain flooded his system. His back. Something was wrong with his back.

Above him, the bright white emergency strobe lights flashed wildly, disorienting him. Dark, oily smoke already clawed its way along the ceiling tile looking for an escape. James tried to push himself up, but the pain in his back was beyond excruciating. *Am I crippled?* he wondered.

Groggily, he lifted his head off the floor to look at his feet. Beyond his shoes, he saw several small fires, the lacquered wood desks and padded cubicle walls aflame. Broken glass littered the floor like confetti in Times Square on New Year's Eve. The world was shrouded in a haze and the ringing in his ears was overwhelming.

He flexed both ankles and wiggled his toes. He wasn't crippled, but his back was certainly injured. James ran through a quick self-assessment, using his hands to feel underneath his spine and around his head. Miraculously, he wasn't trapped under a large piece of furniture or bleeding heavily from any injuries. He knew he had to get out of the burning building so he tried to sit up again.

The pain exploded across his body. He'd wrenched his back horribly when he hit the wall. It was an injury, but not a life-threatening one. Staying inside the tower was life threatening; he had to leave. He tried to push himself up a third time and again, waves of pain passed through his body, threatening to make him pass out. He tried to focus on the need to escape, but his body wouldn't obey his commands.

Slowly, he rolled onto his stomach and began clawing his way toward the exit. As long as he kept his lower back generally straight, he was able to move, but doing so necessitated that he not use his legs. Inch by agonizing inch, James pulled himself along the floor.

By the time he was halfway across the communications room his hands were bleeding from the shards of glass that covered the floor. He turned his head to examine the path ahead. Glass glittered in the light of the fires. He would be cut to ribbons by the time he made it through the room.

He had to clear the way. A quick scan of the surrounding area gave him an idea and he grabbed a dangling keyboard, pulling the cord free of the computer. Using the keyboard, he swept the glass out of the way in front of him, advanced and then swept more of the glass away before crawling forward again.

He had no idea what he'd do when he finally reached the stairwell.

"We'll figure that out when we get there," he groaned.

"Hello! Help me!" Major Leeland shouted weakly from the common area of the branch office.

James pulled himself another few feet, angling toward the sound of the major's whimpers. A mangled pile of cubicle dividers, chairs and various other office equipment lay jumbled against the structural wall. A pale, fleshy hand sticking through the mess moved weakly.

"Tom? Tom, are you in there?" James croaked.

"Here," he whispered breathlessly.

"Hold on. I'll see if I can get you out."

James pulled at the pile, dislodging parts where he could. Every movement was agony. He pulled at the leg of a small coffee table, causing a telephone to fall from above and hit him in the head. He eyed the mass of furniture above him dubiously and continued on, finding a foot that he used as a point of reference to pull himself along until he came to Leeland.

It wasn't good. Dried blood ran in streaks from the officer's ears and his nose was partially sheared off, dangling by a thin piece of flesh.

"Tom, can you hear me?"

Leeland's head lolled to the side, rolls of fat in his neck supporting its weight without effort. He blinked in confusion at James, but made no further attempt to speak.

"Can you move? The building is on fire."

James pulled ineffectively at the bigger man's leg. It was too much. He couldn't gain any type of leverage in his own injured state.

"I need you to try to move, Tom," he ordered calmly.

Leeland blinked at him and then flopped an arm to his stomach, where it fell against something with a dull *thud*. James adjusted his angle to see what he was working with, cursing his back for not allowing him to lift his head higher than a few inches.

Finally, he saw it. The leg of a chair protruded through Tom's abdomen. He'd been impaled through the lower back and the blunt, metal leg emerged from just above his pelvis. There was a surprisingly small amount of blood around the exit point.

That may be worse, James thought. The injury would still bleed. If it wasn't coming out, then it was building up inside his abdominal cavity. If the chair leg perforated his stomach or his intestines, all that fluid would seep into Tom and poison him before help could arrive.

James reached up and shook the chair leg gently. Another leg above them in the jumble of office equipment moved in time with his actions. The leg sticking through Tom was still attached to the seat of the chair. Even if he could move Tom's bulk, the pile would likely collapse on top of them with the shift of an entire chair.

There was nothing James could do for his boss. "I have to go get help, Tom. I can't do this alone."

The man's eyes glittered, reflecting the light of the fires in the office. He mouthed something, but only gurgling sounds emerged.

James pushed himself backward, exiting the pile and leaving Tom to his fate. It was a tough decision. He hadn't liked the man, but leaving him to die a horribly painful and lonely death wasn't right. If his current injuries didn't kill him, Major Leeland would be roasted alive or crushed when the floors collapsed.

The number of fires burning across the city would overwhelm EMS. Even if James made it to safety himself, it was unlikely that anyone would go into the burning building. The best thing that could happen to Tom would be for him to pass out from the carbon monoxide and other toxic fumes produced in the fire, and then never wake up.

The dense layer of smoke creeping along the ceiling flowed out through the broken office windows. It had deepened to a dark, charcoal grey over the course of James' failed rescue attempt and the flashing strobe lights confused him further. If he hadn't worked in the same office for over four years, he easily could have crawled the wrong way. As it was, though, he knew that the exit to the hallway was only about ten more feet and the stairwell was six feet to the left. Then the real challenge would begin.

The crawl to the stairwell took an insufferably long time. When he got there, another challenge presented itself. The push bar to open the stairwell door was at waist-height. Even using the keyboard as an extension, he couldn't quite reach it. He tried once again to get his legs under him, but it wouldn't work. His back was completely locked up.

James looked around the hallway for anything he could use. Nothing. It was your standard Department of Defense office building with no frills in the common areas.

"What the fuck!" he screamed in frustration. All that he'd been through had been for nothing. He was stuck in the goddamned hallway.

An idea came to him and he maneuvered his body around until his feet were near the door. He turned over painfully onto his back and lifted his leg a few inches until he could grab his pants leg. James pulled his leg up, ignoring the grating sound in his back, and put his foot against the push bar. Then, he pushed his body forward and the bar depressed, allowing the door to swing into the stairwell.

His foot fell and an excruciating pain riddled his body, worse than anything he'd felt yet. The pain in his lower body ceased. He lay there for a moment as the pain elsewhere went from the massive spike he'd experienced to a constant level. He tried to move his toes and couldn't; his legs were both totally useless now. He was paralyzed from the waist down.

"Goddammit!" He used his anger to fuel his need to survive and pushed his way into the stairwell. Surprisingly, the lack of feeling in his back made it easier for him to move than the immense spikes of pain at every movement before.

James made it to the stairwell and tried to slide backward on his stomach, but his dead feet got in the way, sticking to the non-skid steps. He had to turn around and ease himself down headfirst, step by step on his belly, pausing at each landing to let the blood flow out of his head.

Ten floors. Twenty-six steps between each floor. He fell, rolling down the remainder of the flight of steps on two different occasions, once from more than halfway up. His hands were bruised and bloody, the skin torn away from the ends of three fingers on his left hand and the palm of his right looked like he'd taken a spill on a bicycle—but he made it.

In the lobby, a security guard outside the building saw him emerge from the stairs and rushed inside. The guard pulled him out of the building and several people that he'd seen in the lobby coffee shop over the years assisted with getting him across the street.

His ordeal was over. He was safe. They'd get him to the hospital and he'd get examined. The doctors could repair his body. Couldn't they?

*****

04 July 2025
Norfolk, Virginia

"Launch everything!" Vice Admiral Sexton screamed. "If they're not armed yet, send them inland. We need to preserve as much combat power as possible."

"Aye-aye, sir!"

"Send word to the *George Washington* and *George Bush* to do the same."

"Aye-aye, sir!"

The carrier's general alert claxons began to sound and the admiral imagined he could hear the pounding of feet on the decks below him. He'd received the emergency report that DC was under attack and started arming the jets on the three carriers docked at the naval base. The planes on the ground wouldn't be able to be armed in time; there was simply too much bureaucratic red tape with keeping ammunition easily accessible on the mainland. They'd have to try and get to an airport somewhere in the interior of the country until the government could coordinate a response—*if* there was a government anymore.

"Target anything in the sky without a US transponder," Admiral Sexton ordered. "I want to shoot a few of these fuckers down before they sink my boat. Tell the other ships that they are weapons free."

The claxons took on a different sound as the Sea Sparrow missile pods activated.

"Tracking inbound targets!" a sailor shouted.

"Kill the bastards, dammit! Don't wait for my order. We don't have time."

The first missile exploded from the pod, sending flames in all directions, severely burning several crew members who hadn't moved away from the system fast enough.

"Fire as soon as you get another lock," he ordered.

Outbound missiles began to stream from other boats, streaking off toward the ocean and unseen targets miles away. They didn't even know what they were shooting at. The radar signatures were completely unlike anything in the computer database and the satellite imagery from DC was inconclusive—the goddamned things were just so fast.

"Reports coming in from DC," a sailor called. "The air defense batteries shot down several of the UFOs before getting wiped out."

"UFOs…" the admiral mused.

He wasn't a believer of alien conspiracy theories until ten minutes ago. Given what he'd seen, though, Sexton had to believe that their enemy wasn't human. There was no way a human body could take the sustained speed and the rapid changes in direction that the craft appeared to take would have caused a human to black out.

"Sir! There are fast-moving boats that just appeared out of nowhere on radar. They are ten miles from shore."

"Put it up on the screen."

The coast of Virginia and eastern Maryland appeared on the bridge video screens. Hundreds of boats appeared, fanning outward from a spot in the middle of the ocean, sailing rapidly toward the coast. They were simply appearing out of thin air.

"Have the *Vella Gulf* and *Anzio* target the origination point with harpoon missiles."

"Sir, there's nothing there."

"Bullshit," the old sailor countered. "There's something there. They're coming from somewhere goddamn it. I'm willing to bet there's some type of stealth vessel out there."

He watched as the radioman talked into his headset. "Sir, both cruisers acknowledge."

"Fire!" he ordered.

Below him, on the flight deck, planes shot skyward from the catapults. Too many of them headed west. They hadn't gotten enough time to arm. *Would they even have ammunition for them at an Air Force installation?* he wondered.

Six large, ship-killing missiles roared away from the cruisers *Vella Gulf* and *Anzio*. He hoped he was right and second-guessed his decision to fire at an empty spot on the radar. "Have the cruisers target the inbound boats."

"Sir?"

"Change the cruiser's target from the origination point to the take out any of the inbound boats that they can."

"Aye-aye, sir."

"Sir, we have visual!"

He pivoted in his chair and followed the outstretched arm of his executive officer. Admiral Sexton picked up his binoculars and lifted them to his tired eyes.

A dark cloud of what appeared to be *UFOs* sped toward the naval base from the east. Too late, he realized there were hundreds of smaller objects streaking ahead of the approaching fighters.

"*Incoming!*"

TWELVE

05 July 2025
Hunter Army Airfield, Savannah, Georgia

"Let's go, Berserkers! Get on that plane before I smoke your asses myself," First Sergeant Thomas shouted.

Gabe grinned in spite of the severity of the situation. His company was loading three of the smaller, propeller engine C-130s for rapid deployment to Washington, DC of all places.

The 82nd Airborne out of Fort Bragg, North Carolina had apparently tried to parachute directly into DC and gotten decimated by the German fighters that controlled the skies above the capitol. The plan to get US troops into the fight was to go overland, so Gabe's company was going to land somewhere in central Virginia to secure a usable airport runway that the 3rd Infantry Division could use to move their tanks and Bradley Infantry Fighting Vehicles northward.

It was a risky move since the Nazis were attacking from the sea. Moving the 3rd Infantry out of Georgia left the entire southeast portion of the United States open to attack with no counterpunch options, but they didn't have other, viable, quick response options.

The capitol was in ruins only a day after the initial attack. The president and vice-president were hosting a breakfast event at the White House to celebrate Independence Day and presumed dead. As such, the Speaker of the House, Javier Sanchez, was sworn into office the evening prior in his home in Sacramento. Sanchez, a career-long adversary of the military, had ordered the overland attack after the failed airborne response by the remnants of the Pentagon leadership.

Gabe checked his watch. They were ten minutes ahead of schedule. He motioned to one of the crewmen inside. She walked down the short steps and looked him up and down before saying, "What is it, sir?"

"Any idea where we're going yet, Lieutenant? I need that information so I can plan how I'm going to secure the site."

"We've been discussing that with the MAC. They're going to use C-5's to transport tanks to whatever location your company secures and those suckers need a ton of runway—eight thousand feet—so every municipal airport is out. That leaves BWI in Baltimore or Richmond International. There are unconfirmed reports that BWI's runways have been rendered unusable, so we're going to Richmond."

"Richmond?" Gabe asked. "How far from DC is that?"

"It's about a hundred miles or so," she replied. "The tanks will drive past the Marine Corps base at Quantico on the way to DC, so they may find a lot of troops whose units were destroyed in the initial air attack. All those Marines just need an enemy to shoot at."

"Thanks," he replied and turned back toward the tarmac where his company had finished loading the other two planes.

Unofficial reports stated that German troops were in DC. It made sense, their fighter planes could inflict terrible damage from the air, but if they wanted to take the capitol, they had to put men on the ground. That gave the Americans the advantage. If they could capture a German, they could discover where they came from, how they got there…and what their objectives were.

"That's it, sir," the first sergeant yelled, holding up his cell phone as he walked along the cargo plane's fuselage from where he'd been standing. "The other two birds are loaded, ready to go. You and I are the last two."

Gabe nodded and grasped the metal pole on the stairs, pulling himself inside. "We're going to Richmond," he told First Sergeant Thomas once they'd settled into the cargo net seats near the front of the plane.

"Richmond, huh?" the noncommissioned officer grunted as he shook out a pair of earplugs into the palm of his hand. "Never been there before."

Gabe marveled at his first sergeant's calm demeanor. The US was under attack and they were flying into position to counterattack. The paratroopers the 82nd Airborne Division tried to send had been wiped out before they had a chance to jump. If the Germans had any type of radar system, there was a very real possibility that they'd detect the airplanes and shoot them down too. The man had ice in his veins.

"It's a lot farther out than we thought we'd be."

"Just means we're gonna get some exercise, sir. We'll be on the move by Wednesday or Thursday."

The first sergeant had a point. It didn't really matter *where* they started from as long as they got in on the action. The tankers and the infantrymen in the Bradleys would have an advantage on the rapid movement piece, but the Berserkers would be in the shit before too long. It was only a matter of time.

*****

05 July 2025
Near Malmstrom Air Force Base, Montana

"*Scheisse!*" Oberleutnant Gregory Wagner shouted in frustration. The remaining twenty-one members of his fallschirmjäger platoon were completely alone without any communication back to Wehrmacht Field Headquarters in Washington, DC or even with Argus Base.

"You mustn't let the men see your frustration, Oberleutnant," Feldwebel Anders stated flatly. "Our situation is not what we'd planned, but we are still a capable German fighting unit and we can continue our mission."

From the moment Gregory's feet had touched down on American soil, the mission had been a near disaster. From his own broken ankle, to the loss of the transport plane and half of his men, the predawn mission hadn't started well yesterday. Additionally, the platoon had suffered a forty percent injury rate that took Schütze Markel the entire morning to repair.

By the time they began movement, they had to be extremely cautious due to the satellite overflight and move slowly toward their target, a nuclear launch site labeled as Yankee Flight on all of his maps. After an arduous day in the blazing hot sun, they'd finally reached the perimeter of Yankee Flight the previous evening.

It was abandoned. Years of neglect and misuse had left the fence in ruins and graffiti covered the concrete bunker. It was easily the biggest disappointment in the oberleutnant's young life.

To compound the problems, he received a frantic call over the wireless that their sister platoon, which had parachuted into Bravo Flight, a site about one hundred and forty kilometers away, was on the verge of being wiped out by security forces at their target. That was four hours ago.

The final chunk of ice on the grave was the loss of their remaining escort düsenjägers. They'd responded to assist with the other platoon's battle and Gregory had listened in alarm as a pilot described the loss of his wingman and the third düsen to the superior dogfighting skills of the American pilots in their inferior machines. The men had gathered around the radio, shielding themselves from the oppressive July heat in the shadow of Yankee Flight's bunker.

The pilot seemed to accept his fate, describing the graceful way the Americans rolled out of his line of fire, never allowing him to get a clean shot. He reported killing one fighter and then the wireless lost signal. Presumably, he'd been killed. And with the loss of his fighter, the long-range transmitter was gone as well, which was why they couldn't reach anyone else.

"What are your orders, sir?" the feldwebel asked as he chewed on a piece of seal jerky.

Gregory stared blankly at the older man for a moment. He didn't know him well, but he knew that Anders had been in the Heer much longer that he had, opting to stay unfrozen and earn promotions along the way before finally being forced to go into hibernation. He knew he should ask the feldwebel's advice, but he'd been trained as an officer. As such, he was in charge.

"We will leave Yankee Flight at dusk tonight and travel to the Bravo Flight location."

"It is a long way," Feldwebel Anders replied, sucking at the gap in his teeth before using a fingernail to pick at a piece of meat. "I don't know if the men will agree to such a long march."

Gregory noticed the way the feldwebel's eyelids dropped low as he glanced sideways at the men sitting a few meters away. He was weighing whether to side with the men or with the officer.

"It *is* a long way, Feldwebel, however, we were trained to enter a nuclear bunker and disable the launch computers so they couldn't use the weapons against our forces. That mission has not changed. Yankee Flight was a poor bit of intelligence work, but the Americans are defending the Bravo Flight location. To me, that means the site is still active and we now have a new objective."

Anders nodded slowly. "Yes, sir. You're right. We can still accomplish what the other fallschirmjägers could not. We will carry the victory for Germany!"

"Yes, of course. For Germany," Gregory replied out of habit. He'd never been to Germany and didn't have any illusions of returning to the Fatherland. The current residents wouldn't welcome the men and women from Argus once the war was over. They'd be worldwide rejects with no land to call their own; an army bred for the singular purpose of carrying out an almost century-old vendetta against the Americans. His illusions of returning to the Fatherland died long ago.

"Tell the men to eat and sleep," Gregory ordered. "We will march tonight and in two days, we'll arrive at Bravo Flight."

The feldwebel saluted smartly and Gregory returned the salute before pulling out his map to plan their route.

*****

05 July 2025
Cheyenne Mountain Complex, Colorado Springs, Colorado

The convoy of SUVs drove into a tunnel that burrowed into the side of a mountain. Barbed wire and heavily armed soldiers lined the roadway and they saluted as the cars drove by. Javier watched through the window with a mixture of interest and disgust at the sheer amount of government

154 | Grudge

funding that must go into a place like this—funds that could have gone to social programs to help America's citizens.

They passed through a comically giant rectangular door that was at least ten feet tall and four feet thick. The door alone made him think this place was built specifically for war, which they were somehow involved in back east. Then they passed through a *second* door of the same design before winding their way deeper underground to a large parking lot filled with gun trucks and more armed soldiers.

The president stepped out of the SUV into a lighted tunnel, surrounded by a full contingent of Secret Service agents that he'd never seen before yesterday. They'd arrived at his home in Stockton, California the day before, waking everyone and scaring his children with their drawn weapons and platoon of Marines outside.

Fortunately, Congress was in a five-day recess and the Speaker of the House was back out west to attend the local Independence Day parade and festival. With the time difference between East and West Coast, Javier Sanchez and his family were asleep; they hadn't heard of the early morning attacks on Washington.

Javier was still wiping the sleep from his eyes when a federal judge arrived and administered the oath of office. He discussed options with the agent in charge and they decided that flying wasn't the safest option since the enemy appeared to have air superiority. They would drive from Stockton to Colorado Springs.

Grudge | 155

The president stretched his legs. Even in the spacious SUV, he'd begun to get cramped on the trip. They'd been on the road for over twenty-four hours, only stopping three times for gas and restroom breaks. Despite the severity of the situation, he couldn't help but grin when he thought of the sleepy gas station attendant in Utah when their ten-vehicle convoy had rolled up at 5 a.m. and the agents swarmed the facility to clear it. That poor guy had no idea what was happening.

"Welcome to Cheyenne Mountain, Mr. President," a military officer stated. He whipped his hand up to his eyebrow for a salute, startling Javier. He hadn't been around the Army much and was naturally distrustful of them anyways.

"Thank you…" He examined the uniform quickly. He had a lot of ribbons and a set of wings like an airline pilot on the chest of his suit. Three stars on each shoulder meant six stars—which told him nothing. "Uh, Captain?" he ventured.

The man dropped his hand and offered it to Javier. "I'm General James Sullivan, sir. I'm in charge of the facility here."

Javier felt foolish as he gripped the general's hand. He didn't know anything about military ranks. *Is a general higher up than a captain?* "So, ahh… This is my wife, Becky, and the boys. What happens in this facility?"

"It was originally built for NORAD back in the 1960s, sir," General Sullivan replied. "The Mountain is designed to protect against a nuclear blast and the entire facility is shielded from EMP. We conduct cyberspace operations and house the US Northern Command, partnered with Canada.

"For now, the most important thing for you to know, sir, is that we can communicate with anyone and this facility is completely secure. My airmen have us locked in tight and nothing will get through."

"Oh, this is an Air Force base?"

He regretted it the moment he'd said it. For a full second, the general looked at him like he was the dumbest person on the face of the planet before he composed himself. "Yes, sir. This facility is owned and managed by the US Air Force. We do have members of all the services working here, but almost all of the support and security functions are conducted by Air Force personnel."

Javier swallowed his pride, telling the general that he knew next to nothing about the military and apologized for his lack of knowledge.

"No worries, sir," the officer replied. "You had a lot thrown on your plate without warning." He glanced back at Becky and the children. "Why don't we go inside Building Two and get your family situated in the apartments there? Is an hour too soon to conduct the initial briefing on what little we do know about our enemy?"

"No. That seems fine, thank you for your hospitality, General."

General Sullivan gestured to a petite woman wearing a similar uniform as his, except with a skirt and not nearly as many ribbons. "This is Captain deBoer. She'll be your military escort while you're here. Anything that you or your family needs, ask her directly. Your security detail will begin working with my security staff to get their billeting arranged as well."

The captain saluted him as well and he awkwardly returned the motion. "Good afternoon, sir. If you and your family will follow me, we have prepared a suite for you."

They walked toward the entrance to what appeared to be a cinder block building inside the mountain. A large number "**2**" was painted on the side.

"So, there are *buildings* inside the mountain?" Javier asked.

"Yes, sir. There are fifteen buildings in the facility, connected by a series of passageways through the granite. Thirteen of them are three-story buildings and two are two-story. It's quite amazing what they were able to do down here before either of us were even born."

The president reached across and gripped his wife's hand as they walked. Becky and the kids hadn't signed up for this. They'd been happy with Javier as a congressional representative for the people of California's 9th District, a social reformer who'd been elected to his fourth term on promises to cut government spending to outdated programs like the military and increase funding to federal social programs. Now, their world had changed dramatically. By some strange twist of the rules of succession, he'd been third in line for the presidency—sufficiently removed that he'd never paid much attention to the practical aspects of the job. He hardly even knew the difference between the Air Force and the Army for Christ's sake.

The suite that Ashley, the military aide, brought them to was nice, not fancy, but clean and well-appointed with an adjoining room for the two boys. She made sure the Sanchez's were comfortable and had some food brought in. Then, it was time for Javier to get the briefing on the situation in Washington.

Captain deBoer brought him to the operations center, a large room filled with enough technology to run a small country. As he looked around the room, Javier wondered how many of these operations centers existed and how much money had been spent creating them. It was a shame.

"Please sit here, Mr. President," the aide said as she indicated the vacant seat at the head of a table in the front of the operations center.

"Thank you, Ashley." He sat and did a quick assessment of the men and women around the table. Except for General Sullivan, seated immediately to his right, he'd never seen any of them. They were mostly military, but a few civilian suits were sprinkled amongst the fifteen members of the briefing.

"I hope the accommodations are to your liking, sir," General Sullivan opened.

"Yes, they are. Thank you, James." He took a deep breath. This was where he was supposed to say something about standing strong and defeating the enemy. He was an excellent public speaker, but he was totally out of his element here. Was he supposed to give orders about where to attack and how?

"Uh… Thank you for taking time out of your schedule to set up this briefing," Javier began. "I'm sure all of you are extremely busy." He looked around the table again. "So, who the hell are we at war with and what are we doing about it?"

The general sighed. "Honestly, you're not going to believe it, sir. It's taken me a lot of video footage and satellite imagery to come to grips with the fact that we're at war with the Nazis."

"The Nazis?" he snorted. "Really?"

"Yes, sir," he paused. "Maybe we should start at the beginning. What do you know about the Joint North American Defense Branch and why it was formed?"

"Literally nothing," Javier admitted.

General Sullivan nodded before he spoke. "In 2020, the attack in Florida killed sixty-three thousand Americans and tourists. It was the largest loss of life on a single day in our history."

"Of course I remember that," the president stated.

"We discovered then that there was an unknown enemy consisting of a rebuilt Nazi army—"

"Rebuilt? As in, this is the *same* Nazi army that we faced in World War Two?"

"Exactly, Mr. President. I apologize that I'm the one who has to give you this condensed brief instead of your National Security Team and that it's out of the blue like this."

"Don't apologize. It can't be helped. Go on."

The general spent seven or eight minutes detailing one of the wildest tales he'd ever heard. The Nazis had established a base in Antarctica during World War Two and we nuked it ten years later. There were more than 150,000 casualties that were removed after the fact and we thought we'd put it to bed until almost seventy years later when they attacked Fort Lauderdale. Since the attack, we'd beefed up our interoperability between the services and added thousands of sailors to the US Coast Guard, expanding their role. All the while, we'd searched the globe to determine where our enemy had originated, but we'd been unable to find anything beyond a lot of odd military surplus purchases with no information on who was buying it.

Now we knew.

"So that brings us to the present," General Sullivan concluded the history lesson. "We have a lot of video evidence from citizens uploading cell phone videos to the internet and camera crews recording images before getting themselves killed. It's the Nazis. They're back, and they have a technology far beyond anything we've ever seen."

Javier resisted the urge to cut in. He'd done that enough, prolonging the meat of the briefing. Part of being a good leader was knowing when to keep your mouth shut.

"So far, we know they have some sort of device that makes their base and larger transport ships invisible to radar and satellite, and presumably the human eye, but we don't know that for sure. The main attack was launched from the Atlantic Ocean yesterday morning. The Navy fired ship-killer missiles at the point of origin and satellite imagery shows a massive debris field in the ocean where the missiles impacted. We don't know what they hit, or how they did it, but they killed *something* out there.

"During the attack, the Nazis targeted DC and the surrounding Air Force and Naval facilities to destroy our rapid response capabilities. They are using an advanced fighter craft—bring up the video," the general said over his shoulder.

A video of a series of sleek, round objects zoomed by the cameraman. They resembled every UFO-conspiracy theorist's definition of what aliens flew around space in. The fighters fired their weapons and rockets into buildings, crowds of people, anything they saw. They seemed incredibly fast and maneuverable compared to anything Javier had seen before. The video lasted for about forty seconds and then began again on a loop.

"This is their fighter jet," the general stated. "It appears to be a multi-role fighter, capable of both air-to-air combat and air-to-ground—you'll notice the rockets they've fired into buildings—and it can also drop munitions on targets. The fighters are extremely difficult to bring down due to their maneuverability, but it can be done. We have reports of several shoot-downs, especially out west where they appeared to be targeting our nuclear launch."

General Sullivan looked over his shoulder at the computer operator once again. "Bring up the tanks."

The UFO video stopped, replaced by a new video of several large tanks driving and hundreds of soldiers walking through what appeared to be the Rosslyn neighborhood in Arlington. The video was shot from an apartment window, so the perspective was a little hard to understand, but the tanks didn't seem to be touching the ground and as they passed over the tops of cars, there was some type of pressure that crushed the vehicles. The tanks fired several rounds into the buildings around them, creating havoc.

"These are their hovertanks. You can see they operate on some sort of lift capability that crushes metal objects underneath them, so it may be magnetic. Our analysts say those guns are 205 millimeter, outclassing anything we have on the ground. It's assumed that these hovertanks can move over water or bypass obstacles, making them a formidable weapon—much like the Panzers of World War Two were extremely dangerous, but not unbeatable.

"As I mentioned, there have also been airborne attacks across the United States on nuclear launch facilities. The attacks seem to be targeting every facility that was operational *before* the 1991 and 1993 START initiatives to reduce the number of warheads. Since then, we've closed more than half of our sites, but those vacant locations are still being targeted. At the locations where we do still have launch facilities, we've been lucky. So far, all attacks have been repulsed, but we believe it's only a matter of time before they gain control of at least one facility."

Finally, the president had heard enough. "Okay, you've given me a quick rundown of everything these bastards are doing *to* us. What's our response?"

"Well, sir, the Air Force was the first to respond, but we're hopelessly overmatched. As of two hours ago, we'd only managed to shoot down thirty of their fighters and we've lost seventy-one of ours—that's not including what was destroyed on the runways and on the three Navy carriers at Norfolk. We're doing our best to calculate where these fuckers—excuse me, sir."

"No, it's alright," Javier assured him.

The general nodded and continued, "We're doing our best to figure out where the Nazis came from. Our analysts think it's either some deep, dark shithole in Africa or they had a second base in Antarctica that we didn't know about when we nuked the first one."

"Sir? If I may," a man with a slightly different uniform than General Sullivan raised his hand from two seats down the table. He had what looked like light blue shoulder pads from his suit on the outside of the fabric instead of the inside. An eagle emblem sat in the middle of the shoulder board.

"Go ahead."

"Good morning, sir. I'm Colonel John Halverson, US Army FORSCOM liaison officer to the Cheyenne Mountain facility. The Army's initial response met with failure as well, but we're going to overcome it. We tried to parachute two Army battalions from the 82nd Airborne Division at Fort Bragg into the area surrounding DC. All ten of the C-17s were shot down, killing nine hundred and eight-seven paratroopers and the crews of the planes."

"So, parachuting a bunch of soldiers into the fight isn't going to work."

"No, sir," the colonel agreed. "Airborne operations are off the table. However, we've begun moving our light forces in from New York, Kentucky and the rest of the 82nd from North Carolina to staging areas surrounding the known landing sites near DC, Baltimore and Norfolk. We'll move cross-country until we can engage the enemy. We've also begun moving heavy troops up from Fort Stewart, Georgia—"

"Excuse me, Colonel," Javier cut in once more. "What are heavy troops?"

"Tanks and Bradleys, self-propelled artillery, air defense vehicles, and mechanized engineers. The Army has both heavy and light forces. The light guys can infiltrate into places, but the heavy guys have a lot more firepower and can punch a hole in enemy formations."

"Okay, I understand," he said. In reality, he understood the tanks and more firepower part; everything else went over his head.

"We're moving tanks up from Georgia by plane to Richmond and then we'll attack over land once they're in position."

"You mentioned the other organizations attacking across country and the tanks attacking over land, are those going to be coordinated movements or is it whoever can get into the fight first?"

The colonel smiled without showing his teeth, reminding Javier of someone who suppressed their true feelings. "It will be a coordinated combined arms attack, sir. We'll use helicopters in the close air support role and they can hide from the Nazi fast-movers. Our tanks will go toe-to-toe with their Panzers and delay their movements further inland. By this time next week, our heavy forces from Texas, Colorado and Kansas should arrive by rail. They'll act as the hammer against the anvil of the blocking forces."

"For all of our sakes, Colonel, I hope our men can do as well as you say they will."

"We'll mop the floor with those Kraut bastards, sir."

"I hope so, Colonel. I hope so."

THIRTEEN

08 July 2025
Anacostia, Washington, DC

"Motherfuckers aren't gonna come into our city and shoot it up!"

"You right, brother!"

"Motherfuckers aren't gonna come into our city and bomb everything!"

"Preach it, brother!"

"Motherfuckers aren't gonna come into our city and murder everyone they see!"

"No, sir!"

Devon looked out over the crowd of men and women seated in the pews of the Union Temple Baptist Church. There were easily four or five hundred of them, including what looked like thirty or so white police officers. Everyone was packed in the church, braving the death squads and the stifling heat and humidity to hear his message. The Nazis were everywhere and they risked being shot on sight just leaving their homes. It was time to send his people forth to wreak mayhem.

He jabbed his finger in the direction of downtown DC, across the river. "Those motherfuckers think they can come into our city and treat us like animals because the color of our skin."

"They's racist, Deacon Johns!" a man yelled from the front row causing him to break his thought process.

"I'm sure they are, brother," Devon conceded. "But don't you think for a minute that they aren't murdering all the white folk too. I saw it with my own eyes when Pastor Kelly was shot along with a bunch of Catholic priests and other Baptist ministers."

The church deacon refocused mentally and continued, "How many of you know about the Second World War? Those Nazi motherfuckers murdered millions of people. People like you and me who were just trying to live their lives and not bother no one. They're doing the same thing here."

He paused as people wailed out, crying over the loss of life. "Now, brothers and sisters, our government ain't never been too good at helping us out, but they ain't in any shape to do so right now anyways. The president and vice-president are dead, a lot of congress is dead, the Army got their ass whooped and we ain't heard nothing about 'em coming back. So, it's up to you and me to fight those Nazi sonsabitches."

The crowd cheered, many of them brandishing weapons over their heads. He eyed the police officers nervously, but they cheered along with the others. They didn't want their families to be murdered either.

Devon patted the air. The last thing they needed to do was attract attention before they were ready to strike. When the crowd settled down, he said, "Now I'm just a simple man of God. I don't know anything about tactics. I don't know how we change from a group of brothers and sisters into an army of soldiers. I need your help. Who out here in this crowd has been in the Army and can help show us the way?"

He scanned the crowd. Most of the people present were locals whom he'd seen over the years in the neighborhoods, some of them regular churchgoers, some of them street thugs and even a few hardcore gang members. None of them raised their hands, except for three of the white police officers.

"That's it? None of you except our fine policemen in the back have been in the military?" He waited again and then motioned the three up to the pulpit. "Alright, brothers. Looks like you have the experience we are desperately in need of." A few boos and hisses accompanied their move toward the front.

"None of that now," Devon admonished. "These men put their lives on the line for our protection before the Nazis showed up and by being here today, they're saying that they're willing to do it again. It don't matter the color of their skin to me. We need to know how an army fights if we're gonna attack and not get wiped out immediately."

He knew what the people wanted to hear, so he gave it to them. "These fine men won't be in charge, alright? I'm still responsible for what we do—and if the death squad shows up, they'll take me. Our friends in blue will be advisors." He turned and looked at the police officers. "Is that alright with you gentlemen?"

All three of them nodded and he turned back to the assembly. "See? They don't want to be in charge of us. They don't want to rule over us. They just want to help take our city back from those motherfuckers!"

The cheers fired him up. He loved the enthusiasm and needed to maintain that, especially once they started taking losses. "Alright, brothers and sisters. We need to spread the word. We're stronger together. There must be a couple hundred thousand of those Nazis and they have tanks and UFO jets…but there are *millions* of us in this city. We *can* fight them. We need to coordinate our efforts or else they're just going to exterminate us block-by-block."

He turned back to the police officers. "Alright, brothers. Teach us what we need to know."

*****

08 July 2025
Virginia Hospital Center, Arlington, Virginia

Another soldier walked by the doorway. Sweat poured from underneath the helmet he wore, and the grey uniform was stained with wetness across his back and in his armpits. The air conditioning had been cut to save as much electricity from the generators as possible, making the hospital unbearably hot since the windows didn't open, for safety reasons.

Once the Nazi had passed, Gloria leaned back down to the bed and whispered to James. "He's gone. Are you sure you're up for this?"

"No, but we can't stay here. It's only a matter of time before they discover who we are and then we'll get a bullet to the back of the head."

Once Gloria had finally made it back home after the Nazi attack on the airport, she'd sat alone, waiting for James' return. The hours stretched by with no word from him as she watched the television footage of the attacks. After living and working in the District for almost twelve years, everything the networks showed was like a piece of her soul being shattered.

Then the call from the hospital came. James' building had been hit and he suffered a spinal injury. He was scheduled for surgery two hours after the nurse called her.

Gloria had to pay triple the normal cost for the taxi over to Arlington because the driver swore that going across the bridge made him a target to the flying saucers shooting at everything from above. By the time they finally made it to the hospital, James was already in surgery. His spinal cord was severed and there was nothing they could do except remove the sharp vertebrae segments and stabilize everything to avoid further internal damage. He'd be paralyzed from the waist down for the rest of his life.

She gripped her husband's hand and kissed his fingers. Leaning forward was uncomfortable for her, but she didn't care. "If they suspect we're trying to skip out…"

"Who cares?" he countered. "If we're leaving the hospital, that's just two less people that they have to keep track of. To be honest, they probably won't even notice."

Gloria leaned back and nodded. "Okay, James. I trust you."

"I know you do, babe. We just have to get out of the city before the counterpunch comes."

The counterpunch, as he called it, would be the military's response to the Nazi occupation of the capitol. It had already been four days, the Army couldn't afford to let the invaders dig in and set up a proper perimeter. If they did that, it would take a lot more firepower to dislodge them.

Of course, they had no way of knowing how extensive the attack was. It had been devastatingly fast and brutal here in DC—were they only here or was New York under attack? What about the coastal Florida cities where they'd attacked before? They'd set up some type of jamming equipment, effectively blocking all cellular signals, data transfers, and television and radio signals. They were blind to the outside world.

James pushed himself up on his elbows, the pain of the effort clearly etched on his face. "Help me," he asked.

She grasped his hand once again and pulled his upper body to a sitting position, then helped him swing his legs over the side. The bed was too high for him to transition to the wheelchair she'd procured for their journey, so she rushed around to the opposite side and pumped the manual foot pedals to lower it.

"Okay, that's low enough," James whispered.

She stopped pressing the pedal and came back around. Between James' upper body strength and Gloria's legs and sore back, they got him into the wheelchair. She began to push him from behind when he gave a yelp of pain.

"Stop!" he gasped. "The catheter."

The tube of his Foley catheter ran from the collection bag on the side of the bed, along the rail and disappeared under his hospital gown. "Sorry," she muttered, unhooking the bag and tubing, dropping it unceremoniously onto his lap.

"Grab a couple more bags," James said. "They're in that cabinet, third drawer down."

Gloria complied, pilfering five more of the fluid collection bags and stuffing them behind James' back. They'd need as many of them as they could get their hands on. James may need to use a catheter for the rest of his life, it would all depend on how much feeling he had internally once the swelling went down.

She pushed him out into the hallway where the realities of the war truly hit home. Injuries of every kind were evident amongst the city's residents and tourists who'd been in town for Independence Day. There were the injuries she expected to see in a war-torn area, the gunshot wounds, and missing limbs from explosions, burns, and so on, but the kids were the worst.

As a student of history, she knew children were often caught in the middle of conflict, but seeing it firsthand instead of in pictures broke her heart. Halfway to the exit, she happened upon a group of three children sitting on the floor along the wall. They all looked similar, probably siblings or cousins. They were dirty, their little faces covered in soot and grime, layered on so thick in places that it was nearly impossible to tell where their clothes ended and the dirt began. While none of them appeared to be physically injured, the vacant stares on the faces of the two younger ones told her that they'd seen far too much for children of their age.

She stopped and knelt awkwardly beside them. The oldest, a small African American child of seven or eight, jumped to his feet and stepped in front of the two girls. He planted his feet wide, thrusting his chest out, and balled up his fists at his side.

"I'm not going to hurt you," Gloria stated.

"You're not a doctor," he replied. His hard eyes stared defiantly back at her, daring her to contradict him.

"No. I'm not a doctor. Where are your parents?"

"Dead. The apartment fell on us." He glanced at the wheelchair and then back at Gloria. "What do you want?"

"I'm sorry about your parents."

"White people don't care about us. What do you want?"

"I—Well, I care about you. What's your name?"

"*Gloria*," James urged from behind her.

She ignored her husband and repeated her question. "I'm Gloria. What's your name?"

"D'onta," he admitted.

"D'onta. Like the football player for the Redskins?"

The boy smiled. "Yeah. I'm gonna be famous like him one day."

"I bet you will be," she agreed. "Are these your sisters?"

"Yeah."

"Are any of you hurt?"

"Phelisha got hit by a brick in the back."

"Can I see?"

He reached down and hauled the youngest to her feet by an arm. She may have been three or four; it was hard to tell with all the grime—which must have been from the apartment building collapse. D'onta spun the listless girl around and lifted up her shirt to show a discolored area on her skin. It would be extremely painful for her to move around for a few days, but she should be alright.

"Thank you, D'onta. I'm sorry about your parents. Do you have any aunts or uncles, maybe a grandma who lives in town that you could stay with?"

Finally, the little boy's tough exterior cracked and he began to cry. "Everyone was over for breakfast. We were gonna eat then go to get a place to watch the fireworks. We," he indicated the two girls, "were outside playing."

"Fireworks?" she asked in alarm. "D'onta, that was four *days* ago. Have you been sitting here since then?"

"No. We was outside playing in the alley and the wall fell on top of us. We got stuck under a bunch of bricks."

"Oh my God. I'm sorry."

He ignored her comment and continued. "They rescued us and gave us some food, then brought us to the hospital. Nobody's talked to us since they told us to wait here for a doctor."

"Are you—D'onta, would you like to come with us? We're going to our home in Dupont Circle to get some clothes and food, then we're leaving the city. You and your sisters can come with us. We'll keep you safe."

"Why? White people don't care about us. What's in it for you?"

She changed her mind. D'onta must have been at least ten years old, his naturally small stature was likely diminished further by lack of nutrition and sleep, and the stress of being trapped inside a collapsed building.

"D'onta, I know that's what your parents told you, but not all white people are bad. I'm not bad. James, my husband in the wheelchair, he isn't bad. We're people, just like you, trying to survive. I'd like to take you with us."

He looked down at his sisters. Phelisha stared down at her feet, the other girl looked back at him hopefully. "I don't know…"

"If you don't have any family, D'onta, nobody is going to get you out of this hospital. They're going to be so busy with everyone else, they'll forget about you, like they already have." She took a deep breath and eased down all the way to her knees. Crouching hurt her belly. "I'll tell you what. You can come to our house, get some food and water, get cleaned up, and if you decide that you don't want to stay with us when we leave the city, you can take your sisters to wherever you want to go."

Phelisha pulled at D'onta's arm, nodding enthusiastically without saying anything. "Okay," he answered. "We'll go get cleaned up, but no promises that we'll stay with you."

"Deal," she replied, holding out her hand.

He shook it solemnly and helped his middle sister up. "This is Lakeisha. She hasn't talked since the explosion, so don't expect anything from her."

"Hi, Lakeisha. We'll take good care of you for as long as you decide to stay with us."

The little girl stared back at her, but didn't say anything, which Gloria understood would take time.

She used the handles of the wheelchair to pull herself up and was surprised when D'onta added his little hands to her armpits to help her up. "Thank you. This baby makes it hard for me to get up and down."

"Oh, you have a baby in your belly? I thought you were just fat."

She laughed. "No, my job makes me stay skinny normally. But thank you for not saying anything."

After introducing the children to James, they made their way out of the hospital. The Nazi guards didn't stop them as she'd feared they would.

Instead, they tried their best to avoid any eye contact whatsoever. Gloria wondered if the men—boys really—had a change of heart about the war now that they were seeing the results of their actions up close. She doubted it, but there was hope.

They walked several blocks from the hospital before they were finally able to hail a cab to take them to Dupont Circle. The driver told them that the bridges into the district were bombed out, except for Memorial and 14th Street Bridges, which were for the occupying force's use only. He could get them to the Rosslyn Metro station and they could travel underground through the tunnel to Foggy Bottom and then walk the rest of the way to Dupont.

It wasn't ideal, and Gloria certainly didn't relish the idea of pushing the wheelchair through the metro—let alone figuring out how to get down the stairs since the power was out to the elevators. It'd been a long time since she'd been on the Orange Line, but she seemed to remember the Rosslyn escalator as one of the longer ones. She hadn't ever gotten out at the Foggy Bottom station, so she had no clue about the escalator there. It was a daunting task.

"What if we didn't go home?" she asked suddenly. "We could just turn west and drive until we were out of the occupied area?"

"The Nazi perimeter was out in Leesburg yesterday," the cab driver offered.

"What about north?"

"I haven't driven there myself, but I've heard it extends all the way to Rockville. Honestly, your best bet is going to be going south into Anacostia. The 11th Street Bridge is still open and they allow people to move back and forth on that one. Word on the street is the folks down there are mobilizing for a fight though, so you may find yourself in a heap of trouble if you go that way."

"We've got to go home and get some supplies," James replied. "We may be able to get some help if we go south. What do you think?"

The thought of the tunnels was terrifying, but it did make sense to go home and get clothing and food for their attempted escape. There were probably thousands of people trying the same thing, so food would be scarce. "Alright. How are we going to manage the escalators?"

The look that passed across his face told her that he clearly hadn't thought about going down into the Metro tunnels and coming back up. "I'll manage somehow," he finally mustered the courage to say. "I made it down ten flights of stairs at the office. I can do this."

She stared hard at him for a moment. What if he couldn't manage it and she had to leave him by himself to go to the apartment? She knew she could do it, but she didn't want to. James was extremely vulnerable in his present state. Any number of things could happen to him. She didn't let herself think about the dangers for a pregnant woman alone in the dark with three kids.

"Alright," she told the patient cab driver. "Take us to the Rosslyn Metro Station."

*****

08 July 2025
Fredericksburg, Virginia

"Vengeance Squadron, if we haven't had the opportunity to meet, my name is Major Schenk. I am your new commander. Oberstleutnant Griese is dead. The last American attack using high-altitude stealth bombers destroyed many düsenjägers that were refueling and killed their pilots and ground crews. These were heinous, sneak attacks by subhumans. We will avenge their deaths."

Oberleutnant Berndt Fischer cheered with his squadron mates. He'd been flying a strafing mission at the Marine Corps base in Quantico this morning when word came over the radio of the attack. In all, the Luftwaffe had lost three-hundred and twelve düsenjägers in the bombing as opposed to the sixty or so that had been shot down in aerial combat since the beginning of the invasion.

It was a disaster and Generalfeldmarschall Mueller ordered the execution of Generalmajor Helmich, the commander of the Luftwaffe, for his incompetence at allowing so many düsenjägers to be parked together in one location.

"Even now, the hour of our revenge is at hand," Major Schenk continued. "The Americans are moving tanks from the airport in Richmond toward Washington. Our mission is to destroy the column before they have an opportunity to threaten the Heer on the ground."

Vengeance Squadron's new commander spent the next several minutes outlining the mission plan. The squadron's forty remaining düsenjägers were to fly south, following Interstate 95, the major north-south highway which ran the entire length of the American eastern coast, until they found the tanks and other armored vehicles. Then, they would destroy them where they sat. It was expected to be an easy run since the Luftwaffe enjoyed air superiority and the Americans didn't have any type of mobile surface to air missiles capable of shooting down a düsenjäger.

"It is time to go," Major Schenk ordered. "Go to your aircraft and prepare for launch."

Berndt saluted and jogged to where Düsenjäger 519 sat parked in the back of a field two hundred meters from any other craft. He was covered in a thin sheen of sweat by the time he finally made it to his aircraft. They'd learned their lesson about leaving the planes too close together and it wouldn't happen again.

He climbed the small rope ladder that they used when the düsenjägers were parked horizontally instead of upright on the transport vessel—not that returning to the ship he'd sailed on from Antarctica was an option. Shortly after Vengeance Squadron had taken off, a missile fired from the naval base at Norfolk sank the boat.

Kriegsmarine officers were still baffled as to how the Americans successfully targeted the shrouded vessel.

Berndt stowed the ladder in the cockpit behind his seat and closed the canopy, securing it with both manual and electromagnetic locks. He followed his handwritten checklist for the startup procedure and checked in on the radio. Within minutes, everyone had answered the commander and they took off.

He experienced a brief moment of weightlessness as the düsenjäger transitioned from sitting on the ground, to hovering and then moving forward. His craft shot up to the collection area over the office supply store where

Vengeance Squadron had set up its headquarters. Once everyone was assembled, they flew almost due south for sixty-three kilometers. That's when he saw his first American tank.

The armored vehicle traveled alone on the side road, not in a long column of vehicles as their intelligence had briefed. As soon as Berndt saw it, the vehicle pivoted and crashed into the wood line along the road.

"*Scheisse!*" he cursed and slowed his düsenjäger's speed so he could open fire with his guns. *How had it known to evade so quickly?* the pilot wondered. It was as if they'd been expecting the squadron to attack.

The rounds from his machine guns chewed up the trees, but he was unsure if the armor-piercing rounds even reached the tank since it was hidden in the trees.

"Vengeance Leader," he grunted into his radio. "This is Vengeance Nineteen."

"Yes?" the major replied.

"I have engaged one enemy tank."

"What do you mean by engaged? Why is it not destroyed?"

"They were expecting us and went into the trees."

"The Americans are fools. They weren't expecting us. Their radar is incapable of detecting our aircraft."

Berndt gritted his teeth. He knew what he'd seen, the tank had been moving at an extremely slow rate of speed, possibly even stopped, he wasn't sure, and the moment they saw him, they went deep into the woods. They'd been watching the sky.

"Vengeance Squadron, come help Oberleutnant Fischer find his lost tank," the squadron leader ordered.

Several düsenjägers appeared in his periphery vision, slowly circling the area where he'd been firing. The feeling of unease grew stronger in his gut. Something was wrong. The Luftwaffe's strength was in their speed and maneuverability. They were doing nothing, hovering over the tops of trees.

A bright flash to his left made him flinch, jerking the aircraft to the right and ramming into the side of a düsenjäger that had drifted too close. Warning claxons began to sound as the hull integrity had been damaged. He fought for control of the craft, but it refused to obey his commands and the ground rushed toward him.

Berndt's düsenjäger crashed into the pavement of the side road near where he'd originally seen the tank. His head slammed into the dash, cutting open his forehead and smashing his nose. Blood poured freely from his wounds as the muted sounds of battle reached his ears.

He twisted painfully in his harness to look over his shoulder toward the sky where his squadron had been. They were nowhere in sight. Several dark plumes of smoke drifted skyward from various places, but there was no indication whether they were from Vengeance Squadron or something else.

Then he saw them. Two helicopters rose from behind the cover of road signs—billboards if he remembered the term correctly. Their rakish appearance seemed sinister and twisted compared to the smooth lines of the düsenjägers. The helicopters fired missiles northward before sinking once more behind their concealment.

Berndt tried to use his radio to warn his squadron mates that the Americans were firing from behind the billboards, but his communication system didn't work. He banged his hand in frustration on the dash and disengaged the locks holding the canopy closed. The aircraft was in danger of catching fire, so he had to get clear of it.

He pushed the canopy aside and it crashed to the ground, shattering the glass. The small rope ladder went over the side and he grasped his pack by the handle. Inside was some food and water as well as ammunition for his pistol and a small blanket. He'd need it all if he was going to evade back to the German lines.

The pilot put his foot on the top step and began to climb down. When his eyes were level with the cockpit, he noticed the yellowed piece of paper with his startup procedure written on it and climbed back up two steps so he could reach inside. He grabbed the paper and hurried down the ladder.

He looked around to determine where his best hiding spot would be. Across the highway, American soldiers worked feverishly to reload some type of shoulder-fired weapon. His heart sank as the man holding it sighted in quickly on a düsenjäger and fired. Even exposed as he was, he couldn't tear himself away.

The missile emerged slowly from the end of the weapon and then shot off at an incredible speed. The pilot never saw it coming as the round impacted behind the cockpit, blasting a hole the size of a small automobile. The aircraft plummeted from the sky and exploded when it hit the ground.

Berndt cried out in grief. The trap the Americans had laid for them decimated his squadron. They'd baited the düsenjägers into slowing down to little more than a hover to search for the tank so their inferior weaponry could be used effectively against the aircraft. Without the advantage of speed, the Luftwaffe aircraft had been easy kills.

He wiped away the tears from his eyes, smearing blood and mucus across his face. He had to put distance between himself and the smoking düsenjäger. It was a beacon for enemy forces to find him once they began searching the wreckage for intelligence and technology. He sprinted underneath the trees, following a broken swath of branches and trampled bushes.

The sound of a large turbine engine roaring to life nearby startled him and a massive behemoth of armor began to move from deep in the woods. Somehow, he'd ended up on the path the tank had torn through the trees when he'd first spotted it.

"Of all the rotten luck," Berndt muttered, cursing himself and his misfortune. He wished he'd received the infantry training like his friend Matthias, maybe then he wouldn't have been stupid enough to follow a tank into the woods. He ducked behind a tree as the Abrams tank rumbled by. The overwhelming odor of sulfur made him gag.

The tank stopped several meters beyond his position and then reversed quickly, the engine's exhaust blowing detritus into the air. He watched in horror as the turret rotated in his direction, the main gun snapping several small trees in its path until it pointed directly at him.

They'd seen him. *How had they seen me from inside the tank?* he questioned as he stared down the large barrel, only two meters from his face.

A hatch on the top of the vehicle opened up and a pair of eyes appeared. "Drop your weapon!" the man inside shouted.

Berndt had been taught enough English to survive in the unlikely event of a crash. So, while he understood the man's words, the massive barrel pointed at his chest told him what he needed to do.

Slowly, so as not to alarm the gunner, he dropped his hand to his belt and unfastened it, dropping his weapon to the ground. He raised his hands above his head and waited.

He could hear the echo of voices coming from inside the tank. Finally, they reached a decision and a dark hand pushed the hatch completely open. An arm appeared, holding a pistol and then a helmet of some sort, followed by the body of a man.

Berndt was shocked to see the soldier's dark skin, like that of an African. He hadn't expected to see an African on American soil. *What's an African doing here?* he wondered.

The soldier climbed out of the beast and trained his pistol on Berndt before jumping down to the ground. In his opposite hand, he carried what looked like a radio cable.

The African stopped less than a meter from Berndt and they stared at each other. This was the first time he'd seen one of them in person. It was fascinating.

"Put your hands behind your back," the African ordered.

Berndt tried to say he didn't understand, but the man cut him off. "Quit your jabbering, Nazi. Put your hands behind your back."

The pilot shrugged in confusion. He didn't know what the African wanted.

"Goddamn it," the soldier muttered. "Quincy! Get out here and help me tie this dude up."

To Berndt's astonishment, *another* African emerged from the tank. Had the Americans formed an alliance with some African nation? It was an amazing discovery, one that his superiors would be interested in.

The second man walked up behind Berndt, causing him to believe he'd be shot in the back of the head to end his miserable existence. He'd die without ever knowing the body of a woman. Unlike Matthias, who'd made it his mission to have sex with as many girls as possible, Berndt had wasted his youth studying to be a pilot.

Even in the stifling Virginia temperatures, he felt the heat radiate off the African as he stepped in close. *This is the end*, Berndt thought.

To his surprise, the man grabbed his wrist, pulling his arm down behind his back, and then wrenching it up painfully. The cable he'd noticed earlier slipped over his hand and the soldier cinched it down tight. He reached up and pulled Berndt's other hand down and tied his hands together behind his back.

I am being taken prisoner, he lamented. The savages had him now. They would torture him and eat his intestines while he watched.

FOURTEEN

08 July 2025
Bravo Flight, Near Lewistown, Montana

The pockmarked concrete façade of Bravo Flight Launch Facility showed signs of recent battle. The electrified chain link fence appeared to be intact, meaning the other fallschirmjäger platoon hadn't breached it. They'd failed before they even started.

Gregory rotated his binoculars slowly, trying to ascertain how the platoon had been unsuccessful. Three days ago, and a hellish journey over vast fields of grass and dangerous rock-strewn hills, he'd received the last radio transmission from his fellow paratroopers. The highest ranking German remaining, an unteroffizier whose name he could not remember, stated that only five men remained uninjured and they were forced to break contact. They would travel west toward Yankee Flight where Gregory's platoon was traveling east. They never heard from them again.

"Who, or what, were they fighting?" he mumbled, searching the area surround the facility.

"Sir?" Feldwebel Anders asked from his position beside him.

The lieutenant glanced over at his platoon sergeant. He held his own pair of small, foldable hunting binoculars. They weren't as powerful as the military-issued binoculars that Gregory had, but were much clearer at closer distances.

"Do you see any indications of what the other fallschirmjägers fought?"

He pointed at a rocky outcrop a few hundred meters from their current position. "There are bloodstains on those rocks. I assume that is where they attacked from—it's a good location."

Gregory turned his binoculars toward the outcropping. He'd been focused on the Bravo Flight facility and not where the others had been. There did seem to be some rust-colored stains on the rocks and the soil was disturbed from soldiers' boots. If that's where they'd been, their bodies and gear had been removed.

"So if that's where they were…" he trailed off as he saw a slight bit of movement beyond the outcrop. A small drone lifted skyward. "Hide!"

His men hunkered down in the rocks, throwing their tan and grey ponchos over themselves for cover. The high-pitched whine of a quadcopter's engines echoed across the wide expanse of the valley as no other sounds disturbed the late afternoon stillness.

He tried to ascertain where the drone was, but he couldn't see anything except the dirt under his nose. Sweat poured in great streams from his hair, down his cheeks and fell to the ground around his nose. His canteen was within reach, would the movement be identified by the drone flying high above the valley?

The dryness in his throat morphed into a tickle near the back of his tongue. He wanted to cough to clear it away, knowing that to do so would be tantamount to suicide. To distract his mind, he thought about the sensors the Americans could have on their drone. If they employed thermal imaging, his men were already discovered. The ponchos wouldn't hide their body heat. However, if it was simply an audio and visual sensor, they may be fine—as long as no one made any noise.

The sound of the drone's engines drifted further away, changing tones as it went. He risked a quick glance and saw that the drone was sinking back to the earth where it had originated from.

He raised his binoculars slowly to avoid someone seeing a sudden movement and examined the point where the drone landed. A small door, camouflaged to be indistinguishable from the surrounding landscape, opened from the side of another rocky area. A soldier's head emerged and he grabbed the drone, then the door closed and disappeared.

"Now we know how the Americans were able to find the other fallschirmjäger platoon," Anders grunted in his ear.

"Yes—and the flanking position was probably how they were able to wipe them out. I wonder if there are other openings in the surrounding area or if that's a small observation post."

"There's no telling, sir. I think we need to divide the platoon and cover that doorway before we attack."

Gregory shifted to look at the launch facility once more. It didn't appear to be much more than a concrete dome with a single door set on the side nearest him. A small collection of antennae and spinning radar panels completed everything he could see.

"What do you make of that one radar dish by itself?" the lieutenant asked his sergeant, pointing to a rectangular dish on the ground and pointed into the valley, not skyward as the others. "Why is it so far away from the others that are all clustered together?"

"It may give off a large signature or maybe it's sensitive and the other equipment interferes with the system."

"Could it be a weapon?"

Anders brought his binoculars up. After a moment, he said, "I don't believe so. There's been no intelligence that the Americans have beam weapons or anything beyond small lasers. The dish is likely segregated due to interference issues."

If he was wrong, it could be a problem. "I want four men to attack the bunker. The rest of the platoon will attack the launch facility. I will stay here in these rocks to direct the battle. I need you to go with the main effort, Feldwebel."

"Yes, sir. When do you want to attack?"

He glanced at his watch. It was 1803. He'd recorded the time of sunset on the previous two nights. They had almost three hours before it sunset. "I want both teams in position by 2115. We will attack on my signal."

The feldwebel saluted awkwardly from his stomach and then crawled away to pass the word to the squads. Gregory stared through his binoculars at the radar dish off to the side once again. There was something he didn't like about it, but it was only a feeling in his gut. He had no evidence that the dish was anything except another radar. Finally, he dismissed the machine. He had to help plan the two-pronged attack on the launch facility and the observation post.

The time passed slowly until nightfall and the drone was flown three more times, almost exactly at the turn of each hour. The Americans set a pattern that was easy to avoid once they figured it out. The 2100 flight ended and Gregory sent his men into action.

First, the squad of paratroopers bounded to the camouflaged doorway and he watched as the grenadier low-crawled to the door. If the soldiers opened it to engage the main attack, the grenadier would toss a grenade inside the doorway. Then, Feldwebel Anders led the main attack cautiously toward the launch facility.

They were twenty meters from the fence when cleverly disguised floodlights lit up, illuminating the entire platoon. "*HALT!* **You are trespassing on US Air Force property. In accordance with the US Department of Defense Directive 5210.56, use of deadly force is authorized. Please back away slowly.**"

Gregory cursed. He didn't know what the voice from the speakers said, but he understood the tone and the intent. They'd been compromised. Anders didn't hesitate more than a moment before his voice range out into the night, ordering the platoon to shoot out the lights.

The fallschirmjägers began firing at the floodlights, filling the valley with the sound of automatic weapons.

Gregory swung his binoculars toward the squad at the observation post. Nothing was happening there.

An alarm of some kind began to sound from the launch facility and a light began to flash near the strange radar dish. **"This is your final warning. We will begin firing in fifteen seconds unless you drop your weapons."**

The words meant nothing to him and his men had knocked out most of the lights. Anders had the platoon moving up, by squad, toward the fence. Then the radar dish rotated, the concaved surface pointed directly at Gregory's men.

He shouted in alarm, but they were too far away to hear him. The radar *was* some type of weapon.

New gunfire sounded near his squad at the observation post. Flashes from muzzles out in the scrub brush told him there'd been another hidden door. The drone, as predictable and visible as it had been, was a decoy. The real outpost was in another location. The four men at the drone site were cut down in seconds.

Blood-curdling screams from the paratroopers outside the launch facility tore his eyes away from the decimated squad. The men writhed on the ground, twisting in pain as their bodies contorted into impossible positions. Others clawed at their skin and eyes, ripping large chunks of flesh away in their madness. One man near the edge of the platoon threw down his weapon and ran, stumbling into the night. He was the only survivor as far as Gregory could tell.

It only lasted a few seconds, a minute at most. Then the shrieks of dying men stopped abruptly.

He peered helplessly through his binoculars at the nearest man, still illuminated in the floodlights' glow. Gregory didn't know how, but the men had burned alive. Their flesh was shriveled and dry in appearance. The men who'd torn open great gashes in their skin were not covered in blood as one would expect, instead, the meat inside was desiccated, completely dry of fluids.

The Americans hadn't used flames or burning petrol—it was that radar dish. He knew it instinctively. The dish had emitted an energy that cooked his men from the inside as surely as if they'd been thrown in an oven. It was a terrifying technology that his superiors needed to know about immediately.

He scanned over to the observation post where his smaller element had been ambushed. Camouflaged men walked among them, checking the bodies. They handcuffed two of his men and a medic began bandaging them. He drew his pistol, intent on shooting his brothers so they wouldn't have to endure torture at the hands of the Americans, but he faltered.

If he shot them, the soldiers would come after him. He'd either die in the ensuing firefight, get captured or commit suicide. All three of those options kept the knowledge of the radar dish weapon from the Wehrmacht commanders. It was imperative that he escape with that information and make his way to someplace where he could establish radio communications with his superiors.

He crammed the pistol back into its holster angrily and threw himself on the ground, pulling the poncho over his body. He'd wait for a few hours until the middle of the night and then make his way eastward. He wept silently to avoid detection by the soldiers only a few hundred meters away.

As he lay in the dirt, Gregory vowed that his men's death wouldn't be in vain.

*****

08 July 2025
Rosslyn Metro Station, Arlington, Virginia

Gloria eyed the four men standing near the top of the escalator with apprehension. They didn't appear armed—the Nazis would have never let them live if they openly carried their weapons—but they could have had just about anything concealed under their baggy clothing.

What do they want? she wondered. They'd set themselves up at the top of the stairs, blocking the way.

"Well, well, well. What have we got here?" the shortest one called out.

"A cripple, a fine lookin' thick white girl, a little brother, and two baby sisters. Peculiar bunch," one of the thugs wearing a white tank top stated.

"It is a peculiar bunch, Stevie. Where do you fine citizens think you're going?"

"We're going home to Dupont Circle, but the bridges are out so we—"

The short one cut her off. "So you need to use our tunnels."

"They aren't your tunnels," James replied.

"Watch it, man. I'll cut you from ear to ear," Tank Top warned.

Shorty grabbed his dick through his pants and strutted up to Gloria. "You need to get home and I need to get laid. I see an easy solution to both of our problems."

"She's six months pregnant, son. Can't you—"

"Keep out this, cripple. It's between me and her," Shorty said. His eyes flicked over to D'onta and his sisters. "What are you doing with these people, kid?"

Gloria saw the other three drifting closer. They still hadn't brandished any weapons, but even without them, they'd be able to do serious damage to everyone.

"They're helping us out. Our apartment building collapsed." The boy, so strong up until this point, allowed his voice to quiver. "Everybody we know is dead. The hospital just left us in the hallway and Miss Gloria said she'd take us with her. They're going to get us out of the city, too."

D'onta's final sentence made the men laugh. They guffawed like idiots, laughing at the Bransons' plan to leave the city. "Boy, you ain't gettin' past them Nazis," Shorty said once he'd finally regained his breath. "You'd be better off stayin' with us here at the Metro than tryin' to leave the city."

"We're going to leave the city with Miss Gloria and Mr. James," D'onta asserted, stepping forward.

"Calm down, Blood. You 'bout to get your ass whooped you go steppin' up like that." He glanced back at Gloria and James. "I ain't about to go bangin' a fat, pregnant lady. Prolly all dried up and gross. What you got to pay the toll?"

"Toll?" Gloria asked. "I don't have anything except five or six bucks."

"You ain't got no wedding ring or jewelry?"

She held up her hands. "I'm too swollen to wear my ring."

"Mother fucker. You people take the cake." He made a show of walking away and then turned back to them, thrusting his open hand out. "Give me what you got and we'll let you pass."

"I—" Gloria chose to shut her mouth and pulled her wallet from the pocket of her maternity pants. She opened it and Shorty snatched it from her hand. "Hey!"

"Shut up, bitch. I'ma just see if you're hiding anything. You'll get the rest back."

He opened it up and the flap with her military ID fell out. Shorty looked at it, then looked at her and back at the ID. "You a lieutenant colonel in the Army?"

"Yes," she answered warily.

"What are you doing to fight the Nazis?"

"I—we," she amended, pointing to James, "—have information about where their base is. We worked on this project for years after the attack in Florida. James got injured in the attack on the 4th of July, so we weren't able to get the information to the Chairman of the Joint Chiefs before we got stranded here. That's why we need to make it out of the city."

Shorty closed the wallet and handed it back to her intact. "I got out the Navy two years ago, ma'am. You really know something about how to stop the Nazis?"

She nodded. "Yes. I have some files in our apartment. We're going to get clothes and make a run south through Anacostia and go to Fort Bragg, North Carolina, where the Army's Forces Command is located. They will put us in contact with whomever the new president is."

He gestured at the other thugs. "You three, help get this wheelchair down the stairs."

"Thank you," she muttered, overwhelmed by the sudden change.

"I don't know how you gonna get back up on the other side though."

"We'll figure something out. This is… You're a true patriot."

"Nah, I just don't want those Nazis around. They bad for business, y'know?"

The men initially tried to have the wheelchair roll backward down the escalator, but James' cries of pain made them alter their plans and they ended up carrying him the rest of the way down.

Including rest breaks, it took ten minutes to get the chair onto the platform. Stevie, who'd been one of the men supporting the weight from the bottom, was glistening with sweat by the time the move was over.

An abandoned Metro train sat on the tracks, all the doors open. In the dim lighting, she could see several people sitting inside. Shorty was already down there and walked up to them, handing her a flashlight.

"Thank you," Gloria repeated. "I don't know how we would have done it without you."

"We got you, ma'am," Shorty replied. He pointed down the tunnel. "That way is downtown. Stay on the little sidewalk beside the tracks and don't go down into the tracks—the third rail is still electrified. Try not to use the flashlight much, the emergency lighting should be enough once your eyes get used to the darkness."

She nodded, more grateful than she could express. "If you run into anyone, tell 'em that you're under Psycho Shane's protection. Understand?"

"Yes. Thank you."

"Go on, get that information to the Army," he said. "Good luck."

She pushed James' wheelchair toward the end of the tiled platform and onto a concrete pathway that stretched into the darkness beside the tracks. *Here goes nothing.*

FIFTEEN

11 July 2025
Richmond International Airport, Richmond, Virginia

"That's the last of 'em, sir. We can expect an Engineer company from the 1st Cavalry Division to replace us within two hours."

"Finally," Gabe muttered, cramming his hard, plastic spoon into the MRE pouch.

Berserker Company had spent the last six days as a combination of airport security and reception element for the 3rd Infantry Division's combat brigades. The units rolled off their transport planes and headed north, directly into battle. There'd been fights only sixty miles away in Fredericksburg, but Gabe Murdock's company hadn't been able to get in on anything.

Now it was Berserker's turn. They were being replaced so the Army could fly in a new division's equipment. The 1st Cavalry Division would secure the airport for themselves, which meant Gabe's company was free to return to their brigade. The problem was the company's entire fleet of troop-carrying trucks was down for maintenance back in Georgia, so they only had four Humvees for one-hundred and fourteen soldiers.

"Any update on transportation?" Gabe asked, giving voice to his thoughts.

The first sergeant grinned and ran his fingers along his scalp through close-cropped hair. "You're not gonna believe how we're getting to battle, sir."

"What did Diego dig up?"

"Two yellow school buses, five pick-up trucks and eight cars ranging from a little Ford Focus up to a Lincoln Town Car."

He laughed. "Where the hell did he get those things?"

"Oh, you know," the First Sergeant Thomas replied. "Good supply sergeants have a knack for finding things and figuring out how to use them for the company's advantage."

"Anything illegal?"

"Nothing you need to know about, sir," the older man winked.

Gabe let that part go. Being a good commander was knowing when to let NCO business stay NCO business and when to assert his authority. This wasn't one of those times. The company needed to go about eighty miles and the Army only gave them four Humvees to do it, so First Sergeant Thomas and Sergeant Diego helped to correct the problem.

He tried to do the math in his head, but came up with nothing useful. "That's enough seats for everyone?"

The first sergeant grunted in acknowledgement. "We can hold about forty-four soldiers per bus with no equipment, or less, with equipment. The trucks can hold between ten and twenty in the cabs, just depends on how close everyone wants to get, plus all the room in the back can have gear from the men on the buses. The cars will hold four each, with gear in the trunk or on the seat, so that's what, another thirty-two? And then our four Humvees hold eight more, plus gear. We're good, sir."

Gabe nodded his head and replied, "Get the men ready to go, First Sergeant. I want the platoon leaders and platoon sergeants here at my truck in one hour for a route brief. That's a lot of moving pieces for one convoy."

"Roger, sir."

He watched his company first sergeant stalk off to finalize the preparations for movement. The commander didn't need to worry about his soldiers having enough ammunition, food or water; that would be taken care of. What he needed to worry about was that an enemy fighter jet didn't wipe them out as they convoyed to the brigade area of operations in and around the Naval Surface Warfare Center in Dahlgren.

Gabe gathered the rest of his MRE trash off the hood of his command vehicle and tossed it in a garbage can before sitting in the passenger seat of the Humvee. He pressed the power button on his Blue Force Tracker, BFT for short, and the position of all known American forces populated on the display. He zoomed in on the area just northeast of his current position. The brigade headquarters was located near the southern shore of the Potomac River. Their mission was to block the Nazis from moving out of the DC area by escaping through southern Maryland.

According to the map, the most direct route would have been by going up the 301, but Gabe didn't want to risk it. Just one bored German pilot could ruin their day. The best route would be to take 360 northeast and cross the Rappahannock River, then shoot up Virginia Route 3, connect with the 218 and take that on into to the brigade AO. It added about an hour to the two-hour trip, but was likely less noticeable. Then again, wouldn't they run into the same potential problem doing that? All it took was one jet to notice the column.

He waffled in his mind, going back and forth several times before finally deciding he'd split his company. The decision went against everything he'd learned as an infantryman. He could hear his old Ranger Instructor, Sergeant First Class Faison, in his head, *Dividing your forces ensures that they'll be defeated piecemeal.* If they ran into trouble with enemy troops on the ground, it would look like a bad decision in hindsight.

The risk of a single column was too great, though. The first sergeant would lead one group across the river on which Gabe assessed to be the safer route, and he'd lead the other. To preserve combat power in the case of an attack, each group would get a bus and a couple of trucks and Humvees to carry gear. The cars would be split evenly, with four for each group.

Gabe sent a few messages to the battle captains and the battalion operations officer to tell them his plan. The S-3 approved his decision to split his forces, saying there'd been several overflights by the Nazi flying saucers, which caused the brigade headquarters and the various subordinate battalion headquarters to relocate into hardstand buildings. It was only a matter of time before they got tired of scouting and began strafing American positions.

He updated his anticipated arrival time so the order could go out to the men on the line not to shoot them when they pulled up and then powered off the BFT. The damn thing drew a ton of juice when the vehicle wasn't running. Twenty minutes on it and the Humvee battery would be dead.

To pass the time, he broke down his pistol and cleaned it, then did the same with his M4 carbine. He wanted to make sure that they were ready to go if they got into a scrape along the way.

A shadow darkened his window and he looked up to see First Sergeant Thomas. "Hey, sir. The gang's all here."

"Oh, the time got away from me," he lied, quickly reassembling his rifle.

The brief only took eight minutes, including questions. His platoon and squad leadership had all worked together and deployed to Africa last summer before he was in the unit. They knew each other and were consummate professionals, likely having already done a map recon themselves before coming to his truck.

"Alright, Berserkers," he said. "I want to be ready to roll the moment that First Cav bird hits the ground. I'll talk with their commander and show him the security points. We aren't gonna get any action just sitting around here with our thumbs up our ass."

"Go," the first sergeant grumbled, lifting both arms from his side toward the air in a *shooing* motion. "Get to your positions. Consolidate all your gear, don't leave any sensitive items behind or I'll have your asses."

Gabe watched the men and women walk back toward their troops. They were in the final stretch and he was finally going to get his revenge against the Nazis for what they did on the beach all those years ago.

*****

11 July 2025
United States Institute of Peace, Washington, DC

"You've cocked this up badly, Oberst Albrecht."

"Forgive me, Generalfeldmarschall, but how is our current situation my fault?"

"Your silly stunt in Florida alerted the Americans of our presence and they prepared for our return. My planners estimated that our perimeter would be at least one hundred and fifty kilometers further to the west and south by now."

"I admit that my attack may have given the Americans an enemy to prepare against, however, we haven't faced ground combat troops at all." Frederick gestured at the collapsed remains of the Lincoln Memorial through the glass front of the building. "The goddamned Luftwaffe spent too much time bombing historical sites instead of strategic positions and they have allowed themselves to become targets of high-altitude bombers by lazily parking their düsenjägers next to each other in neat little rows. They've even proven their inability to adjust to older technologies like shoulder-fired rockets. This—"

"Enough, Oberst," Generalfeldmarschall Mueller ordered, slicing his hand through the air. "*You* commanded the 938th Training Brigade and so *you* are ultimately responsible for the Luftwaffe's failures to adapt. They learned under your leadership."

"Generalfeldmarschall, that is not an accurate assessment. Fewer than twenty percent of the pilots in the cockpit were trained while I was in the brigade, even fewer while I commanded it—and I don't know of any of the squadron leaders who were born before 1985."

"So your belief is that the technology of the Luftwaffe is not the overmatch we had thought it would be?"

"Certainly it is. The Americans don't have anything that can go toe-to-toe with a düsenjäger in the air. They have proved vulnerable to sneak attacks from helicopters that hide in amongst the ground cover and from shoulder-fired rockets—all technologies that have existed for forty years, which should have been accounted for."

Frederick paused to assess his commander's mood. He claimed the problem was with the Luftwaffe, but in reality the problem was with the entire strategy. The attempted seizure of nuclear launch facilities across the American West by the Fallschirmjägers had been an utter failure and a waste of two thousand well-trained men. When he'd heard the paratroopers would be used in a manner that would leave small elements alone and completely isolated from support, he'd protested quietly, but the decision had already been made. The same type of mistake was being made on the East Coast, by not pressing their advantage. If they sat back and waited for the Americans to come, they would.

The field marshal seemed willing to listen right now. He'd even sought council from Frederick, so the colonel plowed ahead. "Sir, what of the Panzer Corps? Our hovertanks have proven to be unstoppable in their limited use in combat so far. Let us release them and destroy the American counterattack that is creeping toward us from both Richmond and Pennsylvania."

Generalfeldmarschall Mueller mulled over Frederick's words, seeming to consider his suggestion. Finally, the field marshal snorted and then laughed. "Why have I handcuffed our forces? The Panzer Corps will wipe the Americans off the map. We must expand our perimeter now and take advantage of the dry summer months before setting up the defenses for the winter campaign."

The man's words soured in Frederick's ears. Winter campaign? The Wehrmacht was originally supposed to attack, destabilize the nation and then return to Antarctica. His wife, Greta, had been dead for five long years, but he still had four sons in the Heer, one in the Luftwaffe and one in the Kriegsmarine. He'd believed that the party's thirst for vengeance against the Americans would be sated by the death of millions.

"Forgive me, Generalfeldmarschall. I thought that destroying the American will to fight was our goal. We have achieved it amongst the civilian population, their television news shows politicians and religious leaders begging for peace. We will destroy their army with your approval to utilize the Panzer Corps. What more could we want?"

"A homeland, Oberst Albrecht," the field marshal sighed. "The Reich's new objective is to establish a homeland for the millions of Germans suffering in the constant cold."

"I—That is a wonderful idea, sir! I hadn't thought beyond our initial occupation and destruction of the American army."

"I know you haven't, Oberst. Since my awakening, I have been continually unimpressed with you. The Americans were prepared for an attack from the sea. They destroyed both of our large transport vessels with missile cruisers at Norfolk on the day of our invasion, leaving us effectively stranded here. Why do you think they were prepared?"

"I... Erm... Is it because—"

"It is because of your ignorance and shortsightedness, beginning with the ill-advised attack in Florida. Your foolish desire to take part in a battle warned them, so they prepared in what ways that they could. Most of our cargo transports that operated outside of düsenjäger-controlled airspace have also been shot down.

"Thankfully," the field marshal continued, "the Americans are too stupid to heed warnings and it appears as if they've done little to prepare their ground forces."

Frederick fumed internally. He'd given up his youth, avoiding the cryogenic chambers to train the Wehrmacht.

Everyone he knew as a boy, all the Heer Henchmen except himself, appeared to be no more than nineteen years old. They had the opportunity to fight against the Americans on the land and in the air above, while he fought the aches and pains of a sixty-year-old body.

"Did you know," Generalfeldmarschall Mueller continued, "that I had every intention of having you arrested today?" He pointed toward the guards standing rigidly at attention several meters away.

Frederick blanched. "No, Generalfeldmarschall. I did not."

"Your recommendation to use the Panzer Corps as a hammer against the American reinforcements saved you—for now." The physically younger man took a few steps and turned back. "Did you know that I met Erwin Rommel once?"

"No, sir. I did not." Rommel was a hero to the Nazis. Frederick grew up studying his tactics with armored vehicles and reading about the man the British called the 'Desert Fox'. The Führer had him discredited during the war, but later Nazi historians restored his name to its rightful place after Hitler's death.

"It was in Italy in 1943—or maybe 1944, the years run together. We'd just shot and killed thirty or forty prisoners from the Italian Army after the Fascists declared an armistice with the Allies. Rommel's staff car appeared out of nowhere and he surveyed our handiwork. He gave each man in my squad a pack of cigarettes and thanked us for our dedication to the cause. Then he drove off and was later given command of Army Group B, responsible for defending the European coastline against the Allied invasion."

"It must have been exhilarating to meet such a great man."

"His panzer tactics are legendary. I want that type of attack to rapidly expand our perimeter."

Frederick nodded, clasping his hands behind his back as he walked a half-pace behind the commander of the Wehrmacht. Given the information he'd been told of his postponed arrest, he had to be careful with what he said. "Rommel's tactics worked well in Europe because the population thought we were only interested in fighting the Army. The American population is well-armed and seem willing to fight to the death against the occupation."

"Then we will have General der Panzertruppe Arnold crush everyone he encounters under his boot," the field marshal thundered. "Frederick, you anger me with your suggestion of using the Panzer Corps and then warning that using them would leave us vulnerable to attacks by civilians. The men will bend their knee and the women will lift their skirts for us. We are the most powerful force on the face of the planet!

"Even the remaining Allies refuse to come to the American's aid. The end of their republic is at hand." Spittle flew from Generalfeldmarschall Mueller's lips as he carried on. "Leave my sight before I have a change of heart once more and have you arrested."

Frederick spun rapidly on his heel and made a beeline toward the headquarters exit. His time in the Wehrmacht was over. He needed to escape before the field marshal changed his mind yet again.

He thought over the few options available to him. He felt that he spoke English passably, having learned from watching television and using the situations presented on the screen to make a connection with the language, so he might be able to escape the city. The closest exit from the German lines was south, across the river and into Virginia.

But what would he do once he made it out of the city?

*****

11 July 2025
Highway 301, near Port Royal, Virginia

Captain Gabriel Murdock's ass hurt, conspiring with the sweat oozing from his pores to make him miserable. The seat cushion in his Humvee was so thin that he could feel the metal frame along the back of his thighs and the heat from the batteries under his seat. He was cramped into the small space on the passenger side with his knees drawn up to the dash while an unstoppable heat poured from broken vents somewhere near his shins. It was decidedly not the glamorous lifestyle he'd imagined as a kid.

He stared out the windshield, his eyes roving between the pavement, the trees along the side of the road and the sky above. It was a matter of life or death to identify any Nazi fighter jets and get the Humvees off the road. The civilian vehicles were probably not going to attract attention, unless the pilot was simply bored.

The Blue Force Tracker beeped, indicating a new message. Far to the east, the blip of his first sergeant's Humvee had pulled off of the King's Highway once again. He'd sent the first sergeant's convoy ahead of his by an hour and a half, choosing to stay behind to ensure the First Cav guys had everything they needed before leaving on the more direct route.

Since leaving the airport, Gabe hadn't seen anything in the air, but the first sergeant repeatedly called a halt due to enemy activity. The BFT showed a decent scattering of friendly forces along the direct route as the Army moved steadily northward, but there was nothing over in the area of his second convoy except his troops.

The further they traveled, the constant aerial passes convinced Gabe that the enemy knew his men were alone.

He tapped the BFT screen with the stylus to open the first sergeant's message, which said:

3 UFO above. Convoy stop.

It wasn't a lot of info, but it gave Gabe enough to make his decision. It was too risky on the roads right now. He tapped out a quick message ordering the first sergeant to get off the road and wait until dark to travel the rest of the way. They'd arrive a few hours later than expected, not a big deal.

He hit send and turned his gaze back to the front, scanning for enemy activity while he waited for an acknowledgement. He waited for what seemed like ten minutes with no response from the first sergeant.

"What the hell?" he mumbled, twisting in the tiny seat to get a better view of the messaging application.

It showed that the message was sent three minutes and twenty seconds ago, but hadn't been opened. That wasn't like First Sergeant Thomas, the man was obsessive about staying in contact with everyone. He said as much to his driver, Specialist Mendoza.

"He probably went to take a piss or shit, sir," the specialist yelled over the vehicle's engine. "You know how much coffee the first sergeant drinks and he's always got a dip in his lip. Both of those things make *me* need to shit."

Gabe grinned and shouted back, "Yeah, you're right. Probably nothing."

He tried to put his belief that something wasn't right out of his mind and scanned for threats, but the feeling persisted. It was made worse by the unit icon flickering a few times on his display. He checked the message history again. It had been nine minutes.

"Okay, I'm calling him," Gabe announced. They were too far apart to reach each other over voice communications, so he pulled out his cell phone and dialed the first sergeant's number. It went directly to voicemail, which could have meant that his phone was off or the battery was dead. There were all sorts of reasons for the call to fail.

He dialed Lieutenant Phelps, it went direct to voicemail as well. Then he dialed Sergeant First Class Peterson. The same thing happened.

"Pull over!" he shouted.

Mendoza complied, pulling the truck off to the side of the road. Behind them, the rest of the vehicles did the same. Gabe noted with satisfaction that the convoy was spread out with at least a hundred meters between vehicles.

"I can't reach the first sergeant," he told the driver. "I tried Lieutenant Phelps and Sergeant Peterson. Nothing. They all go direct to voicemail. Whose number do you have?"

Mendoza pulled out his phone and dialed a few numbers, each time shaking his head. "I got nothing, sir."

"Fuck." The bottom of his stomach dropped out. It was conceivable that the leadership had their phones off to practice OPSEC, but impossible that the privates and specialists that Mendoza tried would have complied as well.

He saw movement in the mirror and recognized Lieutenant Jacob Wilcox's gait. When the lieutenant was beside the rear bumper, Gabe opened the door and stepped out.

"Sir, what's going on?" the platoon leader asked.

"The other convoy. We've tried to reach them through BFT and cell phone. Nobody's answering. I think they're gone."

The lieutenant pulled out his own cell phone and tried a few numbers in futility. "Dammit!" he cursed, jabbing at his phone screen. "Wait. What if they're jamming us, sir?"

Gabe inclined his chin, letting the helmet's weight pull his head toward his chest and stretch out the tight muscles in the back of his neck. "It's a possibility with the cell phones. I don't think it can be done with the BFT though. We use encrypted satellite communications networks that bounce all over the world. It would be hard to get into the data stream."

"So what does that mean?"

Gabe swallowed the lump in his throat. He'd deployed and fought in Syria and Yemen and even spent a few months in Cambodia when his battalion deployed to assist the Cambodian government in destroying a worldwide human trafficking ring. Out of all those dangerous situations, he'd lost three men—one of them a suicide. He couldn't believe that he'd lost half of his company, eighty-one soldiers, in the blink of an eye.

"We continue mission, Jake," he answered. "I'll report up to Battalion that we've lost comms with them and they'll report up to Brigade. If we don't hear from First Sergeant Thomas by the time we make it to Dahlgren, I'm sure Brigade will send a drone down to investigate."

"We could head east and investigate ourselves, sir."

The commander shook his head. "I want to. Believe me, I want to. It's a stupid move though. We've been left alone because the large number of anti-aircraft vehicles and soldiers along this route as they road march from the airport to their staging areas. There's nothing out east…which is why I originally thought it would be the safer route."

Gabe took a breath to steady himself. "I was wrong. I sent those men to their deaths." He wiped angrily at his eyes, the tears that had formed threatened to pour out over his cheeks. "If we go over there too, we're just making ourselves a target. Understand?"

Lieutenant Wilcox punched the side of Gabe's command truck. "This isn't fair, sir!"

"I know, Jake. It fucking sucks…" He trailed off and glanced at the BFT screen. The icon indicating the position of First Sergeant Thomas' vehicle was gone. His BFT was either turned off or destroyed.

"Get back to your truck, Jake. We're leaving in one minute."

SIXTEEN

12 July 2025
Anacostia, Washington, DC

"I hope this is it," Gloria groaned. "I'm so darn sweaty. I think the skin under my boobs is becoming its own ecosystem."

James smiled at his wife's assertion that she was growing something else besides the baby in her stomach. "Is this where we're going?" he asked the rough-looking teenager who'd escorted them from the bridge, pointing at the large, white brick church.

"Yeah," he answered. "Double D will know what to do with you."

It had taken them several days longer to leave the city than they'd planned. Psycho Shane's protective order was as good as his word and there'd been gang bangers on the other end of the Metro tunnel to help carry James and his wheelchair, for which he was eternally grateful. Without the help of those men, he'd still be pulling himself up the escalator, one stair at a time.

After the ordeal of the journey through the tunnels, the stress had caused Gloria to have false labor pains, forcing them to hole up in their apartment for two days. Yesterday, she was feeling better, so they decided to leave, but the Nazis moved a seemingly endless stream of troops and tanks through their neighborhood, causing yet another delay.

Finally, this morning the streets were clear and Gloria was feeling well enough to travel. They'd made their way through the ruined city, crossing the devastation of the National Mall and the surrounding buildings unmolested until they arrived at a Nazi checkpoint on the 11th Street Bridge. Playing on the Germans' racism, his wife had convinced the soldiers that she was a social worker who'd been meeting with D'onta's family when the attack occurred. The children's parents were dead, so she and James were taking them to their grandparents in Anacostia.

The soldiers bought her lie, without much more than a cursory rummaging through their bags, which were full of clothing and a few snacks that they were able to pack. They'd made the hard choice to leave everything but the essentials behind, knowing that they would likely be stopped several times along their escape. The Germans didn't even bother to look at the clothes; if they had they would have realized they were mostly adult sizes and questioned who was leaving.

Two blocks from the bridge, a few local toughs stopped them, demanding payment for passage. Again, the mention of Psycho Shane caused the men to stop. Their leader told James' little party that they had to go see Double D at the Union Temple Baptist Church if they wanted to continue traveling through the neighborhood.

"Who is this Double D guy?" James asked, pushing hard on his wheels to keep up. His hands were in agony from the repetitive motion and his shoulders and forearms seemed like they were about to fall off. But, he'd told himself that if Gloria could make it without complaints, then so could he.

"He's the man who's gonna say whether you live or die, cripple."

"Well, that's just lovely," Gloria muttered.

D'onta helped push James up the small ramp to the church's double glass doors and Gloria held the door open wide. The heat abated slightly inside the building's thick, brick walls. James hadn't ever thought much about the magnificence of air conditioning, but if they survived this ordeal, he would never take it for granted again.

"You wait here," the teen ordered, indicating the general lobby area. He disappeared down a hallway before Gloria could give him a snarky comeback.

"Well, this brought us about half a mile further," James stated, rubbing his palms in an effort to massage some of the soreness away.

"And it was in the right direction," Gloria agreed. "They could have taken us back toward the city, so it's a win in my book."

"Are we still going to be allowed to leave?" D'onta asked.

"Of course," Gloria replied. "They won't keep us here. Mister Double D just wants to meet with us before we go."

James hoped she was right. *People that use a church as a base of operation can't be all that bad*, he consoled himself. *Right?*

Gloria's explanation seemed to work, so the boy led his younger sister, Phelisha, to explore the lobby. Lakeisha stayed near James and Gloria. The girl was extremely shy, and over the last few days she'd refused to leave their side. It worried James. He hadn't been prepared to become a father figure to more than the little one in his wife's stomach, now he had an instant flock of kids that he was responsible for keeping track of.

Whoever Double D was, he didn't seem concerned with people roaming around his headquarters building. The children explored every nook and cranny, discovering a supply of building blocks and coloring books. Lakeisha detached herself from Gloria and wandered over to her siblings where she began to color.

Within ten minutes, the teen returned and ordered Gloria and James to follow him. The kids grabbed several books and a handful of crayons each before they followed behind the adults.

The youth led them to an office labeled '**Pastor**'. Inside, a black man of around thirty sat behind the desk. Several tourist maps of the city were laid open on the desktop, some of them with large circles drawn on them. From his lower vantage point, it looked like some of the circles were around buildings and some were at other locations, like the bridges and street corners.

The man at the desk covered the maps with a few blank pages of paper. "Hello," he greeted them.

"Hi," James replied meekly.

"What's the meaning of detaining us?" Gloria demanded.

Like a goddamned wrecking ball, James moaned in his head.

"I'm sorry," the man answered. "My name is Devon."

He offered his hand and James shook it. "Are you Double D?" Gloria asked.

The man winced. "The street kids call me that. I'm *Deacon* Devon, from the church."

"Oh," Gloria chirped. "I wasn't expecting that." James knew his wife; people seldom surprised her, but this was one of those rare times.

Double D smiled. "I'm sorry. Should I have affected a gangster pose and wore a sideways hat?"

She laughed. "No, Mister Devon. I—"

"Devon is my first name; Devon Johns."

"I meant I wasn't expecting the man to be running the street gangs to be a man of the church," Gloria plowed on through his interruption.

"I don't run the street gangs, ma'am," the deacon disputed. "They choose to work with me so we can get rid of those motherfucking Nazis—excuse my language."

Gloria nodded her head. "Motherfucking Nazis is right, Devon. We're trying to get away from them too."

"Oh, let's be clear, ma'am. I ain't running from them," Devon answered. "I'm gonna do whatever I can to make sure they get what they deserve for attacking my city."

James crossed his arms over his chest and said, "So, you're not a gang member then?"

"No!" the deacon said, standing rapidly and then cramming his hands in his pockets. "I am not a gang member. I am a community organizer; I lead our community in organized resistance. I didn't want the role at first, but when they murdered Pastor Kelly, the Nazis forced that on me."

Devon stared out the window, through the bars. "What is your story?" he asked. "How did two white folks with black children get the blessing of Psycho Shane?"

"We needed help getting from the Rosslyn Metro Station to the other side of the river because of James' wheelchair," Gloria answered. "Shane helped us get the wheelchair down the stairs and his men got it out at the other end."

"What did you have to pay him off with?"

"Nothing—" Gloria stopped. "You don't approve of his ways, do you?"

"Of course not. The man is a lunatic. This church stood as a beacon of hope for our youth, giving them a shot at education and fellowship without joining a street gang. We were bitter enemies with the gangs until the Nazis came; now we're in an uneasy truce. I've got the police and a lot of military members—"

He stopped suddenly. James thought he knew why. "We're not collaborators, Devon," he offered. "We hate them just as badly as you. Those three children are without parents... I'm crippled for life... Hundreds of thousands of people are dead. All of that happened because of those *motherfucking* Nazis. You don't have to worry about us."

"You still haven't answered my question," Devon stated, sitting back down. "What did you give Psycho Shane in exchange for his help?"

"I'm an officer in the US Army," Gloria replied. "He was trying to shake us down and saw my ID card. He used to be in the Navy and offered to help us, free of charge."

"No joke? That guy was in the Navy?"

"That's what he told us," she confirmed.

"We could use more military leadership. Would you be interested in joining our cause?" Double D pointed at Gloria's stomach. "Obviously, not in the field, but you could help out with planning and tactics."

She shook her head. "I'm sorry, Devon. I have to leave the city and get in touch with my leaders."

Gloria stopped and looked sidelong at James. He nodded. "It's okay."

"I may have information about where the Nazis came from so we can nuke them into oblivion."

The words hung in the air and the silence was palpable.

"You know a way to end this earlier?" Devon asked.

Gloria grimaced. "I *may* have the information, based on historical data. They were definitely there at one point, but they may be gone now."

"Anything is better than nothing." The conversation ceased once more and Devon folded the corner of a piece of paper. He was worrying over something.

Finally, he said, "I—we—have a favor to ask you."

"What is it?" James asked guardedly. He wasn't in the habit of agreeing to favors without knowing what was being asked of him.

Devon stood and said, "I'll be right back. Hold on."

He rushed out of the room and closed the door behind himself. James glanced back at the kids to see what they were doing. They sat on the floor, coloring the books they'd taken from the lobby. He turned back to Gloria. "What's that all about?"

She shrugged. "I don't know. It has something to do with our knowledge about the Nazi base though. I'd just about guarantee that."

There were two quick knocks on the door and Devon reappeared. "Sorry to keep you waiting—although you're probably better off waiting until the morning to leave. We can keep you safe here overnight."

"What do you want from us?" Gloria asked. "You weren't all that willing to help out until you heard about my occupation and why we wanted to leave the city."

Devon ducked his chin and turned slightly back into the hallway. He reached out and then gently guided an older man, thin with age, into the doorway. "Let me introduce you to Colonel Frederick Albrecht. He's a Nazi defector and he knows what they're planning to do."

*****

13 July 2025
Naval Surface Warfare Center, Dahlgren, Virginia

"You need to snap out of it, Gabriel. There's nothing you could have done. This is war; shit happens."

Gabe looked at his commander as if he'd never seen the man before. He wasn't dumb enough to get mouthy and then get in trouble, but *shit happens*? That's what he got for losing eighty men. Men whom he was responsible for; some of them, like First Sergeant Thomas, had been his friends.

The brigade unmanned aerial systems had finally been able to fly down to Montross, where the first sergeant's convoy had stopped when they saw the Nazi planes. They'd found the burnt-out wreckage of two Humvees, a big yellow school bus, four sedans and one pickup truck; there was no sign of the second truck. Bodies were clearly visible as the UAV dropped lower and decreased its speed enough to keep it aloft, barely.

Gabe wanted to scream obscenities at the callous man standing beside his truck. "Uh… I get it, sir," he replied instead. "I know that it was all a matter of luck, but I'm still the one who ordered them to go that way."

"Then believe that it was me who ordered them to go," Lieutenant Colonel Calhoun offered. "I'm the one who told you to come to Dahlgren. Blame me. Do whatever you need to do to get your head back in the game because I have a mission for you."

The captain's head snapped up. "A mission?" *Revenge*, he thought.

"Yeah, it comes all the way from the President of the United States. Division was given the mission to secure a high value asset. Seems the Nazis have a senior defector who knows their capabilities and their battle plan. We need to go get him before they snatch him back up. Division gave the mission to our Brigade, Colonel Graves gave it to me, and I'm giving it to you, Gabe. This is a matter of national importance, if you can't do it, then—"

"We'll do it, sir!" Gabe replied hastily. If he could get his hands around the neck of one of the senior Nazi officials, he'd wring every bit of information out of him that there was. In the flash of an instant, he imagined himself as an interrogator, leading the defector through mental and physical anguish in order to get the needed information.

Colonel Calhoun slapped a large, meaty palm on Gabe's shoulder, stirring him from his victorious musings. "Good, I knew I could count on you. This is top priority, so I'm giving you the battalion eighty-ones and our snipers. I know you lost half of your heavy weapons, so Alpha company is giving you soldiers to round out your company."

Gabe held up a hand. "Sir, that's what got my men killed the first time around. If there'd only been a handful of them, the Germans probably wouldn't have even noticed them. I think going up as a full company is a bad idea."

"Well, give me your suggestion, then."

"No more than a platoon—in civilian clothing, with civilian vehicles. Once we get within twenty or thirty miles of the city, we dismount and go in on foot. I doubt many people are driving *toward* DC, so it would send up a warning immediately. We go in with a very small footprint, pick up the defector and then get the hell out of there."

Calhoun rubbed at the day's stubble on his chin. "In and out quick, like a Ranger platoon, huh?"

"Yes, sir. Just like the Rangers." Gabe knew his commander didn't mean to compare Berserker Company to the Rangers—who'd taken one hundred percent casualties in the first days of the war attempting to parachute into the city.

"It sounds good on the surface, but what if you run into—hell, into just about any size enemy element?"

"We'll have our FO and I'd want the battalion JTAC," Gabe replied immediately, saying that he had his own company artillery observer, but he also wanted the battalion Air Force Joint Tactical Air Controller, or JTAC, to control close air support.

Calhoun shook his head. "I can't give you the JTAC, Gabriel. The belief that you could call in fast movers would be potentially disastrous. So far, the only thing our jets have been able to do against the Nazi UFOs is get killed. Until we can figure out a way to gain air superiority, the Air Force isn't flying."

"So no CAS," Gabe muttered. "I can live with that as long as the long guns are up and ready to go."

"I'll get with Spartan Six immediately after this and try to get dedicated artillery…" Lieutenant Colonel Calhoun trailed off, staring at a spot on the ground. After a few seconds, he slapped the hood of Gabe's Humvee. "Alright. Approved. I want you to pack body armor and helmets though. Their benefits outweigh the risk. Pick your men. You have the pick of anyone in the battalion. I don't think you're going to want to take the 81s if you're humping it; your company 60s can handle the job. But, I want you to take a sniper team."

"Yes, sir. I'm also gonna need some 240 gunners and A-gunners, but other than that, I should be good to go. I'm taking Lieutenant Wilcox's platoon."

"His dad died at the Pentagon, didn't he?"

Gabe nodded. "We think so, sir. He was a colonel on the Army staff and at work when the building was destroyed."

"Does he have any other family?"

"A mom in one of the DC suburbs, but he doesn't know if she's alive either."

"This is a shitty mess, any way you cut it," Calhoun stated. "I'm gonna go tell the Three that you're in the planning stages of your mission and make that phone call to Spartan Six."

Gabe's commander walked a few steps and then turned back. "You need to be on the road by tomorrow morning, zero eight hundred. Good luck, Gabriel."

"Thank you, sir," he replied and grabbed the radio handset once the older man was gone.

"Jake, it's Berserker Six. We've got a lot of planning to do. I need you and your platoon sergeant at my victor in five minutes. We're going after those sons-a-bitches."

*****

13 July 2025
US Port of Entry, Loring, Montana

Gregory stumbled and sat heavily on the ground, scraping his elbow on a rock. If he were honest with himself, he'd actually fallen, but he would never admit that it happened. *Fallschirmjägers don't get tired. Especially from insignificant things like exhaustion, dehydration, hunger, and sunburn*, he told himself as he wiped the blood onto his trousers.

He'd traveled nearly three hundred kilometers, 190 miles according to the road signs, from Bravo Flight near Lewiston to the Canadian border. He'd quickly shed his uniform top, hat and all but his pistol, which he kept in the holster under his shirt instead of on the outside. Gregory absently patted the weapon to ensure it was still there, instantly regretting it as his hand brushed across the chaffed skin around his waist where the nylon had dug into his unprotected skin.

Growing up inside Argus Base hadn't prepared Gregory for the heat and the dangers of the sun. He didn't even know that a sunburn was possible. Within hours of his initial flight after his platoon was roasted alive by the secret American weapon the skin on his arms, face, and neck was bright red and hot to the touch. In places, he even had blisters filled with fluid. He figured out that it was the sun on his bare skin and sought cover. Since that day, he'd traveled only at night, paralleling the road steadily northward.

And now he'd made it to Canada and freedom.

Gregory pulled the binoculars from his pack and scanned the large, squat building less than half a kilometer away from where he sat. Big, black block letters on the front of the building stated that it was the United States Port of Entry. His English was passable, but he had no idea what a "port" was. He determined it must be another word for building and put the thought out of his head. It wasn't important.

He looked at the parking lot to see if there were any vehicles present. It looked like there were only two; one sedan and one of the smaller lories the Americans preferred to drive—although as far as Gregory could tell, they rarely carried anything in the cargo area.

"So, two vehicles," he mumbled aloud. "That means there could be six or seven people in the building."

His mind worked the math. He had twelve bullets in his pistol and three more magazines in his pack, bringing his total number of rounds to thirty-six. More than enough to kill seven guards, but they likely had rifles for standoff distances as well as other defenses. He shuddered at the memory of his men roasting, their skin bursting open as the meat inside of them cooked.

Gregory watched the station for a few more minutes with interest. No one entered or left the building and besides the vehicles, there didn't appear to be anyone present. He shifted his view, following the road beyond the building. There was a checkpoint of sorts, with a draw arm that was painted with the colors of the American flag. Beyond that was another draw arm painted with the Canadian colors. Both were lifted out of the way of traffic, indicating to Gregory that the border was open.

The border-crossing site seemed incredibly welcoming, surprising Gregory. As a child, he'd learned the Americans were some of the cruelest creatures on the planet—the weapon at Bravo Flight was certainly indicative of that—while the Canadians were hapless tree farmers, dragged into the war by their treaties with England. The only martial thing about the entire border crossing point was a three-meter tall barbed-wire fence, which ran for about a hundred meters on either side of the road before terminating as if both parties thought the entire attempt at security too tedious to continue.

He checked his watch. There were only two hours until daylight, so if he was going to make the crossing, it needed to be done soon. Walking through the checkpoint would probably alert a lot of unwanted attention, especially since he had no papers of any kind. If he was stopped, they'd detain him immediately and then they'd quickly discover that he was a German paratrooper.

That meant the checkpoint wasn't a valid option, so that left the open fields on either side of the checkpoint. The US-Canadian border was thousands of miles long; he could simply begin walking in one direction and cross over at any point, away from watchful eyes.

Gregory decided that's what he'd do. He dug into his pack and fished out his canteen. He'd filled it from a cattle pond two days ago. Since then, he'd sipped at it sparingly, unknowing when he'd get another opportunity to fill the bottle. He shook it near his ear. It sounded empty.

He unscrewed the cap and tilted it up into the air above his outstretched tongue. A few droplets fell into his mouth, but that was it. He was out of water.

Gregory cursed his luck at being assigned an impossible mission. He'd trained his men hard, waking months before the regular Heer soldiers, and it was all for nothing. They'd not captured the launch facilities. Hell, he didn't even know if they'd even *seen* the launch facilities or if they'd only encountered the security buildings. As far as he knew, he was the last fallschirmjäger in the entire Wehrmacht. The Americans were prepared for the attack—unlike what his superiors had estimated.

The canteen went back into the pack and he rolled onto his hands and knees painfully, and then pushed himself up like an old man. He *felt* old. Too bad Schütze Markel was dead; Gregory could have used a quick injection of the serum to give him the energy to carry on.

He glanced back at the Port of Entry building to ensure no one observed him. It was as quiet as it had been the entire time, so he plunged into the grass, walking roughly parallel to the barbed wire fence. The sound of his boots crushing the brown grass underfoot filled his ears.

And yet… There was another noise echoing in his mind. It reminded him of something he'd heard before, but he couldn't quite place it. He stopped and the sound seemed to magnify as it became the only noise to fill the night.

It came from somewhere high above him in the pitch black sky. Something was up there. It was something familiar.

"*Scheisse!*" he screeched. It was a drone, like they'd used at Bravo Flight. He was sure he'd been spotted.

He turned and lumbered toward the Canadian border. The whir of the drone's rotors became louder and he knew it was descending.

Faster! Faster, you idiot! he chastised himself. He knew enough about international boundaries to know that if he could make it over the border he'd be safe. The Americans couldn't do anything to him once he set foot in Canada.

Shouts of alarm and the barking of dogs came from his left. He risked a quick glance. Flashlights bounced as men ran out of the building. It was more than seven.

The drone sounded as if it were right behind him and then his body suddenly went rigid. He couldn't stop himself from falling as electricity coursed through his body, causing his muscles to shake violently.

He screamed in pain, embarrassed at his reaction. Then the feeling of being electrocuted stopped and he tried to sit up, but his body was slow to follow his commands.

Dimly, he heard the dogs getting closer. He drew the pistol and crawled awkwardly toward the border. He'd been so close. If he could make it, they wouldn't be able to do anything.

A vicious growl was the only warning he had before canine teeth sank several inches into his calf muscle. The dog shook its head, tearing away flesh. Gregory screamed again and fired blindly into the darkness behind him.

He was rewarded with a yelp and the filthy creature released him.

Then another set of fangs closed around his wrist, crushing the bones there. The pistol tumbled away uselessly. The dog jerked him violently, causing him to fumble his recovery attempt for the weapon.

Rough, angry voices filled the air as the bones in his wrist continued to be ground into jagged shards. The shape of a man appeared in the inky void above him and he had half a second to realize that the soldier's arm was drawn back. Gregory threw up his free hand to shield himself.

The blow fell quickly, smashing into the arm that wasn't held by the dog. The border patrol agent repeatedly hammered his baton down on the paratrooper until the arm fell away and it connected solidly with his head.

Oberleutnant Gregory Wagner, Fallschirmjäger Platoon Four commander, knew no more.

SEVENTEEN

14 July 2025
Marine Corps Base Quantico, Triangle, Virginia

"Driver, back!" Staff Sergeant Meyers shouted into the microphone on his helmet. "Gunner, identify."

"Tank, uh…hostile," Sergeant Gaines said, unsure of what to call the giant vehicle they'd managed to ambush.

"Load sabot," Meyers said calmly. They'd rehearsed this thousands of times, shot hundreds of main gun rounds together. He wouldn't let his crew hear the fear he felt at participating in the first tank-on-tank battle in over twenty years. If he got off a clean shot, they'd take the German tank right in the side. "Aim for where the turret meets the hull, Gunner."

"On the way!"

The tank shook violently as the depleted uranium round shot out of the 120mm main gun of Meyers' Abrams tank at 5,700 feet per second. The round impacted directly where Meyers had ordered Gaines to shoot, right in the weakest spot of any tank. Much is said about the engine compartment or the underside of tanks, but the area where the turret met the hull was thin metal by comparison.

Smoke began to pour out of the hovertank's turret as the inside of the German tank caught on fire. Within seconds, flames shot out of every possible opening and then the optics in the Abrams fuzzed out from a massive explosion that sent the turret flying several feet into the air.

"Hot damn! Her rounds cooked off!"

"That's what I'm talking about!" Gaines cheered.

Meyers opened the hatch above his head, letting the fresh air pour into the cramped interior of the tank. "Keep an eye out, Gaines. I'm gonna go up and see what there is to see."

He pulled his body up onto the seat and stood with his upper body exposed. The Abrams' optics were second to none, but he got tunnel vision looking through them. There was an entire world of danger around them, especially in the air above and the ground behind, where they were blind.

They sat at the edge of a wood line, several feet back from the open area they'd prepared to cross when they identified the German tank. Their aerial overwatch, an Apache helicopter, flew overhead. He watched as rounds poured out of the 30mm cannon underneath the nose.

He couldn't see what they were firing at, but it was clear that they shot across the horizon instead of the ground. The helicopter juked straight up and began firing again. "What are they shooting at?" he wondered out loud.

Meyers' glasses were covered in specks of dirt. *More likely*, he corrected himself, *overspray from my gunner's spit bottle*. He pulled them off and looked at the lenses. There didn't seem to be anything on them, but he rubbed them on his coveralls just to be sure.

When he put them back on, they were clear until he looked up at the helicopter. Black specks surrounded the bird and he realized what the Apache gunner had been firing at. "Drone swarm!" he shouted.

"Huh?" Sergeant Gaines asked, opening his own hatch and popping up.

Meyers pointed into the air around the helicopter just as several of the small, unmanned drones impacted against the rotor blades. The drones shattered under the immense power of the rotors, but more flew in, replacing those that were destroyed.

The helicopter jerked hard to the side and the blades destabilized. Meyers watched in shock as one of the blades impacted against the fuselage, shearing the end of it off. One of the engines caught fire as the helicopter plummeted to the ground, hitting with a deadly crunching of metal and glass.

"Holy shit!" Gaines shouted over the tank engine. "I can't believe we just saw that."

"It was a drone swarm," Meyers repeated into his helmet communications system. "They've been briefing us for years that an enemy could do something like that to bring down a helicopter or plane, but wow…that was quick."

A shadow darkened the ground at the edge of his vision and he tore his eyes from the sky. Something was out there. "Gunner, identify!" he shouted, dropping back into his tank to press his face against the sights.

"Tank, 1,200 meters!" Gaines yelled back, already in position.

Too late, the crew saw the massive German hovertank as it turned its turret toward them.

"Driver, back!" Staff Sergeant Meyers managed to say. Then he tried to order the loader to chamber a round, but his mouth didn't work. His brain registered a bright flash and then everything was gone.

*****

14 July 2025
Anacostia, Washington, DC

The sirens from passing emergency vehicles blared outside and gunfire rattled the ancient windows of the historic home where Gloria's party holed up. They'd been set to leave the city when word filtered in to Deacon Johns that the Army was sending a unit into the city to extract the colonel. Devon convinced them to stay, that way they didn't miss the soldiers on their journey south. Gloria agreed with him. Both she and James needed the extra rest, so it didn't take a lot of convincing.

That was yesterday.

Overnight, the Germans launched a full out offensive into the neighborhoods of Anacostia with the intent of wiping out the resistance. Frederick retained his radio and warned Devon of the attack, earning him the eternal gratitude of the community organizer, who was able to set up a rapid defense against the Nazi forces at the river.

Gloria pressed the power button on her cell phone, praying that the battery still had enough of a charge to turn on. It did, but after a few seconds, it was clear to her that the signals were still jammed, so she powered it off quickly. She wanted to tell her mother that she loved her one final time before the end.

"Stop it," James chastised.

"Hmm?"

"Stop thinking that we're not going to make it," he clarified. "You've tried your phone at least five times today. The damn battery is gonna wear out."

"I just want to say goodbye."

"You don't need to. We're gonna get through this and you'll see her before you know it."

"I don't know," she replied. "This feels different. The Nazis are attacking on the ground—that hasn't happened before."

"That's because there wasn't an organized resistance to attract their attention before. Devon and Psycho Shane have an army of men and women who are armed to the teeth and ready to fight for their homes."

"Be thankful the panzers have not come," Colonel Albrecht grunted from the corner where he sat on the edge of a box.

"Excuse me?" Gloria asked. She was already annoyed with the smug German. He rarely spoke, except when it was to praise the technology of the German Army and Air Force.

"The panzers," he repeated. "They are moving to the southwest in attack formation." He held up the radio. "I have a few hours of battery life remaining. The panzers are—how do you say—*knocking up* the American armor."

Gloria suppressed a giggle, intent on being angry, but it eluded her attempts and came out anyways. "It's 'knocked out'. Knocking up means…well," she pointed to her stomach.

"Ah, it means with child. How silly I must sound," Frederick said. "The reports are that the Americans are very good at setting traps and ambushes. When they attack a panzer from an ambush position, they can kill it—if the angles are right, of course. However, they are quickly destroyed by the panzer's wingman."

More of the advances in German technology. Gloria stared at him, attempting to bore holes through his forehead. "How did your technology advance so rapidly? You guys couldn't have had many resources locked away down there on Antarctica."

It was the German's turn to flinch. "How do you know—Who are you? Do you work for the C-I-A?"

She placed both of her hands on her hips. His elaborate pronunciation of the three letters infuriated her even more. "I don't have to tell you a damn thing. Why don't you start with telling me why you're defecting? Are you planning on betraying us? How do we know that you're not transmitting our location right now, or that you aren't going to do so once we take you to the field headquarters? Maybe you're a suicide bomber or something."

He chuckled and pointed to his own body. "Do you think we'd rely on such a frail old man to be a suicidal bomber? I think not." He sighed and rubbed his palms on his thighs to clear away the sweat.

"I am sentenced to death by our commander, Generalfeldmarschall Mueller."

"Why? What did you do?" James asked, coming into the conversation.

Frederick glanced at him and then looked back at Gloria. "I am the commander of the 938th Training Brigade. For the past forty-three years, I have been training our soldiers to fight against the Americans, waiting for the day when our revenge would come. I—"

Gloria interrupted him. "How did you feed all of those people? It must have been nearly impossible."

"Ah, but you see, there were never more than three hundred thousand or so awake at any given time."

"Awake?" James repeated. "What do you mean by that?"

"Our soldiers are divided into age groups and go through training together as a group. They are encouraged to breed with as many women as possible before their seventeenth year. When the age group turns seventeen, they go through a lottery. Less than one percent stay to become trainers, the remaining members of the age group are administered a regeneration serum and then cryogenically frozen, stored away in the deepest parts of the base until it's time. Now they are all here, including the training brigade soldiers."

Gloria opened her mouth and then closed it. Was he attempting to fool her? He certainly looked serious. "I, uh… Are you being serious or are you joking?"

"I am not joking, Miss Gloria," he answered. "As a man who was not frozen, it is heartbreaking to see your friends and your children packed away when their time comes. I did my duty to the Reich, sacrificing everything, only to be told that because we have experienced setbacks that it is my fault due to ineffective training. What about poor leadership from that old fool, Mueller!"

The German sprung up, surprisingly spry for an old man, and then leaned heavily against the wall. "I am the fool," he wailed. "Six children. I have six children, all of whom are in the Wehrmacht. I attempted to seek them out, but only found two of them. They barely recognized me. I've aged so much without the regeneration serum."

"How did your scientists work through the problems of freezing and reanimating human beings?" James asked, obviously fascinated. "I mean, we've tried it with animals, but nothing makes it through without dying."

"The Aryan gave us the formulas, unlocked the secrets of regeneration and assisted with the design of our hovertanks, the düsenjägers, the shrouding devices that allowed us to arrive undetected… He's advanced our technology by centuries."

Gloria's mind reeled. The survivor from the crash in the Bavarian Alps in 1938. She remembered the day she met James in the Pentagon. She told him of the UFO crash in the Alps and he looked at her like she was insane. Now, this man was reinforcing her research. It was real.

"I knew it! I knew the Aryan survived the crash. What else has he told you—more importantly, why?"

"I am not certain, miss. The Aryan was helping German scientists long before I was born. The düsenjägers were an old technology by the time I was old enough to choose whether I would train as a Luftwaffe pilot, join the Heer, or, God forbid, the Kriegsmarine."

"He has to have a reason for doing it," Gloria pressed. "Why?"

"I don't know. He and I had a falling out years ago. At the time, the bulk of the Wehrmacht was still frozen and I was the highest ranking officer not sleeping. I wanted to know the same things you're asking, but he refused to tell me, publicly questioning my loyalty to the Reich."

"So you accepted help from someone you know nothing about?"

The German stared at his feet, whether in contemplation or embarrassment, Gloria wasn't sure. "Yes," he answered after some time. "The Führer trusted the Aryan completely and Generalfeldmarschall Mueller was his man. So, the Reich listened to him, following his designs and recommendations for weaponry and medical advancements—allegedly based on what he could remember from his own society."

Gloria nodded. It didn't seem to be Colonel Albrecht's fault that they blindly followed the Aryan. "I'm sorry if this is difficult for you—"

A loud explosion nearby made everyone jump. Little Phelisha screamed and ran over from where she'd sat coloring to bury her face in Gloria's armpit. Automatic weapons fire responded to the explosion.

Frederick tilted his head, listening. "Those are MG98s—the machine guns that our heavy weapons platoons carry. They sound much closer than they were previously."

Gloria looked to her husband. "Should we try to get out of the city before we get surrounded again?"

"I think we're probably better off staying put in here," he answered. "We're underground, for the most part. Even if we were to get searched, there's nothing linking us to the resistance."

"Except him," Gloria replied, pointing at the German.

"Except him," James acknowledged.

She thought about it a little longer and decided it was best to stay put. James couldn't run and hide like everyone else if the Nazis came close and they were immeasurably more safe underground in the basement.

"Alright," she said, sitting down on a folding chair. "We'll stay put. But if the Germans come down here, we don't know the colonel. Understood?"

James nodded and Gloria looked back at Albrecht. "Before that interruption, you said the Führer trusted the Aryan. Hitler? You're talking about Hitler, right?"

"Of course," the German replied. "There is no other Führer."

A ripple of excitement coursed through Gloria. "Did he… Did he commit suicide in 1945 like everyone believes?"

"No. The Führer would never have done anything so cowardly."

"I knew it!" she said, clapping her hands. "How'd he escape? Was it a deal with the Russians?"

"No, he hated the Slavs until the day he died."

"Oh. He's dead? I thought you just got done saying that you had a regeneration serum and everyone got frozen."

"That is true. However, Adolf Hitler died in 1946. The serum was not finished until the mid-1960s."

"So he died before Operation Highjump," Gloria stated, intrigued by the new information. "Didn't you say that the Aryan had the formula? Why didn't he give it to Hitler?"

"Because it was not ready…"

"But the Aryan must have had some to copy the formula from—what did Hitler die of?"

"A heart attack."

"Hmmm…and you say it was almost twenty years later that the serum was available?"

"Yes. Roughly that."

"Long enough for all of the senior leadership of the Third Reich who'd made it to Antarctica to die of natural causes," James surmised as if he'd read her mind.

A look of confusion passed across Albrecht's features. It seemed to be a line of thought that he'd never explored. "No. It just took that long to duplicate the serum in our labs. It was…" He faltered, unable to continue.

"I think it's entirely possible that this Aryan fellow is playing his own game," Gloria concluded. "One that he didn't want any of the original members of the Fourth Reich to discover. He must have waited for them to die of natural causes."

"Generalfeldmarschall Mueller has been there from the beginning," Albrecht said, ignoring the machine gun fire that erupted once more. It sounded like it was directly in the front yard. For all they knew, it was. "He was the man who shot the Jews to fake the Führer's death. He is as connected as any man could be."

"Was he a senior party member at the time?"

"No. He was only an oberjäger."

"Quite a meteoric rise in rank," Gloria stated. "That's what, a sergeant in the German paratroopers? All the way to the highest ranking officer."

The colonel smiled. "I'm impressed, Miss Gloria. You know a great deal about the Wehrmacht and secret German history. What do you do for the Army?"

"Frankly, that's none of your damn business, Colonel."

He held up his hands in front of himself. "I'm not meaning to be difficult. It's simply that the ranks within the fallschirmjäger formations is fairly obscure, probably the least understood of any German unit. You're something of an expert on the fallschirmjägers, are you?"

"I'm a generalist," she stated truthfully. "I just happen to be interested in early airborne operations, which, as we all know, the fallschirmjägers perfected."

He nodded. "Well, I can't tell you exactly how Mueller rose to power, he was our leader and already frozen by the time I was just a few years old."

"So—"

A loud explosion shook the basement walls, raining down dust and particles from the old ceiling tiles. Gloria held her breath and covered her nose. The older tiles contained asbestos and the basement didn't look like it had undergone and renovations over the years, so they were likely the original tiles. She didn't need the baby getting that mesothelioma cancer bullshit from asbestos.

When her air supply ran out, she pulled her shirt up over the bottom part of her face and breathed through the fabric. It took a few minutes for the dust to settle, everyone content to listen to the sounds of battle outside, which alternated from sounding near to far away.

Finally, the air looked clear enough to talk, but Gloria kept her shirt up, not giving a damn that the lower part of her stomach was exposed. "So, as I was saying," she began. "It seems like the Aryan is using your people. An entire generation of people fooled into believing that he has your best interests in mind—*generations* of people apparently."

"Sixty-seven generations to be exact. Although only fifty-six are in the invasion force."

She glared at the German. "Why are you defecting again, exactly? You said you'd been sentenced to death, but it's obvious that you love your country, or homeland, or whatever you call it. Why are you willing to betray them?"

"My home is called Argus Base, but we still refer to the entire continent as Neuschwabenland," he answered, infuriatingly polite. "And, yes, I love my people without question. However, even though I am distrustful of the American government's motives and was raised to believe that you were savages, I do not agree with the wonton sacrifice of German life to carve out a new Fatherland."

James snorted. "*We're* savages? Have you ever heard of Auschwitz? Birkenau? Buchenwald? Hell, fifty other places just like them?"

Albrecht tilted his head in thought. "The names sound familiar. Were they training camps or—no, wait, they were prisons in old Deutschland, correct?"

"Concentration camps," James amended, "where your precious Führer ordered the murder of *millions* of Jews, Poles, political dissenters, homosexuals and the like. The Nazis are the savages. Americans liberated those camps, rescuing the ones we could. I may be in a wheelchair, but I'll kick your German ass if you dare say that we were the savages."

"You Americans are so self-righteous," the colonel scoffed. "*You* are the only nation in the world to use nuclear weapons in warfare, dropping them as a test run on the Japanese and then again in Neuschwabenland, destroying our primary base and condemning us to live in the cramped Argus location and forcing us to freeze people alive so we wouldn't starve."

He stood and pulled down on the ends of his uniform jacket. "Don't talk to me about savagery." The colonel stalked off to the farthest corner of the room and sat back down, obviously finished with the conversation.

"Well, looks like he's done talking," Gloria muttered.

"And he still didn't answer the question about why he was defecting," James added.

"No, I think he alluded to it. He said he didn't agree with their methods to create a new Fatherland. The Nazis are planning to keep what they've taken."

*****

14 July 2025
Anacostia, Washington, DC

Devon's hands shook uncontrollably. This was different than the tremors that went through him when he was scared, and unlike the tingle that ran up his spine when his wife nibbled on his ear. It wasn't even the same type of feeling when he shivered in the darkest days of winter, waiting for the bus. Although, he *was* cold. So cold—and thirsty.

"I— Water," he moaned.

"I don't think it's a good idea, Double D," one of the kids he'd helped to raise said.

"T-thirsty," Devon managed to croak. He tried to stop shaking, to make it seem like everything was alright. He even held his hands over his stomach to hide the stain, so they'd give him some water. But the blood continued to come up from his stomach as he burped, trailing down his dark skin.

Deacon Johns had been shot in the stomach during the last Nazi attack. They'd come at the defensive line that his men created to keep them in from breaking out of the city, firing thousands of rounds into the old neighborhood. Finally, the defenders had forced the Germans back and they had a few minutes reprieve.

Devon knew they couldn't hold out against the entire German Army for long. Soon enough, they'd bring their tanks and UFOs to the fight and it would be game over for the resistance and all of the Anacostia residents, regardless of whether they'd fought—or not.

He could feel air seeping into his stomach. That was why he continued to belch. He just needed a little bit of water to quench his thirst, and to clear his throat of some of the blood. Devon reached out a trembling hand and laid it on King's arm, imploring him with his eyes to give him just a sip. A few drops were all he needed…

"Dammit, King," a voice behind him cursed. "Give him the fucking water. It don't matter what we do for him. He gonna die."

No, I'm not! he wanted to yell. Instead, he bucked his shoulders against the man's leg in protest. Interestingly enough, the pain had subsided and all he felt was cold.

A plastic bottle of water appeared in his line of sight and someone pressed it against his lips. He drank, swallowing the warm liquid greedily.

"Stop!" the voice behind him said. "All it's doin' is going down his throat and them pouring right out the back of him."

He felt himself lifted on his side and the person whistled. "His back blown open. He ain't got no stomach for the water to go to."

No stomach? he thought. *That's not right.* Of course he had a stomach. He'd been a healthy man, serving the

Lord for his entire adult life. There was nothing wrong with—

Then he remembered being shot. Someone had shot him. Shot him in the stomach. He needed a doctor. Instead, a bunch of street thugs and gang bangers who'd banded together under his leadership surrounded him. There were no doctors. Only certain death.

He batted weakly at his pocket until one of his men noticed what he was doing. The gang banger reached inside, pulling out a scrap of cardboard with a quickly jotted note written across it. Devon had received instructions to move the colonel this morning, but he hadn't returned to the safe house to tell them where to go.

He wanted to tell the man what to do with the note—he also wanted to get up and walk away, which he knew would never happen. He'd have to trust that the instructions would make it to the woman and the colonel.

A calm settled over Devon and he knew that his work on Earth was done. He spent his remaining time in prayer, communing with the Lord above. He prayed for his family and the community, and for the end of this horrific occupation. Most of all, he prayed for the redemption of his soul.

EIGHTEEN

15 July 2025
Fort Ricketts ruins, Anacostia, Washington, DC

His men spread out along the crumbling walls, forming a perimeter of modern weaponry. Getting through the overgrown weeds and underbrush had been harder than Gabe would have expected when they were ordered to go to this site and await contact with the Nazi defector. Dozens of scratches and cuts of dubious origins covered his bare arms, making him wish he'd chosen long sleeved civilian clothes instead of the t-shirt and jeans he wore now.

He'd grabbed a pamphlet from the historic site marker on the way into the woods, stuffing it into his pants pocket. There was no telling how long they'd be in position, so he figured he might as well have something interesting to look at. Surprisingly, the unkempt wilderness around them had been a defensive position during the Civil War, part of a ring of forts built to protect the city. Now, it was a place where murderers dumped their victims and druggies hid from the world, while prostitutes sold their bodies for a few dollars.

"Get a drone in the air," Gabe directed Lieutenant Wilcox. They needed to have a bird's eye view of the immediate area to avoid any surprises.

"Mendoza, get Spartan Six on the horn," he ordered his driver, now radio operator. He needed to tell Higher that they were in position and attempt to determine how long they'd be in this mosquito-infested "park."

"Hey, sir. Saw you slappin' at your neck," Sergeant Kelley, one of the two snipers that battalion gave him, said. "I've got some bug juice in my pack. Hold on."

Gabe accepted the insecticide repellant gratefully, spraying his exposed skin and the shirt he wore with a dense layer of DEET. He hoped it would keep some of the bites down, he sure as hell didn't want a mosquito bite from a bug that had just been sucking on a hooker.

"Here you go, sir," Specialist Mendoza said, holding out the radio handset.

He waited until the radio crackled with the brigade commander's voice. "This is Spartan Six."

"Sir, Berserker Six. We're in position at the rendezvous point."

"Good work, son. We got the message to our contact two days ago. Zero communication since then, so we don't know if the asset is on the move."

Gabe chewed at his lip in frustration. That's the same thing he was told yesterday when they dismounted their vehicles and began walking toward the rendezvous point. They didn't have any updates in twenty-four hours?

"Understood, sir. Any change to the situation in DC?"

He could hear sporadic gunfire coming from the northwest, in nearby Anacostia proper. Farther away to the southeast, likely across the river, the echoes of large, booming explosions rolled across the land.

"Satellite imagery shows street fighting all across southeast DC, unknown combatants, and we're in a tank fight out near the Occoquan. The damn Nazis are using drone swarms to take out our helicopters, which is taking away some of our momentum. Otherwise, we're doing good. Hold on."

The colonel paused and then said, "Alright, Berserker. The asset is holed up in the basement of a house on 14th and V as in Victor Street and he can't get out without support because of the street fighting. It's just a hair over a thousand meters to the northwest of your current position. I need you to go get him."

Gabe pulled his cell phone out and tried to bring up a map, but there wasn't any signal in the middle of the park. "Roger, sir."

He checked his watch. It was about ninety minutes to an hour until darkness. "We'll begin prepping and move out within the hour."

"Solid copy, Berserker. Spartan Six, out."

He passed the handset back to Mendoza and called out, "Lieutenant Wilcox, change of mission. I need you and Sergeant Cheng over here now."

The lieutenant and his platoon sergeant walked rapidly to where he sat on his ass with a paper map close to his nose. The damn thing was printed off the internet before they left the brigade area and the finer details—like street names—were hard to make out. He wished he got some type of cell reception or that the BFT in his pack wouldn't light him up like a Christmas tree to a German signals interception unit.

"Shit, I can't see anything on this map," he admitted, handing it to Wilcox. "Your eyes are better than mine; can you make out V Street or 14th Street? If we can get one of those, we'll have an idea of where to start."

"I'll look, sir," Jake Wilcox replied, taking the map.

"What are y'all seeing on the drone?" he asked the noncommissioned officer.

"We're alone in this stretch of woods as far as we can see, sir. There's a lot of activity over that way," he gestured toward the heart of the city, "but we can't make out what it is yet. We were gonna start expanding the perimeter and flying the drone in a large circular pattern. That should get us a better picture."

Gabe didn't want to tip anyone off that they were here. "Hold what you've got. Let's not take the drone wider than the immediate area just yet."

"Roger, sir."

"Uh, sir," Wilcox muttered as he examined the map. "You said we had a change of mission. What is it?"

"Yeah, sorry," Gabe replied. "The asset is holed up in a house in Anacostia and can't meet us here like originally planned. We're going to need to go the rest of the way and pick them up."

A long burst of nearby automatic weapons fire interrupted him. He waited until it was finished and continued. "As you can hear, there's street fighting all around us."

"Who's fighting, sir?" Sergeant First Class Cheng asked.

Gabe shrugged. "Before we left, there was talk of some kind of organized resistance against the Nazis, but to be honest, we don't know who's fighting right now. It could be the resistance fighting against the Nazis or it could be rival street gangs duking it out now that the police aren't a concern. Satellite imagery can only show us so much. The colonel said the tanks were fighting out near the Occoquan, which is a river to the southwest, and didn't say anything about armor in the Anacostia neighborhood."

"I think I've got it, sir," Lieutenant Wilcox said. "I can see 13th and 16th, but can't make out what's in between them. It should be 14th, though."

Gabe looked where Jake had indicated on the paper. If he squinted his eyes he could make out the street labels that the lieutenant pointed out were there. He cross-referenced the location of Fort Ricketts and measured a thousand meters northwest from the park.

"Somewhere on this block," he stated, drawing a circle around a small area, "is where the asset is located."

He held it out for the two men to see. "We need to get there without drawing attention to ourselves, get the German defector, and get the heck out of there."

"Damn, we're close, sir," Sergeant Cheng stated. "We could try sending a couple of guys up there, it should take less than an hour for them to go get the guy and come back—as long as they don't run into any problems."

"That's what I'm worried about," the commander replied. "I like your idea of a smaller force though."

Gabe paused and thought about his options. He had forty-six men with him, but a smaller force would be less likely to draw attention from enemy drones or spotters. A few men, maybe a squad-plus, could provide enough firepower to break contact if they got into a hairy situation. The rest of Berserker Company could stay here to secure the ruins. They'd use the cover of darkness to slip out of the city and beat feet as far as the defector could make it. Then they'd find a place to stay for the daylight hours.

"Okay, I've made up my mind. Jake, you're going to stay here and secure Fort Ricketts. I'm taking Sergeant Paredes' squad with me to the target. I want the sniper team ready to move out ahead of the squad to find a position they can provide overwatch."

"Got it."

"I should be going, sir," Jake protested. "I can go get the guy and then come back here. Easy as pie."

"It's not that easy, Lieutenant." Gabe hoped that Jake would catch the subtle change in his voice. He sure as hell didn't need an argument with Wilcox. "I need my ass covered by men that I trust. We don't want some group of Germans—or street thugs for that matter—sneaking up and shooting us in the back. We're close enough that you could respond quickly if we run into trouble. I need you back here, Jake."

"Understood, sir," the lieutenant grumbled. "When are you leaving?"

"I told Spartan Six that it'd be within the hour. I want to make it to the edge of the park while there's still a little bit of light. Then we'll wait until dark to move into the neighborhood."

Gabe waited for any more discussion, when there was none he told the Lieutenant Wilcox and Sergeant Cheng to prepare Paredes' squad to move out and the rest of the platoon to secure the patrol base.

*****

16 July 2025
Cheyenne Mountain Complex, Colorado Springs, Colorado

"Mister President?" Captain deBoer asked, knocking softly. "We have an update from the East Coast."

"Dammit, Ashley," he responded. "I'm going to the bathroom. Can this wait five minutes?"

"Of course, sir."

Her footsteps retreated down the hallway a respectful distance. The novelty of being the President of the United States had worn off over the past two weeks. Javier couldn't even take a dump without someone trying to give him an update about the war.

Javier sighed and pressed the off button on his phone. To be sure, he wasn't ungrateful and the Nazi invasion was the single most significant event to happen to the United States since the Civil War, but he just wanted ten minutes to do his business in peace and play solitaire on his phone while he did it.

"Looks like I won't extend that winning streak after all," he grumbled, setting the phone down on the counter beside the toilet so he could clean up.

When he finished washing his hands, he slipped the towel back onto the hook and stepped out of the bathroom quickly, leaving the light on to keep the ventilation fan engaged.

"Alright, Ashley. What is so important that you felt you needed to interrupt my precious few minutes of privacy?" Javier asked the blonde military aide standing in the hallway.

She started to walk toward him, but stopped, allowing him to walk to her and then turned to follow along beside him. "Sorry, sir. There've been a few developments out east."

He stared at her profile as she walked, willing her to glance his way. When she did, she grimaced. "Of course, sir. You know the update is about back east."

The president nodded sarcastically. These military people needed to loosen up. "Let me guess: We won and everyone can go home now?" he offered.

"Uh, no, sir. The Germans are using drone swarms to bring down our helicopters and regain air superiority."

"Huh?" he asked in confusion.

"You may remember that the Apache gunships were working in tandem with men on the ground using shoulder-fired Stinger missiles to shoot down the German saucer jets…"

"Yes, I remember," he stated—although, admittedly, the myriad of different types of tanks, planes, and guns confused the hell out of him. "The Germans are doing what now?"

"They're flying a whole bunch of drones together like a swarm of mosquitos. They fly them into our helicopter rotors and turbine intakes to foul up the engines, causing them to crash. Uh, think of it like a bird strike that happens to a plane engine every so often at an airport. It's the same principle, except the drones are purposefully trying to bring down the helicopter instead of a bird accidentally getting sucked into an engine."

He appreciated her using simpler terms that he understood instead of relying on military jargon that so many of them fell back upon when pressed for answers. "I haven't really heard anyone talking about the enemy using drones before this. Is that a new development or was it just something that hadn't filtered up to my level?"

"We believe it's a new development, sir. They appear to be civilian drones—which would make sense if they're sustaining themselves from general merchandise stores in the DC area. Plus, there's a drone manufacturing plant on the Eastern Shore, so they may have access to thousands of them if they found that place."

"Why aren't you shooting them down?"

"We're trying, sir," she replied.

Javier realized that he still thought of his relationship with the military as 'them versus us,' his political party versus the establishment. He couldn't change an entire lifetime of thinking in a couple of weeks, but it sounded harsh to his own ears.

"What are *we* doing?" he asked, accentuating the word slightly.

"The idea of a drone swarm is not new," the aide replied. "We've been working on countering it for more than a decade, but there is no practical solution. The most reliable and effective method is an electromagnetic countermeasure. We flip a switch on a device and everything with power falls out of the sky."

"Sounds great."

"Not really, sir. It also affects our helicopters. So, it's perfectly suited for use as a defensive measure around structures or facilities, and has even proven effective as an offensive capability as long our birds aren't in the air. We can also target specific frequencies and jam those, but that one is a crap shoot and doesn't work at all if they're flying set routes by GPS."

"So what about blowing them out of the sky?" the president asked. He thought back to the WWII documentaries he'd been watching over the past couple of weeks. "Isn't that what the Germans did to us with their damn flak guns?"

She nodded, opening the door to his office and standing aside to let him proceed. He waved at the two secret service agents off in the corner. "Bill. Ted," he greeted.

They accepted his comments without response. Once he'd learned that the black-haired one was named Ted

Logan, it didn't matter what his blond partner's name was. They would forever be Bill and Ted to him.

He sat at the cheap, office furniture store desk and Ashley continued. "Flak is an effective measure against drone planes due to stability issues, sir. Unfortunately, those aren't what we're seeing. Quadcopters are what the bulk of ground forces and civilian hobbyists—and now the Germans—use. They are much easier to control and incredibly durable. As long as the flight control module and the battery is intact, they can fly. A quadcopter can stay airborne on only two engines and having entire sections of the frame blown off doesn't affect them like you'd think it would.

"Lasers work much the same way as the air burst munitions—the flak guns," she amended when she saw his confused look. "They're effective against plane-type drones, but the lasers slice off pieces and parts of the quadcopter and the damn things keep flying. We've tried all sorts of stuff, from aerial nets to crashing our own drones into them. Heck, we've even tried using sniper rifles, which have been largely ineffective, minus a few lucky shots during experiments when the quadcopter hovered and didn't move."

"So you're saying there's nothing we can do?" Javier asked.

"Not against drone swarms, sir. Unless we ground our helicopters and then fire up the electronic attack systems, we have to ride this out."

"So the military has been working on this for more than a decade and all you've—all we've come up with is recommendations to weather the storm?"

"The simple nature of the quadcopter works against us, sir. Like I said, we can certainly knock them out of the sky, but our helicopters and drones can't be anywhere near the signals because it will affect them too." She paused and then added, "Of course, this is all information that I learned my senior year at the Academy and what I've picked up working in the operations center, sir. I can see if we can find a counter-unmanned aerial systems expert to provide a brief to you."

"Yeah, that sounds good," Javier agreed. "Okay, so we can't reliably shoot down all of their drones. You said the Germans are using it to gain control of the skies?"

"Yes, sir," Ashley replied, clearly relieved to venture back into territory that she was prepared to discuss. "So, as noted earlier, the Apache gunships work in conjunction with Stinger missile teams on the ground. Between that combination and high-altitude bombing, we've destroyed approximately six hundred and forty of their saucer jets. We estimate that to be more than half of their fleet. Their losses have been so severe that they stopped using the saucers in support of ground movements, choosing instead to engage in long-range missions that result in one or two ships shooting up cities all across the nation."

"We've had a few of them out here," the president muttered.

"Yes, sir. However, now that the drone swarms are knocking out the gunships, their pilots are once again returning to the close air support role, which is hindering our advance to take the land back from them."

Javier nodded. He didn't need the five-minute lesson in tactics and capabilities; he needed an answer. "So what are we going to do about it?"

"We're rushing soldiers and Stinger missiles to the front, sir. We're doubling, even tripling, the number of shoulder-fired missile launchers in the maneuver elements. Early estimates from the bean counters are that we'll likely use double the amount of ammunition than we would have previously."

"I don't care about expense," President Sanchez replied. "I want those heathens out of our country."

The aide's lips thinned as if she were suppressing a smile.

"Yeah, I don't know why I used the word 'heathens' either," he stated with a grin. "Okay, what's next? The counterattack is stalling; I got that part. What about that defector that knows all their secret plans and whatnot? What's his status?"

"*Um…*" She thumbed through several pages of briefing notes until she found the one she wanted. Javier had almost no faith in the defector and told his staff as much, so it moved farther and farther down the priority list. "It says that he's stuck in a house in Anacostia because of the street fighting still raging between the Germans and local resistance forces. The commander on the ground in Virginia made the call to send a small unit into the city to retrieve him."

"*Hmpf*," Javier grunted. "Like that movie about the couple of soldiers who went up against the Nazis to rescue a guy when all of his brothers were killed."

"Sort of, sir," she acknowledged.

"How long until they can rescue him?"

"It will depend on the situation on the ground. They should be able to close in on the target house tonight and get out by morning, but that doesn't account for the Murphy factor."

"What can go wrong, will go wrong?" he asked.

"Exactly, sir. No matter how much you train for an operation, Murphy always sneaks in and throws a wrench in the works."

Javier chuckled. The members of the military that he interacted with in the complex were a superstitious bunch overall. The idea that some mythical entity waited around specifically to interfere with military operations was preposterous.

"Well, I'm sure things will go fine."

Captain deBoer took that as her cue to move on to the next topic. "We've captured several of the newer types of German weapons, from machine guns to their saucer jets. As you were previously briefed, you know that we have an intact airframe, similar to what they are using. Our scientists and engineers have worked for decades to repair or replicate the propulsion system, but we've been largely unsuccessful because the technology was simply too advanced and our ship was too damaged. Now that we have several of the German jets with their propulsion systems intact, we are confident that we can replicate them within a few months."

"Good Lord, Ashley!" he groaned. "The Army doesn't expect this to go on for *months*, do they?"

"It's unknown, sir. We believe that the Germans are cut off from resupply. There have been no new large cargo planes or boats, so it would seem that the soldiers who are here are the ones we need to worry about. We hope to recapture DC by the end of August, but it's prudent to plan for the long haul."

"Your prudent planning just about gave me a heart attack. I haven't done anything as the president except receive reports about how the war in DC is going. I need to make this country work again. I have a cabinet to appoint— Dammit, I guess I can't get a cabinet confirmed without a Congress, can I? The United States needs to hold elections, then confirm a cabinet, then we can begin the recovery process. We need to overturn several of the previous administration's laws and ban weapons of mass destruction so things like this won't ever happen again. We need to revamp our medical system, which starts with medical malpractice and insurance costs; citizens shouldn't have to take out loans to pay for life-saving care."

Javier stopped and blinked. He hadn't realized that he'd stood as he talked about setting his administration. "I'm sorry, Ashley," he said as he sat heavily. "I know you don't care one bit about my plans for policy reform. None of this is your fault and the only reason you're even acting as my military aide right now is because you happened to be stationed here when we made this our temporary home."

"It's not a problem, sir," she replied.

"I know you'll deflect negative comments and agree with anything I say. That's what you've been trained to do. I just—"

"Excuse me, sir. If I may?" Ashley said, holding up her hand.

"Uh, yeah, go ahead." He wasn't used to being interrupted, especially not since he'd been sworn in as the president.

"Just because I'm polite and respect the office of the President of the United States does not mean I'm some ditz who will smile and nod, no matter what. The Air Force—actually, all of the US military—respects the opinions of our people. We're not an internet startup, so everyone doesn't get a vote, but we do allow subordinates to voice their recommendations and then the commander, you in this case, makes a decision based upon those recommendations.

"You may not have wanted to be the president, sir, but you are. Now that you are, you may want to push your agenda and follow through with years of campaign promises and drastically alter our current form of government…but there won't be a nation to correct the policies of if we don't first stop the Nazis.

"Stopping them doesn't just mean pushing them back into the sea," she continued. "We need to annihilate them. The prisoners we've taken have been indoctrinated from birth to hate Americans. The Nazi leadership will stop at nothing to destroy our country, so it may not be palatable to you, personally, but we must destroy every last remnant of them—both here on our soil and wherever it is that they came from. Otherwise, they'll just return in another eighty years and my grandchildren will have to fight them."

She stopped talking and Javier considered her words, looking at her in a new light. The woman he'd thought of as simply an aide who followed orders blindly appeared to be anything but.

"Do you really believe that there's no negotiating with them?" he asked. "That the answer is annihilation of their women and children?"

"Yes, sir. They will come back for us," she asserted. "The prisoners are adamant that if they were given the opportunity, they'd strike out against us—regardless of what happens to them. They consider Americans to be subhuman and savages. Their words, not mine. When asked where they come from, the prisoners recite a litany of names, heroic Nazi soldiers from the past as if that is all they are. They will not surrender."

His advisors had briefed Javier on the odd behavior of the few prisoners his forces had captured, most so badly injured that they were incapable of killing themselves. They purported to believe that they were descended directly from a host of World War Two-era Nazi soldiers, even that some of their leadership, non-combatant scientists, and engineers were secreted away from Germany toward the end of the war when it became apparent that the Axis powers would lose. Given their supposed ability to cryogenically freeze men, it was feasible…if not completely insane.

Not a single one of them had given up the location of their base, though. Regardless of the interrogation techniques that were employed before Javier found out about them and put an end to it, the prisoners remained tight-lipped about their home. Even though he had little faith in the information that the defector may have, it was the main reason he'd authorized talks to carry on with the man. Otherwise, he'd have left him to the rebels in DC.

"Alright, Ashley. You've certainly given me a lot to think about. I'm getting tired and I'd like to eat dinner with Becky and the boys before I need to read this report that General Sullivan's people dropped by today." He held up a thick binder full of briefing charts and recommendations about funding for the Air Force.

Even during a catastrophe, the Air Force knew how to take advantage of a situation. Most of the members of congress were dead or missing and the flyboys wanted an increase to their base budget for the following year.

It was going to be a long night.

*****

16 July 2025
Holloway Office Complex, CIA Black Site Three, Reston, Virginia

Berndt looked forlornly at the vertical bars of his cell. There were twenty-five bars spaced approximately ten to twelve centimeters apart, making the cell two-and-a-half meters wide. Since the room appeared to be square, he assumed it was the same depth. The only fixtures in the room were the mattress on the floor that wasn't long enough for his entire body to fit onto, a low sink and the toilet.

The Luftwaffe pilot didn't know how long he'd been in the prison. Sleeping wasn't an effective measure of the passage of time since there was nothing to do except sleep. He didn't even think his meals were delivered on a regular basis. His best guess, based on bowel movements, was that he'd been in captivity for a week or more.

He tried to do calisthenics to keep himself healthy and sane, but he found himself tiring too quickly to get any real satisfaction from the exercises. Besides calculating the size of his cell, the only other thing he could do to entertain himself was talk to the prisoner in the next cell. The man hadn't been there as long as Berndt had. He was captured far away in the American West. Their conversations were surely being recorded, although no one questioned him regarding his interactions with the other prisoner.

Berndt wasn't sure if his newfound friend was completely sane, though, and often wondered if he spoke the truth. He told wild tales of terrifying weapons and said that their American captors beat him for no discernable reason other than he was a fallschirmjäger. Berndt himself had never been physically harmed, but his friend often returned from his sessions with obvious signs of abuse.

They'd taken the man next door for another session what seemed like hours ago. Time seemed to stretch away from him as he focused and unfocused his eyes on the wall across the way. As a game, he began to try to find shapes and patterns in the painted brick. Several düsenjägers appeared and there was one creature that mostly resembled a lion. Everything else was just an uncomprehending jumble of texture.

Berndt heard the commotion before he saw any evidence of what caused it.

Shouting drew his eyes from the wall to the edge of his vision outside of the cell. He stood and pressed close to the bars for a better view. The dull thudding sounds of batons impacting against flesh made him cringe, shying away from the bars to sit on his bunk. Then, the noises quieted and two guards appeared across his limited field of view. They dragged a semi-conscious prisoner by the armpits between them. His friend's head lolled to the side and his eyes fixed on Berndt. He smiled, causing blood to pour from his lips.

That brief glimpse was all he had of the man whom he'd come to know over the past few days. The guards opened the cell next door and it sounded like they threw him to the floor. The prisoner shouted obscenities at them in German.

The giant brutes were likely too stupid to understand what he said.

Berndt waited until the guards disappeared and a door slammed nearby, letting him know they'd returned to wherever it was that they went between sessions. He also knew that he was next.

"Gregory!" he hissed. "Are you awake?"

"Yes, brother. I am alive."

"I didn't—never mind. What did they ask you?"

"The same questions as always: Where did we come from, how many troops do we have, what is our goal, how many people did I kill—and other questions along those lines."

"What did you tell them?" Berndt asked, curious if the man's story would change.

"That *they* were the savage beasts, not us. That machine…" Gregory trailed off and Berndt worried that he passed out from the beating he'd received in the hallway.

After the long pause, Gregory began again. "That machine was pure evil. My men screamed in agony as they were cooked alive and their skin split open like an animal cooked over the fire too long. They died horribly. Everything we were taught about the Americans is true; they are monsters in human form. But, they will not break me. I will resist."

Berndt smiled at the man's insistence that he would stay true to the Reich. "So you didn't tell them anything?"

"No, of course I haven't," the paratrooper asserted.

"That is good, brother. They do not know where our base is, otherwise, why would they continue to ask?"

A wet slap on the opposite side of the wall meant that Gregory hit the concrete block with a bloody palm. "If they discover its location, then that is the endgame for our people. I failed in my mission to seize control of the nuclear launch facilities and at least one other platoon did as well. They can still destroy Ar—"

"Watch out!" Berndt warned, fearing the man would accidentally mutter the name of Argus Base, which was named for the Argus Dome eighty kilometers away. The Americans had proven time and again that they were unafraid to use the nuclear option. Hiroshima. Nagasaki. Neuschwabenland. Regardless of their assertions that they were the good guys, they were certainly not.

"Thank you," Gregory mumbled. "I almost said it."

"I know. They are recording us. Even though we can't see the cameras or the microphones, it is as sure as the sun will rise that they are there."

"You're right, Berndt. It was a momentary—"

"*Back away from the bars!*" a voice ordered in German through the speaker in the hallway. Berndt stepped back rapidly. It meant that the guards were coming to take another prisoner to the interrogation room. He wasn't sure how many Wehrmacht soldiers were captive in this facility, but he'd seen at least five different men cross in front of his cell, including Gregory. How long could they continue to resist?

Not that Berndt had been treated harshly, of course. The interrogators were cordial with him. He'd only been hit once. They were returning him to his cell when a person opened a door which he'd never seen open before. He stopped, seeing a massive room beyond, filled with people and large television screens. The guards hit him behind the ear, knocking him unconscious. He awoke on his bunk.

Gregory, on the other hand, seemed to get beaten every time they took him. He'd never known the man before, since Luftwaffe and Heer rarely trained together after their duty assignment, but he seemed to revel in making problems for himself. He told Berndt that for three consecutive sessions he'd refused to say a single word, so they didn't even know what to call him. He often caused trouble, trying to incite the other prisoners to resist or to actively work at escaping. Berndt would escape if the opportunity presented itself, but until then, he would cooperate and avoid unnecessary hardship.

"*Oberleutnant Berndt Fischer, prepare for interrogation,*" the speaker directed.

He stood in the middle of the small cell, placing his hands on his head where the guards could clearly see them. In seconds, the men appeared to take him to the interrogation room. One man opened the cell while two others, dressed in thick green uniforms that looked as if they were designed to absorb bites from the prisoners, moved quickly into the room, flanking him with clubs drawn.

It was their standard procedure. It had startled him at first, but he'd grown accustomed to it as this was his fifteenth interrogation—maybe it was the twentieth, he could no longer remember how many times they'd taken him for questions. The guards were not rough with him, per se, but one of them applied firm pressure against his spine with the club to get him moving. These men did not speak German, so asking them for directions was useless.

He waited until they handcuffed his wrists behind him. When they were finished, he walked through the open cell door and turned left, leading the way toward the interrogation room. The guards fell into step behind him, ready to bash him in the back of the head if he deviated from the path.

It was a relatively short walk. The prison corridors were nowhere near as long as those in Argus Base. He stepped into the room where he'd been questioned on multiple occasions and sat in the chair facing the door. He waited for the man with the glasses to come into the room.

Berndt was surprised when a dark-haired woman entered instead of his normal interrogator. *This is different*, he thought as he appraised the newcomer's appearance. She was thin, but appeared well-endowed; pretty without being one of the women that he would have imagined to be in a beauty pageant.

"Good morning, Oberleutnant Fischer," she stated flatly.

He smiled. It was the first time he'd seen a woman up close since before he was frozen. He'd seen some Americans from far away at the airfield, but it wasn't like this. He could have reached out and touched her—if he'd dared.

"Good morning," he replied, not realizing that she'd spoken in German until he responded in kind.

"My name is Megan. I'm going to ask you a few questions. What is your unit?"

"I fly—flew—Düsenjäger 519 in Vengeance Squadron, Fourth Reich Luftwaffe," he answered truthfully. There was no sense lying about things that were inconsequential. Plus, it helped him to keep his stories straight.

"Very good, Oberleutnant." She made some annotations on a piece of paper in a folder. "What was your mission?"

"To attack the advancing American forces."

"Were you successful?"

Berndt thought about all the bombing runs he'd conducted and the two jet planes that he shot down on the first day of the invasion. Yes, he'd been extremely successful.

"I carried out my missions with honor, ma'am."

"Were you successful in attacking American forces?" she repeated.

"I did my duty, yes."

"What about against the civilian population? Were you successful in carrying out that mission as well, Oberleutnant?" the woman asked, her pleasantness dropping away. "Did you know that our current estimates of dead or dying civilians is up around four million? That's a lot of innocent lives lost."

"I— I did my duty to the Reich, ma'am. If I was directed to attack a target, then I did so." He did not like where this line of questioning was headed. The male he'd spoken to previously never discussed the fact that innocents likely died in the düsenjäger attacks. Berndt thought of the children that he never fathered, regretting that he was not more like his friend, Matthias, who'd bedded many women.

Faster than his mind could process, the woman across the small table lashed out, punching him directly in the nose. He cried out in pain, hunching over as blood flowed freely from both nostrils. Another blow landed on his ear and he fell from the chair to the floor, unable to defend himself with his hands secured behind his back.

"Those 'targets' were my family!" the woman screamed, as she came around the table and kicked him in the kidney.

Dimly, he heard the door handle rattle as her foot connected with the back of his head. "Doctor Sanjay! Stop immediately," a familiar male voice shouted.

Berndt turned to see the original interrogator standing in the doorway flanked by several guards. As he did so, the woman's booted foot impacted against his cheek, slamming the back of his head into the concrete floor. His blurred vision began to swim and he was fearful of passing out. If he did, the woman would kill him.

"I'm done," she answered, her boots retreating to the other side of the table.

"What you did is against the Geneva Convention for dealing with prisoners of war," the man with the glasses stated. "Oberleutnant Fischer did nothing to provoke your attack. You are relieved for the day, you may go home."

"My home is gone, Jeff. Everything is gone because of the Luftwaffe."

"That may be, but this man did nothing to you. Guards, escort Doctor Sanjay from the room and then return the oberleutnant to his cell."

Berndt rested his cheek against the cool concrete, seeing his dark red blood spread in a small stream toward the drain in the floor, covering several preexisting rust-colored spots. *Dried blood*, he thought. Then, another odd thought occurred to him as the bespectacled man's shadow darkened out the overhead lights.

He tried to think straight, but his mind was fuzzy. Had he imagined the interaction between the two doctors? Surely he must have. His brain must have created the dialogue in an effort to distract him from the beating.

Berndt knew he imagined it because the doctors had spoken to each other in German.

NINETEEN

17 July 2025
Anacostia, Washington, DC

Gabe knelt beside Staff Sergeant Paredes in the deepest shadows of an old brick church. They'd picked up V Street and followed it northwest until the road intersected with 14th Street. It had been much slower going than he'd anticipated. The snipers, Sergeant Kelley and Corporal Hicks, had to reposition twice because buildings interfered with their view of the squad. Their last move brought them to the fire station across the street from where the captain rested on his knee.

Gabe glanced around at their surroundings, trying to determine if the asset was to the north or south along 14th Street. Spartan Six said that he was in the basement of a house on 14th and V, as in Victor. To the south along 14th Street, it only appeared to be more of the larger buildings like the church and the fire station. To the north, the road split around a small median with apartments and another church on one side, and single-family homes on the other. He was willing to bet that those homes were where the asset was hiding.

"Alright, we need to move up to those houses," Gabe said, gesturing toward the row of homes on the same side of the street. "We'll have to knock on doors until we find the right place, and hope that nobody has dogs or an itchy trigger finger."

The latter part scared him more than the dogs. It was the middle of the night, and there had plainly been fighting nearby as little as an hour ago, so people were bound to be wound tight. He didn't need a friendly fire incident.

"What if we try looking in the basement windows before we knock, sir?" the NCO asked. "We can avoid knocking on *any* door until we see something that interests us."

"Good idea," Gabe said, keying up his throat microphone so everyone could hear. He didn't know why he hadn't thought of something so simple. "I'll take Griffiths and McCoy to peek in the windows of the houses on this side of the street. The remainder of the squad will keep watch to make sure nobody comes creeping up on us. The snipers will provide direct overwatch of my team as we try to figure out which house the asset is located in."

"*Got it*," Sergeant Kelley replied over the radio and Staff Sergeant Paredes gave him a quick thumbs up.

"Griffiths, McCoy, on me," Gabe ordered. He saw the squad's heavy machine gunner stand and run toward him while another soldier slunk through the shadows. The second man had an M32A3 Multiple Grenade Launcher for suppression and a pump-action shotgun as his primary weapon.

Once both men were at his location, Gabe gave a quick brief on what they were going to do. They'd use their night vision to sneak through the darkness and peek through the basement windows. If they found a house that looked promising, *then* they'd knock on either the door or window and ask about the German colonel.

The men acknowledged their understanding of the plan and the captain stood, prepared to cross the street to the first house.

"*Contact*," Corporal Hicks stated over the squad frequency.

Gabe froze and then quickly scooted back into the bushes beside the church. "Where is it?" he whispered.

"*Far end of the next street. I count three—no, four men—coming toward us. Looks like Germans.*"

"*Berserker Six, this is Berserker One,*" a new voice came over his headset.

"This is Six. We're a little busy, One. What is it?"

"*You're about to have company. We count eight men moving your way. We can't tell whether they're hostiles or civilians.*"

He glanced skyward. Somewhere up there was Jake's drone, keeping watch on them from the sky to provide the full picture of the area of operations. "Our snipers just saw them too," Gabe replied.

"*Recommend you stay hidden. Drone has a twelve-pound shape charge that we can drop on the newcomers if it comes to it.*"

"Roger. We're going to wait them out." Gabe passed that message over the squad frequency. The men were mostly combat vets, but there were two privates who'd only conducted live fire training, not any situations where the enemy shot back at them. If they panicked, then the whole operation could be in jeopardy.

"Powell and Sweeney, this is Captain Murdock. You boys need to stay calm and don't initiate a firefight. Understand?"

"*Yes, sir,*" they replied in unison over the net.

He had to hope they'd keep their cool. Next to him, Griffiths and McCoy prepared their position silently, shifting behind old bricks and pressing as close to the dirt as possible. He did the same.

The group of men came closer, all eight visible to Gabe's squad. They were too far for him to make out any type of uniform or features. Then, he noticed something.

"Corporal Hicks, this is Six," he said into the radio.

"*Yeah?*"

"Are those black guys?"

"*Roger, sir. Looks like…seven black dudes and a white guy wearing a cop uniform.*"

"Everybody, listen up," Gabe stated. "Those are Americans. When they get close, I'll call out to them and go out to meet. Maybe they can tell us where we're going." A few grunts of acknowledgement reached his ears without the need for the earpiece.

They waited until the lead man was even with the stop sign across the street and then Gabe called out in a whisper.

"Friendlies."

The point man must have jumped three feet into the air, firing a round into the church behind Gabe.

"Goddammit, stop!" the captain shouted, all attempts at being quiet hopelessly lost with the report of the point man's pistol. "We're American soldiers."

"William, put that thing away, you fucking idiot!" someone whispered harshly from the group of newcomers. "You're an American?"

"Yeah," Gabe answered, still under the cover of the bushes. "We're up from Georgia, sent here to take back the city."

The cop pushed his way through the group. "Come on out, then."

Gabe glanced at his men and then nodded. This was the most opportune time for him to get shot. "Alright, I'm coming out now," he stated.

"We won't shoot ya."

He stood, hunched over in the bush and parted the branches in front of him so he could get out. "Holy shit! You're either a real soldier or you've got way too much time on your hands," one of the guys laughed. "Look at all that gear you got on."

Gabe shrugged. Besides being in civilian clothing, the only thing he wore different from the standard grunt was the range extender for his radio, everything else was what they wore on a daily basis. "I'm coming across the street," he said, holding his hands up so they could see he didn't have anything.

"Come on, then."

He closed the distance quickly and pulled his glove off before shaking everyone's hand. "Captain Gabriel Murdock, commander of Berserker Company, Three-Seven Infantry, Third Infantry Division. We're here to link up with a man named Deacon. Have you heard of him?"

The police officer frowned. "Well, sir, you're a couple days too late. Deacon Johns was killed two days ago fighting against those Nazi bastards near the bridge."

"I'm sorry to hear that," Gabe answered truthfully, mimicking the cop's frown. "He had something in his possession that we needed, something that could turn the tide of the war."

"You mean the German and that family in Lucretia's basement?" the point man asked.

"Ah… The German, yes—if he's the one I'm hoping for. Is he a high-ranking Nazi?"

"I guess so. He's a defector and Deacon Johns seemed to think he was important," the police officer stopped, glancing behind Gabe. "You can put that away, fella. We ain't gonna shoot your boss."

Gabe turned to see the barrel of Griffiths' machine gun bristling from the bush. He nodded and patted the air down to try and get the men to understand that the newcomers were alright. "This is Berserker Six," he said, thumbing his throat mike. "Everyone come out. Sergeant Kelley, Corporal Hicks, stay in overwatch position."

"*Roger.*"

Sergeant Paredes' men materialized from the darkness, fanning out behind Gabe. "We're in a hurry, *uh*, I didn't catch your name."

"I'm Jerry," the cop replied. "You've met William, let's see," he pointed at the man farthest away and then indicated each individual when he called out their name. "That's Skinny. Next to him is D'Andre, then Tyson, Michael, Chris, and uh… Oh yeah, and Anthony."

Gabe acknowledged each of the men before repeating his statement. "Nice to meet everyone. We're in a hurry. We have orders to get the German out of the city tonight, so we can have him back to the headquarters by tomorrow evening. They'll get all the information that they can and hopefully, we can use that to defeat the Nazis once and for all."

"Hey, sir. This is Berserker One."

Gabe held up his index finger to Jerry and the others, and then turned away, placing his hand up to his ear—more for the civilians to realize he was on the radio than out of need. "This is Six. Go ahead."

"We've got a second drone inbound. Coming from the city."

"Shit," Gabe said out loud. "The Nazis have sent up a drone. It's coming our way."

Jerry cursed under his breath. "They probably heard William's gun go off. Come on, let's get you to the house where the defector is staying." The civilians turned and began walking without waiting to see if the soldiers would follow.

"They fly a drone over the area before they send in troops," the cop called over his shoulder. "It's a good bet they're already on their way."

"Alright, Berserkers, let's go," he said, waving his men on.

"*Sir, what about us?*" Sergeant Kelley asked.

He'd temporarily forgotten about the snipers. "Ah, can you get on top of that fire station? I'd like to maintain overwatch."

"*Eh, we could get up there, but the drone would see us pretty easily. Especially if it's equipped with infrared.*"

"Dammit, you're right," he conceded. He wished they had some time to prepare a hide site for the snipers so they could keep an eye on things, but it couldn't be helped. He'd have to rely on Lieutenant Wilcox's drone to give them updates. "Alright, let's go. Everybody."

They shuffled along quickly behind Jerry and his men to the fourth house on the block, a narrow, grey siding-covered house with wide concrete steps that reached all the way to the sidewalk. They rushed up onto the porch to try and get under the overhang.

"Hold on, fellas," Jerry ordered. "We can't all fit under here. Let me unlock the door and then we can get off the street."

Despite the seriousness of the situation, Gabe smiled at twenty grown men trying to fit onto a porch designed to hold two chairs and a small side table.

Jerry produced a key from his pocket and unlocked the door. He twisted the knob and called out into the darkness behind the door, letting the occupants know who was coming in. The police officer disappeared inside.

"*Six, that drone is only about two blocks away. You need to get under cover now!*" Lieutenant Wilcox radioed.

"We're working on it, One," Gabe replied, glancing unconsciously skyward. It wouldn't do any good; he'd never be able to see a tiny drone against the night sky.

Jerry reappeared. "Okay, come on in."

The squad filed in quickly and Gabe was grateful to be off the street, even if it meant they were temporarily holed up without any eyes on the surrounding area.

*****

17 July 2025
Anacostia, Washington, DC

Gloria heard the door upstairs open and several pairs of feet tramped across the hardwood. She glanced at her watch; it was only 3 a.m. What were so many people doing out at this hour?

Then the realization hit her and her stomach dropped. It was the Nazi death squad. They'd found out about Frederick and were here now. They'd shoot everyone because of the colonel and leave their bodies rotting in the streets.

"James! James, wake up," she hissed.

"Huh?"

"Nazis!"

"What?" he asked, becoming more awake.

"Upstairs. Nazis. I'm going to wake the children and have them hide."

"Yeah, okay."

She sat up awkwardly on the lumpy mattress and put her feet down on the rug. In her haste to reach the children, she stumbled blindly into the wheelchair, sending it crashing to the side with an audible *clank* when it fell against the concrete floor.

Gloria fell with it, crying out in pain as all of her weight landed on one hand, spraining her wrist. She pushed herself up determinedly and stumbled to the main room where the children slept, guarding her injured wrist.

Frederick crouched at the base of the stairs with a pistol of some sort.

"What are you doing?"

"I'm not going to be shot in the back of the head with my hands behind my back," the German replied. "If I die, I want to die fighting."

"You'll get us all killed, you idiot."

"You're dead anyways. Everyone inside this house is dead."

She shook her head as more boots clomped across the floor above her. Gloria turned her back on the German and rushed to the couch where D'onta and his sisters slept. The little boy's eyes were already wide, their whites showing in the basement darkness.

"They found us, didn't they?" he asked.

"Yeah, sweetie," she replied, nodding foolishly since he couldn't see her. "The bad people are here. I need you to hide in the back of the storage closet like we practiced."

"Okay. We'll be quiet."

D'onta gently shook his sisters awake and whispered that they had to go to the closet. Gloria willed them to go faster, eyeing the stairs as she picked up Phelisha and carried her to the closet.

The children were quiet and didn't complain when she stacked up the few boxes that the homeowner had. It wouldn't survive much more than a cursory inspection, but she had to hope that they would be satisfied with the adults—especially Frederick. She closed the door quickly and rushed back toward the room she shared with James.

"This is Jerry," a man's voice drifted down from the stairwell. "It's okay, we have US Army soldiers with us."

"Jerry?" Gloria blurted out much louder than she'd meant to.

"Yes, ma'am. I know you're armed, please don't shoot us."

"Put that thing away, Frederick," she ordered the German, who still stood at the base of the stairs with the pistol.

"How do we know that he's telling the truth? No one was supposed to be back inside the house until the morning."

"If they wanted us dead, they'd just toss a few grenades down the stairs," James said from the doorway where he'd dragged himself.

"Put the gun down." Gloria was getting pissed at the German. He knew they were waiting for a link-up with an Army unit, why wouldn't they choose to come at night? It made perfect sense to her.

Frederick reluctantly put the gun in the holster under his arm. "I have secured my weapon," he called up the stairs to Jerry.

"Alright," the police officer replied. "We're opening the door. Again, I have a US Army unit with me. They're armed."

"Oh, for Heaven's sake," Gloria muttered, storming back to where Frederick stood.

"Jerry, it's Gloria. Come down. He put the pistol away."

"Alright, thank you, Gloria," Jerry answered and soon the sound of footsteps thumping on the old wooden stairs filled the basement as several men came down.

A white guy in civilian clothes wearing all sorts of military gear stepped out from behind Jerry and extended his hand to Frederick. "Oberst Albrecht?"

"Yes, that is me," Frederick responded, grasping the soldier's hand.

"I'm Captain Gabriel Murdock, from the US Army 3rd Infantry Division. We were sent here to escort you out of the city so you can tell us what you know."

"I know many things," Frederick stated.

"Uh, yeah. Okay, that's good," the officer replied, looking around the basement. He noticed Gloria and said, "Hello, ma'am. Is this your house?"

She laughed. "No, it's not, Captain Murdock. I'm Lieutenant Colonel Adams-Branson, US Army Center for Military History over at Fort McNair."

He took her hand lightly. "Ma'am. Uh… If this isn't your house, what are you doing here with the colonel—if you don't mind my asking?"

"So that must mean that we never came up," Gloria surmised.

"No, I… Ah, I don't think so, ma'am."

"We were leaving the city and got caught up with Oberst Albrecht when Devon Johns was coordinating to get him out of the city. Devon wanted us to take him with us since he can't read English and would need a guide of some kind. We agreed, came here to wait to leave the city under the cover of darkness. Then, the Germans began expanding their lines and the Resistance pushed back. We got stuck, waiting for a break in the fighting. Devon said he contacted the Army and that the new plan was for us to wait until you guys arrived.

"That was four days ago," she finished.

"Hmm," the captain mumbled. "I'm authorized to bring Oberst Albrecht back with me, but not you."

"It's not just me," Gloria amended, realizing that she hadn't introducing her husband. "My husband, James, is the Deputy Director of the Joint North American Defense Branch, which was responsible for coordinating the US defense after the attacks in Florida a few years ago."

"Did you say 'Florida'?" Frederick asked, seeming to come to life.

"Yes," Gloria replied. "I met with James and some others after the German sneak attack in Fort Lauderdale—"

"It was hardly a sneak attack," Frederick scoffed. "It was a tightly controlled, limited test of the German capabilities, using inexperienced pilots and soldiers."

"Limited test?" Captain Murdock whirled on the German. "I was there, you son of a bitch. Sixty-three thousand people died."

"I did not know my mother," Frederick answered casually. "She may well have been a bitch."

"What's your game, man? Why are you helping us if you don't care about what happened?"

"On the contrary, Captain. I do care. I ordered that attack to determine whether the Reich was ready to begin thawing our soldiers or whether we needed to develop more advanced technology. The American response was pathetic. There was no resistance. I knew it was time to wake everyone and seize our opportunity. It—"

The buttstock of the captain's rifle impacted solidly into Frederick's nose, crushing it and ending his haughty statement. The older man crumpled to the ground and Gloria was dimly aware of the soldiers using zip ties to secure the German's hands behind his back.

Her mind reeled at the implications of what Frederick said. He'd admitted to ordering the attack in Florida. *He was the reason for everything that had happened since that day.* She'd slept twenty feet away from a mass murderer…

Gloria's vision began to swim and she had to sit down on the arm of the sofa.

"Are you alright, ma'am?" the captain asked.

"Yeah, I just need to— I just need to—"
Gloria passed out, falling backward onto the couch.

TWENTY

17 July 2025
Holloway Office Complex, CIA Black Site Three, Reston, Virginia

"Wakey, wakey. Hands off snakey," a guard said, tapping on the bars of Berndt's cell, waking him from a fitful slumber.

"I am tired," he protested. "Please leave me alone."

"We ain't leaving you alone, ya filthy Kraut," the second guard replied. "It's time to go see the doctor."

Berndt tried to remember how long it had been since his last interrogation. Was it two meals ago or three? The time truly ran together in this place. The last time he'd spoken to anyone besides Gregory—whom he was now convinced was insane—had been when the woman beat him.

The door to his cell opened and he pushed himself up. "May I use the lavatory first?" he asked.

"Oooh! Good idea!" Gregory's voice lilted through the hallway as if he were singing a happy tune. "That way you don't piss yourself when they shock you!"

"Shut up, Wagner," the first guard ordered.

"You can't do much more to me! No, no, no! Only I know where the base is, but it's locked away forever...*in my mind*," Gregory's voice changed to a hoarse whisper, like the sound of ice chunks grating against one another. "You'll have to kill me and look through my skull for the answers!"

"How's about we go over and dig it out through your ear right now?" the meaner of the two guards, the one who always wore a hat with the letter "**B**" embroidered on it, asked.

They closed his door with a loud *clang* and the two of them disappeared in the direction of Gregory's cell. The man was a fool, bringing more misery upon himself than was needed.

Berndt stumbled to the lavatory to relieve himself since the guards hadn't told him that he couldn't. They were too occupied with Gregory anyways. The last time he'd returned, he'd been a bloody mess, much worse than any time before. Berndt had tried to ask him what they wanted, but the other man's mind had clearly been broken during that session. He babbled incoherently about different ways to keep secrets and men being cooked in giant ovens.

It made Berndt wonder why the interrogations were so incredibly different between himself and the paratrooper. They were both officers, allegedly protected under the Geneva Conventions of 1929—and while the Reich didn't sign it, the Geneva Convention of 1949 should have governed the United States as well, which granted even more protections to prisoners of war. Torture was expressly forbidden.

"They're going to lie to you, düsen-driver!" Gregory screamed as the sound of batons impacting against flesh echoed down the hallway, causing a few other prisoners to grumble about trying to get sleep. The man cried out in pain as they did who knew what to him behind the cinderblock wall.

Finally, they stopped and returned to Berndt's cell. "You wanna come along or we gotta convince you, too?" the hat-wearing guard asked.

"I'm ready, sir," Berndt replied truthfully, waiting patiently in the center of his cell.

"What is it about you Krauts? Half of you is polite as can be and the other half do everything they can to fight us."

"It must be the different year groups and how long someone was frozen," Berndt answered. "I've noticed that the longer a solder is in cryogenic hibernation, the more aggressive they become." Of course, he had no way of knowing if that held true in Gregory's case or whether he was simply an ass.

"Good to know," the first guard said. "Come along. Time to see the doctor."

"They're the animals, Berndt!" Gregory croaked. "Not us! Them! They did this to us!"

The guards ignored the paratrooper's comments this time and led him, handcuffed, down the hall to the familiar interrogation room. As he shuffled in, Berndt noticed that there was much more dried blood on the floor than in his previous visits. He wondered if this room was used for multiple people, like Gregory, or if that was his blood that hadn't been cleaned.

He sat in the chair with his arms over the back, as always. This time, he was surprised when they wrapped a chain around his waist to secure him to the chair.

"Gentlemen, I assure you, this is not necessary."

"On the contrary, Oberleutnant Fischer, it is." The familiar voice of the bespectacled doctor came from behind him as the guards secured his legs to the chair as well.

"We're going to try a different tactic with you today."

Berndt cringed internally. *So this is it. This is the day they begin the torture.* They'd tortured the others; apparently it was his turn. "I will not betray the Reich," he managed to say, sounding much more convincing than he felt.

"That may change when you learn the true origins of your Reich," the doctor stated. "I am on your side, Berndt. I have stopped my superiors from ordering your torture like they have done to the others."

He sat in the chair opposite the pilot. "So I am not going to be tortured?" Berndt asked hopefully.

"I am doing all I can to keep them at bay. You must understand that the longer this war lasts, the more bloodthirsty they will become. Like my hot-headed companion said the other day, we estimate four million Americans have died in the Nazi attacks. That's a tough pill to swallow, Berndt."

He stared at his lap. "I never wanted innocent people to die. I did my duty to the Reich, attacking targets where my superiors ordered. I'm truly sorry that the woman's family was killed."

The doctor slapped the tabletop loudly, making Berndt jump and look up at him. The man pointed a finger at him, saying, "And *that's* why you're different. You're remorseful for the accidents and horrors of war. Many of the others are not. It is an interesting theory you have about correlation between the length of hibernation and the level of aggressiveness. It's possible that the brain is degraded somehow…"

The doctor trailed off, not realizing that he'd casually given away the fact that the cells were indeed monitored. Berndt had guessed that everything he discussed with Gregory was being recorded, but now he knew for sure that it was. He'd been alone with the guards when he made the statement about the freezing process.

"Regardless," the doctor continued. "I am going to show you what your Nazi ancestors did during the Second World War. I speak with many prisoners, all of whom talk about the American savagery during the war—even you. Logically, I understand that the information was drilled into you as children and it's all you've ever known. Even the ones who squirreled away a television in the darkest chambers of your secret base only saw the programs that their Reich masters allowed to be seen. So you have no ability to see how the world viewed what the Nazis did during the war, or even to hear dissenting views from your own."

"I don't understand," Berndt stated. "I'm sure there were incidents, warfare is not glamorous to those who experience it. Just as the doctor's family was killed accidentally."

"Did they teach you of the concentration camps?"

"The gulags?" Berndt asked. "Yes, they did. Thousands of German soldiers were taken to the Siberian camps and worked to death—even after the war was over. I often wondered why our first target was America and not the Soviet Union."

The doctor chuckled. "For one, the Soviet Union doesn't exist anymore. You are correct about the gulags, though. They were terrible, but hardly the worst part of World War Two. No, your government, the so-called Third Reich, was responsible for the death of almost forty *million* people between the gas chambers in their concentration camps and the mass starvation of Russian civilians."

"That is not possible," the pilot disputed. "That many deaths would have been purposeful, not the occasional accidental destruction of an occupied building or errant bomb. I do not believe your lies, Doctor."

"Very well. You've all been deceived by your Reich. Slaves who were taught only what your masters wanted you to know."

He reached into the pocket of the white coat he wore and produced a rectangular object. "I have put together newsreel footage and several documentaries on the war for you and several others like you whose brains are not corrupted."

The doctor pointed the object at the wall behind him and pressed a button. A projector, hidden somewhere where Berndt couldn't see it, began playing black and white footage that he recognized from the war. He'd seen similar footage thousands of time in Argus Base.

"I'll leave this playing, Berndt. I want you to watch and absorb the lessons of history from an unbiased and unfiltered source."

The doctor left after that. For several minutes, Berndt didn't listen to the broadcast, instead, he fumed internally that his captors were trying to subvert his reality by saying that his forefathers were the architects of chaos, not the Americans or the British. The doctor had even glossed over the horrors of the Soviet gulags, where German prisoners of war disappeared, never to be seen or heard from again.

As time stretched on, Berndt found himself drawn in by the words and images on the screen. Sometimes the message was lost as the narrators spoke too quickly in English for him to understand it all, but the pictures and videos completed the story. It was a story of hate, ultra-violence, and outright genocide. It was totally different than anything he'd learned of the past.

They left him strapped to the chair until he could no longer hold his urine and he was forced to relieve himself, soiling his clothing.

And still the disturbing images continued.

*****

17 July 2025
Anacostia, Washington, DC

"She's waking up, sir," Specialist Olshefsky, the squad's combat lifesaver, stated.

Gabe nodded, cursing himself for not bringing the company medic with him. Olshefsky did what he could to make the colonel comfortable, but he only had a week of lifesaving courses, which basically consisted of how to put a tourniquet on and learning to give IVs—not much help for a pregnant woman who passed out for no apparent reason.

Her eyes blinked a few times and she turned her head slightly until she saw Mr. Branson and the children he'd ushered out of the closet while she lay on the couch. "Ahh... Hello?" she mumbled.

"How are you feeling, ma'am?" Olshefsky asked. "You passed out, but lucky for you, you fell back onto the couch."

She tried to sit up, but the crevasse between the couch cushions and her stomach conspired against her, so she reached a hand out. Gabe took it and helped to pull her into a sitting position as she swung her legs over the edge of the couch.

"Where's Frederick?" Lieutenant Colonel Adams-Branson asked warily.

"He's over there," Gabe replied, gesturing toward the far corner where the German sat, his arms still handcuffed behind him.

"I don't want him near the children," she said. "He's a murderer."

"I am not, you wench!" Frederick Albrecht shouted. "Everything I did was in the interest of my nation, during war. I am not responsible for your people's lack of preparedness."

"Please, sir, and ma'am," Gabe hissed, raising his hands to get their attention. "We don't know if the German troops are walking by out in the street. We need to remain civil and most importantly, we need to keep quiet."

"I will not stand by and allow a *woman* to insult my integrity and honor," the colonel snapped. "Tell her to be quiet and I will do the same."

Gabe shook his head. How the hell were they supposed to travel with these two at each other's throats? His orders didn't exclude him from extracting others, but regardless, there was no way he could leave the pregnant woman. She was his superior officer and had a makeshift family to take care of. If he left her, he'd be miserable for the rest of his life.

Her husband was going to be a problem though. The wheelchair wouldn't make it through the woods back to Fort Ricketts. He'd need to devise something else to get the man back to the fort and then overland to their transport.

"Berserker Six, this is Berserker One."

"Go ahead, One," he replied.

"We've got hostiles inbound. Looks like there was a second drone up that we didn't see."

Their position was compromised. "Shit. How much time do we have?"

"Maybe a few minutes. They're moving your way from the northwest about three blocks away. Looks like they're moving cautiously, so they know something is up."

"Yeah, they heard that shot for sure," Jerry said, glaring at William. "They'll spread out like ants all over the neighborhood, trying to find out where it came from."

Gabe shook his head. "Second drone saw us come in here," he replied. "Does the Resistance have any troops to fight with?" Gabe asked.

"Sure, we got troops all over, but every time we've tried to stand toe-to-toe with the Krauts, they've kicked our asses. The best thing to do is ambush small units, and then get the hell out of the area before they send reinforcements."

"We don't have time for that," Gabe replied. Into the microphone, he said, "One, I need to verify that our route back to Fort Ricketts is clear."

"As of right now, yes, sir."

Gabe made his decision. "Lieutenant Colonel Adams-Branson, I'm going to follow through with my mission to extract the German. You're welcome to come back with us—and we'll help you and your husband—but, we're leaving now."

"Now?" she answered. "But, James can't make it up the—"

"Non-negotiable, ma'am. My orders are to secure the colonel. My men can carry your husband up the stairs and we can run for the cover of our patrol base at Fort Ricketts, and then get out of the city. But I need to get him out of here before we get trapped behind their lines."

"Captain, I'm ready," James replied, rolling his chair closer to the stairs.

His wife stood and went to him. They spoke in hushed tones for a few seconds and she nodded, her blonde hair swaying wildly as she did so. "Alright, Captain. We're going to take the opportunity you're giving us." She looked to where the children sat huddled on the floor. "Kids, put your shoes on. We're gonna go for a little run."

"Already on, Miss Gloria," the boy said, displaying his feet proudly.

"Okay, let's do this," Gabe said. "I need some of you guys to carry Mr. Branson up the stairs, somebody else grab his wheelchair. Then we're going to go back out the way we came in. Sergeant Paredes, designate some men to take turns pushing the wheelchair. We'll go as fast as the chair can go."

The squad sprang into action, two men picked up Mr. Branson and carried him up the stairs, while Private Powell picked up the wheelchair and followed them up. "Oberst Albrecht we're leaving now," Gabe said when he saw the colonel sitting in the corner still.

"I heard. I'm just resting my legs for as long as I can."

"Time's up. Your friends are out there hunting for you and it's a good bet that the second drone saw us come in here." He paused and then added, "Let's go, sir."

It took a minute to get everyone up the stairs. "One, Six. Time hack."

"They're two blocks away and closing, Six."

"We gotta make our lead count," Gabe shouted. "Let's go."

They jogged slowly down the street, setting an easy pace for the motley crew they'd inherited. In addition to the wheelchair, Gabe had a sixty-year old man whom he'd removed the zip strips from, a pregnant woman and three kids, each of them presented a unique challenge and had to be handled carefully. *Oh yeah, then there are the goddamned Germans who are closing in from behind*, he grumbled to himself.

The sharp whine of turbofan blades told him that the German drone saw them and was closing. "Paredes, DroneDestroyer. Now!" The Germans knew they were here, no sense trying to keep it a secret any longer.

The squad leader pulled something that resembled a rifle off another soldier's back and spun around, taking a knee as he did so. He brought the electronic warfare device up to his shoulder and turned it on, initiating a tracking system that acquired the drone's signature quickly. Several bursts from the device scrambled the drone's frequency and it tilted sharply. It went sideways for a half of a second, then went completely upside down and burned into the ground.

Gabe congratulated Sergeant Paredes and then added, pointing to the DroneDestroyer, "Keep that thing out. There's more of 'em around."

They ran after the rest of the squad, who'd followed the company's standard operating procedure and continued moving. Since the engagement lasted less than a minute, the others hadn't gotten far.

The squad jogged in silence and Gabe began to feel the tickle of sweat running down his skin in the empty space between his lower back and the heavy tactical vest he wore. He waited to hear Lieutenant Wilcox warning of an imminent attack any moment, but he didn't come up on the net.

Finally, he'd had enough of guessing. "One, this is Six. Status?"

"They've stopped temporarily. Probably trying to figure out who you are since you just blasted that drone out of the sky."

"Good. How much further until we reach Fort Ricketts?"

"Uh... Looks like about a tenth of a mile. You're coming to the green space now."

Thoughts and plans warred in his head for supremacy. On the one hand, he wanted to continue moving and get everyone out of the city as soon as possible. On the other, they could defend the fort against a ground attack—until they ran out of ammo or the Germans brought up one of those hovertanks.

It didn't take long for him to decide. "Berserker One, prepare your platoon for movement. We're going to move through your lines and continue toward our next assembly area." They'd established several link-up points along the way from where they ditched the cars in case the platoon got separated. Gabe had just ordered the abandonment of Fort Ricketts in favor of the Naylor Road Metro Station about a mile away.

Up ahead, Sergeant Kelley called a halt. They couldn't push the wheelchair anymore along the rutted path leading through the nature area.

"I got him," Corporal Hicks said as he scooped Mr. Branson up on his shoulder into a fireman's carry.

Private Powell once again moved to the wheelchair and pressed some button or knob with his foot. The chair collapsed, folding in half. A couple of the guys clapped him on the back and Gabe heard him say, "I've got a grandpa that has one of these."

They moved along the path and he slid up the line near Lieutenant Colonel Adams-Branson. "How are you holding up, ma'am?"

"I've felt better, Captain," she replied, supporting her stomach on interlocked fingers underneath. "I'm not going to complain though. Let's get as far away as we can."

He nodded. She was a trooper; she'd make the best of it. He moved forward to where the colonel struggled, picking his steps carefully over the rugged terrain. "How are you doing, sir?"

"Is this what Americans call a rescue mission? Where's the helicopter?"

"It's too dangerous. All it would take is for one of your flying saucers to notice the bird and then we're all dead. This is much safer."

"Flying saucer? Oh, you mean a düsenjäger. Yes, they are much more superior than your helicopters."

The captain dropped back. The man rubbed him the wrong way. From his arrogance to his assertion that everything German was superior, Gabe couldn't help but wonder why the man was willing to betray his people.

"It's because he's pissed off their boss," the woman stated as his pace slowed.

"*Hmm?*"

"The look on your face is plain as day, Captain Murdock. You want to know why he's offering to help us, right?"

"Yeah. How'd you—?"

"I work with all men. My entire career, I've been the only woman around, so I know a lot about how you guys think. That man is an opportunist. From what I could gather by talking to him the past few days as we were stuck in that basement, he got himself into trouble with the German commander somehow and now he's been sentenced to death. He took off before they could carry out the punishment. The only reason he's helping us is for self-preservation."

"He's sentenced to death? For what?"

"We never got him to admit why. He said that he didn't agree with their leader's plans to create a new Fatherland, but I've given it some thought and I'm not sure. Why did he spend all those years training the Reich's soldiers if they weren't planning on attacking and staying off that miserable continent?"

"Miserable continent?" Gabe asked. "He told you where their base is?"

"I already knew where their base is," the woman replied. "I knew five years ago after the attack in Fort Lauderdale."

"Well, where the hell are these people from, ma'am?"

She glanced over at him and then looked ahead. "Is that Fort Ricketts?"

He looked up. They'd made it to the perimeter of the old fort. "Yeah. We're only stopping to drink water and grab our packs."

She nodded. "Their base is an underground complex in Antarctica."

Gabe stopped, watching the squad file into the base. Of all the places in the world she could have said, he never would have imagined she'd say that. There wasn't anything to eat there. How'd they survive?

*****

19 July 2025
Holloway Office Complex, CIA Black Site Three, Reston, Virginia

How long have I been here?

The air smelled of stale piss and sweat. He lifted his leg from the chair. The dried urine had crystalized, forming sharp little flakes that dug into his skin. Preventing dehydration and the loss of electrolytes was something the Wehrmacht drilled relentlessly into its soldiers. The crystals meant he was losing salt in the room's oppressive heat—not good.

"I'm ready to talk!" he shouted. "I will tell you where our base is! Please, just stop the videos."

His eyes drifted to the projector screen. Yet another program was playing. This one showed Allied troops liberating another Nazi concentration camp. Mounds of rail-thin nude bodies were piled high, covered in some type of white powder, waiting to go into the fires. There had to have been thousands of them.

"At least the dead's suffering had ended," the narrator droned on. *"More than half of the liberated prisoners died within a day or two of the Allied soldiers' arrival. Well-meaning men shared their rations with prisoners. The sudden influx of nutritious vitamins and minerals sent their bodies into shock. The psychological trauma of believing that they were saved, only to die by the hundreds after liberation, was terrible."*

"Why!" Berndt wailed. "Why would anyone do this to another human being?"

The hours continued to stretch by as one documentary ended and another began. This was one following the Waffen SS, recorded by what appeared to be Nazi cameramen. These men carried out their assigned missions with glee. Their enthusiasm made him sick and the sight of their uniforms, which were the exact same as his, destroying the last vestiges of his loyalty to the Reich.

His predecessors were evil. Pure, unadulterated evil.

He tried to come up with stronger words, but his mind failed him. The word was sufficient enough, he supposed. It conveyed his feelings of hatred for the

Germans who came before him. It boggled his mind that all of what he'd been shown had been hidden from him for his entire life.

"Please, turn it off!" he begged. "I will tell you where the Nazi base is. I will work for you—yes! That's it. I'll work for the Americans *against* the Nazis. Anything, just—"

The video stopped abruptly and a black screen replaced the older footage. A small shape appeared in the center of the screen and got larger until a circular blue emblem filled the center of the screen. Inside the circle was a white shield with what appeared to be a compass rose emblazoned across it. The head and shoulders of a bird of prey—likely an eagle, although Berndt had truthfully never seen one before—rose above the shield over a red and white bar. Along the bottom was a yellow scroll that bore the words he recognized as '**United States of America**'. There were more words above the eagle, but Berndt never learned to read English, only to speak it haltingly.

"*Germany today*," a female voice announced, surprising him. Up until now, all the videos he'd been shown were narrated by men. Easily thirty or forty hours of dull, monotone male voices speaking softly for the benefit of their listeners had trained him to expect the same when the new video came on.

This video advanced rapidly in color, another stark difference between the other films. It showed what the Fatherland looked like today, eighty years after the end of the war. Germany had one of the strongest economies in the world and was a staunch ally of the United States. The people they showed seemed to be happy and the nation appeared to be truly prosperous. The architecture was grand and imposing, like the pictures young soldiers were shown during their education, except different. This was newer, more cleanly defined than what he'd seen.

The realization that *everything* about the outside world was a lie hit him hard. He'd known that a lot of it was rhetoric to stir up the masses, but there hadn't been a single shred of truth in anything that he'd learned as a child.

The video of *Germany Today* ended after segments on each of the vastly different cultural regions of the nation. The lights turned up, making him wonder when they'd been dimmed.

The door handle jiggled behind him and a rush of fresh air entered the room as the doctor came in. He sat in the chair and wrinkled his nose at the stench coming off of Berndt.

"You are ready to talk?" the doctor asked.

"Yes! Yes, sir. I've seen the wickedness of the Nazis. I don't want any part of that."

"So, you want to cooperate with the United States, is that what I'm hearing?"

"Yes. Those people were treated worse than animals." He jutted his chin toward the screen. "That's not humanity. The Reich lied to all of us. They need to pay for what they did."

"This will not do," the doctor stated, surprising Berndt. "Guards! Come in here."

He twisted in the chair, trying to see behind him, but it was no use. The movement sent spasms of pain through his aching body.

"Yes, Doctor Grossman?" a familiar voice asked.

"Please, take Oberleutnant Fischer to one of our guest suites and help him change out of his filthy clothing." Doctor Grossman looked back at him. "Berndt, the guards are going to take you to a room and let you shower and get a few hours of sleep. Then we'll talk about what we need from you. What *you* can do to help us make this right—and to make the Reich pay for their transgressions against the Jews, the Poles, the Russians and the Gypsies."

Berndt nodded his head. The Nazis were likely the most terrible thing to have ever happened to this planet and he was ashamed that he'd believed their lies. He vowed to himself that somehow, he'd make it right.

The doctor sat, watching as the guards unwrapped the chains securing him to the chair and helped him to his feet gingerly. Agony enveloped him when they released the handcuffs from behind his back. His shoulders screamed in protest as the muscles in the front of his body contracted after having been stretched wide for so long.

The guard with the embroidered red letter B on his hat leaned over and said, "I'm sorry, Oberleutnant, but I'll have to secure your hands in front of you."

He carefully positioned Berndt's hands in front and reattached the handcuffs. The pilot was amazed at his changed nature. "This way, sir," the other guard said, gesturing the *opposite* direction from where he'd gone previously to return to his cell.

They led him to an elevator and went up several floors, then got off on the sixth floor. Three doors from the elevator, a doorway stood open, with light flooding into the hallway. The guards indicated that he should go in, so he did.

It was a bedroom of some sort. There was a bed, a couch, a television and a *window!* It was nighttime outside; the stars twinkled softly through the glass.

"The bathroom is off to the left here, sir. You'll find towels, soap, shampoo, and a toothbrush. There are clothes in the drawers under the television and we'll have food delivered to the room in about fifteen minutes. Any questions?"

"Yes," Berndt replied. "Did I fall asleep watching those horrid documentaries? Please don't wake me from this dream."

The hat-wearing guard smiled. "Welcome to America."

TWENTY-ONE

19 July 2025
Hillcrest Heights, Maryland

Gloria needed sleep. Real sleep, not the half-assed in and out of consciousness that she'd gotten the past two nights.

Across the parking lot, only five hundred feet away, was a Budget Inn. Her aching back longed for the beds that the small motel offered and the possibility of running water for a shower seemed appealing as well. Instead, everyone who wasn't on watch tried to rest wherever they could underneath the platform's roof. Gloria had learned to hate the hard, red hexagon tiles. They'd been stuck in the Metro station for two days as scores of German soldiers patrolled the area, searching for their quarry.

The night they fled Fort Ricketts, the platoon had engaged in a harrowing game of cat and mouse. The only reason they lived was because of the drone that kept watch over their surroundings, telling them when it was safe to travel and when they needed to hide. Once they made it to the Naylor Road Metro Station, Captain Murdock assessed that it was too dangerous to continue moving that night and ordered them to hunker down in the Metro station.

It turned out to be a brilliant tactical decision, but a poor strategic one. The elevated train platform offered very little in the way of protection from the elements or from observation, so the Germans dismissed it as an entirely unlikely location for a group of soldiers to pick as a base. They were left alone and the overhead cover provided concealment from enemy drones that crisscrossed the sky above, but they could see the patrols searching the surrounding houses and run-down businesses. They'd missed their opportunity to get away before the noose tightened. Now they were stuck.

"Alright, it looks clear. We're going to send up the drone," the captain whispered loud enough to be heard by Gloria's entire group. He'd been good about keeping them informed. Apparently, his parent brigade was sending a relief element toward them since getting the colonel's information—and hers—was one of the most important tasks besides killing the Germans.

The whine of the drone's four engines filled the platform and the small vehicle shot skyward at the farthest point away from the stairs coming from the first floor. When possible, the platoon flew the drone every two hours to see what was going on around them. It wasn't perfect, but the batteries needed time to recharge in the sunlight.

"Alright," Jake Wilcox mumbled, sticking his tongue out slightly as he pivoted the camera around for the best views of the immediate area. "Looks like we're still alone, sir."

He flew the drone north, and then circled around toward the east for half a mile before heading south. It was roughly the same path, near the end of the drone's frequency range, that he'd flown almost twenty times. She wondered if they should change up the pattern so their moves weren't choreographed. Once the Germans figured out where to look, they could easily follow the drone back to the platform—

"Ahh…wait," Jake said.

"What is it?" Captain Murdock asked.

"Looks like someone flashed the quadcopter with some type of light, like a laser pointer."

"What does that mean?"

"I don't know, sir. It could be somebody trying to signal us, or it could be somebody trying to blind us. There's no way of knowing for sure."

"Can you trace the point of origin for the laser?"

He concentrated as the drone fought against winds up at the higher elevations. "This is where I was when—" The camera washed out with a series of red and green prismatic bursts.

The light continued to dazzle the drone's camera lens for several seconds until the lieutenant rotated it away. "That's a defensive counter-UAV measure," Sergeant Cheng stated from beside her. "We faced the same thing in the Ukraine back in 2016 and in Syria a few years later. It's not very effective since the drone can just fly away from the laser, but it can temporary hide the activity in a certain location."

"The Germans didn't use drones the first few days they were here," Gloria said, thinking out loud. "They probably don't have any defense against a technology they didn't anticipate."

"Shit," Jake mumbled, "I just got dazzled from another direction."

She spun on her heel, looking to where the colonel sat glumly on a bench a few feet away. "What are they doing?" she demanded.

"It's safe to assume that they know we have remained in the area," the old man replied. "You are right, Miss Gloria. We examined the use of drones a decade ago and decided they were not worth the effort required to acquire the systems or the time to train on them. You must remember that our system focused on formal education, training in your assigned combat occupation, and then freezing so the next generation could use the same limited space—not to mention the difficulty in securing food supplies from our allies—not learning to use toys that have no practical application to warfare."

"Allies?" Gloria repeated, her eyes narrowing. It was a piece of the puzzle that she'd wondered about, but often got sidetracked trying to glean information from the old man.

He chuckled. "You have been duped. Our allies in Argentina, who worked in conjunction with the Venezuelans for oil, supplied us with food. But our greatest ally has always been the Japanese government. They provided the raw materials for our weapons and assisted with the düsenjäger technology."

"No." She was truly shocked. Not about the Venezuelans, or even the Argentinians, the Japanese though… They made it seem as if they'd given up their warlike ways, cowed into submission by the atomic bombs America had dropped. In reality, they hadn't given up anything.

"History lesson's over, ma'am," Gabe said, slipping between her and the colonel. "What are those Nazi bastards doing?" he demanded of the old man.

"They know we remain. They are using the lasers to blind your camera so they can move troops without being observed. It's a low-tech solution, but as I said, the use of drones—and defense against them—is not a line of effort that we spent much time developing."

"So, we should expect an assault?"

"Most likely."

Gabe stepped away, issuing orders to his men. Gloria asked, "Did the Japanese know that you planned to attack the US?"

"The ones I dealt with personally did. I can only speculate that the arrangement was made *before* the Führer left Europe."

Gloria sat down beside him, her mind wandering back through time to the spring of 1945. Only a delusional, schizophrenic sociopath like Adolf Hitler would believe the Germans had any hope of winning the war, or even of fighting to a stalemate at that point. In the Pacific, the Japanese had lost all of their expansionary claims except China. Tokyo was firebombed in early March, killing between seventy-five and two hundred thousand, and in April, the US landed in Okinawa, the first of the Japanese home islands. The writing was on the wall for them as well.

The fact that the German base in Antarctica was a joint effort between the two nations should not have surprised her as much as it did. Certainly, the governments of the 1930s and 40s had collaborated somewhat before the war, but she'd always been under the impression that their communications during the war was limited due to the distances between them. That appeared to be false now.

Several feet away, she heard Captain Murdock requesting immediate support and exfiltration. The time for tactical patience had passed; the Germans were closing in.

"Sir, I've got a squad of Nazis at…four hundred meters."

Gloria glanced at the sniper, Sergeant Kelley, who'd whispered the warning. His spotter peered through an oddly shaped scope on a stand that allowed him to adjust it higher or lower. Corporal Hicks' free hand unconsciously trailed the length of his own rifle, which was shorter than the sergeant's weapon, and sported a smaller scope. Hick's rifle resembled a traditional hunting rifle, while Kelley's had all sorts of military enhancements that she didn't know anything about.

"What are they doing?" Gabe asked.

"They're pointing toward our position, sir," Hicks answered.

"Are you sure?"

"Yes, sir. Ah, shit…"

"What?"

"Their officer is looking at the metro station with binoculars."

"Hey, sir," Lieutenant Wilcox called, regaining Gabe's attention. "I've been flying around trying to see who was dazzling the camera. We've got about a hundred, hundred and fifty, Nazis inbound on our location from the north and northwest."

"Goddammit!" Gabe grumbled. "Sergeant Kelley, take out that squad to the south as quick as you can, then reposition to the north side."

"Understood, sir."

Corporal Hicks put his spotting scope to the side and picked up his rifle. He slid the suppressed barrel forward until the tip protruded through a small gap in the concrete wall.

"Hicks, I've got the officer, you take one of the others," Sergeant Kelley stated. "Try to find an NCO."

"Target identified," Hicks replied.

"On my mark, then weapons free."

"Roger."

"Three… Two… One."

Gloria jumped slightly as the muffled sound of both rifles firing nearly simultaneously startled her. Each man worked the bolt action on his weapon quickly, chambering a new round, before aiming and firing again. Their sequencing quickly became separated as the sergeant fired more rapidly than Hicks. Gloria wondered if it was the fancy rifle or experience that made Sergeant Kelley faster.

She watched in amazement as the two snipers killed men right in front of her, snuffing out their lives before they even knew anything was happening. Part of her felt as if it weren't fair to the Germans, while another part of her cheered that each round the men fired likely meant one less soldier trying to kill them in the next few minutes.

Sergeant Kelley dropped the magazine on his rifle and slapped a new one home. He pushed the bolt forward and aimed again. Then it was Hicks' turn to swap out magazines. Before either of them had cycled through their second five-round magazine, the sergeant said, "Clear."

They displaced to the opposite side of the platform to the second position they'd prepared and set up. Other members of the platoon occupied their previous location just a few feet from the bench where Gloria sat with the colonel.

"Where are the hostiles, LT?" Hicks asked.

"Bounding this way from the north," he replied. "You should see them soon."

"Contact, three hundred meters!" someone yelled, forgetting about the need to remain quiet.

"Dammit!" Gabe cursed again. "Sergeant Cheng, your men are authorized to begin firing. Do whatever you can to keep them away from the station."

Slowly, the men began firing at unseen targets and Gloria rushed the children over to the nonfunctioning escalator. They were surrounded on three sides by a concrete railing which provided the best possible cover on the platform. Down below on the first floor, men spread out, facing south to defend the station's only entrance.

The sounds of incoming rounds impacting against concrete, tearing through metal poles and shattering glass erupted around them as the Germans began to return fire. Within seconds, the litany of sounds was drowned out by the company commander's shout, his voice cracking at the effort to be heard above it all.

"Medic!"

*****

20 July 2025
Holloway Office Complex, CIA Site Three, Reston, Virginia

Berndt stretched his hands above his head languidly. He felt like he'd slept for days, but the sun shining through the window this morning told him that it had only been one complete night. He pushed his head down into the pillow, enjoying the softness. He'd never felt a bed so soft, it was comfortable beyond belief. It felt as if he were floating on a cloud.

There was a knock on the door and a woman entered without being invited. She pushed a cart ahead of her into the center of his room. A silver dome-like object was the dominating item on the cart. Additionally, there was a silver container that resembled a tea kettle, a coffee mug, a small plate, and utensils.

"Good morning, Oberleutnant Fischer," she said. Her voice was soft, sounding very much like the women in the television programs he'd seen as a child.

"Good morning," he replied.

"Anna," the woman stated, lifting away the dome to reveal a massive plate of food underneath. "My name is Anna. I've brought you a breakfast of ham and cheese omelet, bacon, a side of oatmeal, some assorted fruits, and of course, coffee."

"*Real* coffee?" he asked. "We got a little bit of it after the initial invasion, then we pushed outside the city and it wasn't as easy for our supply personnel to find."

She smiled. Her teeth were straight, and white—far whiter than anyone's teeth in Argus Base had been. "Of course, sir. We wouldn't think of giving you anything but the very best. After all, you're going to be a hero."

The smell of the bacon made his stomach rumble. "May I?" he asked, gesturing toward the lavatory.

"Of course, Oberleutnant. This is your room."

He started to stand and realized that he'd slept naked. "Ah, I'm sorry. Could you?"

"Oh! Of course," Anna said, smiling devilishly before turning her back to him.

He rushed to the lavatory to relieve himself. When he was finished, he shrugged into a white robe hanging on the back of the door.

"Ah…much better," Berndt muttered as he came out of the bathroom.

Anna sat in one of the two chairs that made up the small sitting area. The top two buttons on her blouse were undone, but Berndt was positive that they hadn't been before—or had they been? It seemed a strange thing to focus on.

"You should eat. I made that omelet for you myself," she directed. "It's special; it'll give you lots of energy."

"Hmm. Thank you, ma'am."

"Oh, no. You should call me Anna." She leaned back, arching her back in a stretch that pressed her breasts against her shirt.

Berndt picked up the plate and sat at the table a few feet away. He cut a section of the omelet away and shoved the fork into his mouth. After a moment of chewing, he decided that Anna was right; the omelet was exceptionally good. She watched him expectantly.

He swallowed. "You make a very fine omelet, Anna."

"Thank you," she blushed. "Now, eat up." She stood, walking to the cart. "How do you like your coffee…Berndt?"

"Um, one cream and one sugar? I think that sounds about right."

She leaned over the cart, busying herself with preparing his coffee. She didn't realize that the angle she was at gave him a perfect view down her shirt. He felt himself stirring and she glanced upward, catching him looking at her breasts.

"Hey, what do you think you're doing?" she asked, not quite sounding like she was offended to Berndt's inexperienced ear.

"I'm ah… Sorry, ma'am. I didn't mean to—"

"Yes, you did, Berndt," she stated, walking over to the table and setting his coffee down. She pushed her hand into the pocket on her trousers and emerged with a blue, diamond-shaped pill. "Here, take this vitamin. You weren't taken very good care of during the interrogation phase and your health suffered from lack of nutrition. This will help introduce some of those vitamins back into your system."

He stared at the pill for a moment, trying to determine if it was a cyanide capsule or some other form of poison, but dismissed the idea. If they wanted to kill him, they would have done so long ago and skipped the charade of a nice hotel room, a beautiful room attendant, and a marvelous meal.

Berndt picked up the pill and popped it into his mouth, followed by a sip of coffee.

Anna smiled again. She seemed to do that a lot more than any of the girls he'd been around in Antarctica. "So, Doctor Grossman tells me that you're willing to make amends for the wrongs of the Reich."

He sipped the coffee once more, relishing the rich flavor that he'd only experienced a few times in his life. "Yes. Those videos of the war opened my eyes to their wrongdoings. I still have a hard time coming to terms with how completely I was fooled by them."

She slipped off her shoes, which were the oddest things he'd ever seen. A long spike ran from her heel to the ground. It must have been impossible to run or march for long distances in them. The carpet made an odd *swishing* sound as she rubbed her bare feet back and forth on it.

"I think it's wonderful that you've decided to help America—to save America, really."

"I'm sorry, what's that?" he asked, moving on to the oatmeal.

"You know, that you're going to carry out this mission and save the United States from the Reich."

"What mission?" he asked guardedly, feeling an odd tingle in his crotch.

"We can't talk about it here—secrets, y'know?" she stated. "But just know that I know, and it's a very big turn on to be in your presence."

He frowned. "I'm not sure I understand you. What am I turning on?"

"Me," she breathed.

"Uh… I'm not sure how you were turned off. Why do you need me to turn you on?"

She giggled, unbuttoning another button on her blouse. Berndt definitely was beginning to feel something underneath the robe. "You're funny. I like you."

"I like you too," he answered. "You have a very pretty smile."

"Thank you, Berndt." A look of worry crossed her face.

"What is wrong?"

She leaned back heavily against the back of the chair. "It's just… Oh, it's silly of me to say it to you."

"No, go ahead," he prompted.

"It's just that… I'm scared. The Reich is expanding their position, pushing beyond where they used to be. I don't want them to do the same things that they did in Europe over here."

"There are different leaders now," he countered. "The Führer is long dead. That couldn't happen again."

"Are you so sure? Before two days ago, you didn't even know the Nazis were responsible for the largest ethnic genocide in human history. Where are all those soldiers and Reich members going to live? They'll move into the homes of the average American citizen and eliminate the occupants. All the support personnel and everyone from your base, they'll need places to stay as well. I think that Generalfeldmarschall Mueller plans to keep the territory they've taken."

Berndt's mind raced to remember whether he'd ever mentioned Generalfeldmarschall Mueller, but stopped. Of course they knew, there were several prisoners, if even one of them mentioned the commanding officer, they'd know about him.

"Do not worry. He will not—" He stopped, considering what he'd learned about the Nazis of the past and what they were capable of. "On second thought, given what I know now, he *may* attempt to cleanse the Washington, DC area to keep as the new Fatherland."

A small, suppressed sob escaped Anna's lips. "Please tell me you will stop him like Doctor Grossman believes."

"Stop the generalfeldmarschall? How am I supposed to do that?"

"I don't know!" she exclaimed. "You're the military officer. You've got the training, not me. I'm just a scared girl who wants the war to end and all the suffering to stop."

"I don't know what I can—"

She surprised him by rushing to his side. The feeling of arousal down below was almost unbearable. "Promise me, Berndt."

"Promise you what?"

Anna sank to her knees, reaching out tentatively to slide her hand between his robe lapels, her fingers tickling the hair on his chest. "Promise me that you'll be the hero."

"Hero?"

"You're a hero, Berndt. You just need to accept that fact. America needs you to defend us. *I* need you to."

"What is it that you think I can do?"

Her fingernails scraped lightly across his ribs, sending his body into a frenzy. "You are going to kill Generalfeldmarschall Mueller and end the war."

"I'm what?" he asked incredulously.

Anna's opposite hand trailed along his thigh under the robe. "You are going to be America's savior. *My* savior."

She leaned up and kissed him. "But first, I'm going to show you my gratitude for what you're willing to do. What *every* woman in America would be willing to do for a hero, such as yourself."

TWENTY-TWO

20 July 2025
Hillcrest Heights, Maryland

Gabe had given up trying to reach the brigade. They continued to tell him that help was inbound, but it wouldn't matter. In a few hours they'd be dead. The only reason they'd survived the night was because of their night vision devices—standard issue for American infantrymen. It seemed the Germans didn't have the same capabilities, yet another advancement in the technology of warfare that they'd chosen not to pursue.

He would have asked the colonel whether the Nazis had night vision, but Specialist Olshefsky hadn't been able to save him. The German took a bullet to the throat in the first few minutes of fighting, drowning in his own blood until the medic put in a chest tube to drain the fluid. Then, the blood loss led to shock, which led to a heart attack and finally, death.

The platoon's mission was a failure all around. They'd failed to exfil without alerting the enemy, they'd failed to extract the asset, and they'd failed to get the location of the Nazi base directly from the colonel. On the positive side, they still had Lieutenant Colonel Adams-Branson, who claimed to know that the base was in Antarctica, and with the exception of the German, they hadn't lost anyone else.

That would change, though. His men were already at less than half of their expanded combat load of ammunition.

Gabe high-crawled to where Jake Wilcox tinkered with the drone. "When can you get that thing back in the air?"

"I don't know, sir. One of the rotors is completely destroyed and the frame is bent, making it all wonky when it flies."

"I don't care about it listing to the side like a drunken sailor, Jake. I need it up in the air observing those Germans."

"Got it, sir. I've had Privates Powell and Sweeney working the crank charger non-stop for about an hour, so the battery should have enough juice to stay airborne for about forty-five minutes."

"Good," Gabe said, glancing eastward toward the lightening sky. "We need it up in the sky. They'll attack once they can see."

"Got it. It'll be up in the next ten minutes."

"Good," he repeated, slapping the lieutenant affectionately on the back. "You've done a hell of a job, Jake. We'll get through this."

"Thanks, sir." Lieutenant Wilcox paused and then added, "It wasn't your fault the colonel got shot. I saw him; he was standing up, like he was trying to see the action. It was his own fault."

"I know, Jake. Doesn't make it any easier though."

Gabe dropped the conversation and crawled to the stairwell where his new high-value asset rested with her family behind the protection of concrete walls. "How are you holding up, ma'am?"

She rubbed her stomach absently as she responded. "I'm doing alright. James won't say so, but he's in a lot of pain. I can tell. The doctor only gave him enough pain meds for a week because he was supposed to return for a follow-up. Now he's out of drugs only two weeks after he became paralyzed."

"I'm sorry to hear that, ma'am," Gabe replied, unable to do anything about the narcotics he'd likely been given. "I can have Olshefsky give him a bunch of Motrin, that's about it."

"Would you mind? Like I said, he'd never admit to weakness, but he needs something."

"Of course. Anything else I can do for you?"

She smirked. "You can tell me that the cavalry is on its way."

"It *is* on the way."

"That's what they told you two nights ago when we stopped here initially. I just hope we haven't been written off because the colonel's dead."

"They wouldn't do that."

"It's wartime, Gabriel. The military has done much worse during war."

Gabe decided that he didn't like talking to her very much. Conversations with her almost always ended with some way that the past was coming back to haunt them in the present.

"Well—"

The report from an M4 at the far end of the train platform cut him off. He gave the lieutenant colonel a thumbs up and crawled back to the bench he'd designated as his command post. He had to try to get the brigade on the horn. Gabe's driver, Specialist Mendoza, already had the radio handset ready to hand over to him.

"Thanks." Into the handset, he called, "Spartan Three, this is Berserker Six, over."

"Berserker Six, this is Spartan Three November, over."

The Operations Sergeant Major. Gabe's hopes soared. The Three and even the Six were worried about their next job in the Army. Getting more troops killed trying to rescue troops in combat was always a slippery slope. It was the right thing to do, but oftentimes military panels of inquiry decided that rescue attempts were misguided and poorly-planned. As a result, officers tended to over-plan and tried to make sure the conditions were perfect *before* they acted. The noncommissioned officers, however, had spent their entire career on the line. They knew the importance of immediate assistance.

"Three November!" Gabe shouted, holding the transmit button down for a couple of seconds so the sounds of gunfire would transmit. "We have troops in contact, request immediate extraction, over."

"Roger, I understand. *TIC.* The Three Actual got called away to a meeting. I'll send a runner to tell him, over."

"Sergeant Major, we ain't gonna last long. We need immediate exfil. Can't you call your buddies over at the Aviation Brigade?"

"I can, sir, but I'm not authorized to do that, over."

"Sir," Lieutenant Wilcox yelled. "The drone's up. There's a hovertank coming our way!"

"Dammit, Sergeant Major!" Gabe shouted into the handset. "They're bringing armor into the fight. We can't do shit against that thing. Take some fucking responsibility and get us the fuck out of here."

"You keep your men alive, sir. I'll see what I can do, over."

Gabe wanted to throw the handset, but it was their only lifeline; without the radio, it was a guarantee that they were done for. Around him, men screamed for medics, cross-leveled ammo, and called out targets to one another as the fighting renewed. The time seemed to slow and he realized that they were all going to die at the Metro station.

Calm settled over him. There was nothing else that he could say to headquarters to spur them into action. He needed to get on the line and fight beside his men. Gabe pressed the button to transmit. "Thank you, Three November, do what you can. We're amber ammo. One *KIA*, multiple *WIA*. Berserker Six, out."

He gave Mendoza the handset. "Monitor for any further traffic from headquarters."

"Roger, sir."

"Give me your extra magazines. Keep three for yourself."

Mendoza dug through his bag and produced five thirty-round magazines of ammunition and pulled another four magazines from the pouches attached to his body armor.

"Thanks, Mendoza. You're a great soldier."

Gabe high-crawled to the north side of the platform, handing Mendoza's magazines out to the men there. They'd seen the heaviest fighting and needed ammunition more than the others. Once that was done, he crawled to a bloody spot in the line of men where someone had been shot. Out of the corner of his eye, he saw that Olshefsky had dragged the injured man to the concrete wall and was busy slapping bandages on him.

Gabe pressed the butt of his rifle against his shoulder and peered through the ACOG site. Men in dark grey uniforms, wearing the same mixture of helmets that he remembered seeing that day on the beach, appeared in the ACOG. He turned off the feelings of abandonment and the responsibility of leadership. For now, he was simply another rifleman on the line.

He squeezed the trigger, satisfied that he was finally able to do something for his men.

*****

20 July 2025
Skies above Virginia

The düsenjäger's controls felt familiar in Berndt's practiced hands—and yet, somehow different. He couldn't explain it. *He* felt the same, and yet different. He'd been trying to figure it out since Dr. Grossman told him that he'd be flying the captured düsen back to the capitol.

The feelings of contradicting loyalties assaulted him as he walked with the doctor from the hotel room he'd shared with Anna that morning. He was a German, through and through, raised to hate Americans and prepared to sacrifice his life for the revenge that the Reich had fostered inside of him—except, his experiences in captivity made him feel something that he hadn't felt in all his years at Argus Base. He felt hope.

It was an odd sensation because in all likelihood, he was flying to his death, but he knew the truth now. His ancestors had committed terrible atrocities and the Americans, along with the Brits and Russians, were the only ones who'd been able to halt the reign of the Third Reich. Now he was fighting on their side, flying headlong toward the US National Mall, where he knew Generalfeldmarschall Mueller made his headquarters.

The ground sped by underneath him. It would be a short flight and he needed to work through his feelings in the few remaining minutes.

He was a changed person. The knowledge of what his people were capable of, and what they'd *done*, made him sick to his stomach. He'd been lied to for his entire life. Everyone he knew had been lied to. He wanted revenge. They'd taken his youth and injected him with the regeneration serum, which, if the men who'd been kept in the cells beside him were any indication, may be responsible for mental derangement over time.

Ahead, he saw a group of German hovertanks traveling in a single file line down a wide, six-lane highway. They were completely unaware of his presence above them, content in the knowledge that the Wehrmacht owned the skies. He briefly considered firing upon them. The düsenjäger's cannons would make short work of their lightly armored hatches. The move would save the lives of countless American soldiers and civilians.

The desire to contribute something that would be an immediate benefit to the men and women on the ground was strong, but Berndt knew that it was a foolish train of thought. If he killed the hovertanks, word would get out that there was a rogue düsenjäger pilot on the loose, jeopardizing his ability to land without clearance. The success of his mission depended on his ability to make it to the generalfeldmarschall's headquarters without alerting his former companions.

The hovertanks disappeared behind him and he passed the smoldering ruins of the American Pentagon building. It had continued to release toxic fumes and smoke for more than two weeks as the decades of paper and secrets were destroyed.

Then he was over the National Mall. The skeletal remains of most buildings were the only indication that there'd been anything there at all. He took a deep breath and thumbed the radio transmit button.

"This is Vengeance 519 requesting immediate clearance to land at Wehrmacht Headquarters."

"Vengeance 519, this is Luftwaffe Control. What is the nature of your emergency?"

"I, uh… I have information that Generalfeldmarschall Mueller must hear."

"What information, Vengeance 519? I'm showing your düsen as destroyed and the pilot killed in action. What is your name, pilot?"

"My name?" He faltered. *What if I can't do this?* he doubted himself.

So many people were depending on him. The doctor had told him that the American war effort relied on him accomplishing his mission, which would destabilize the German leadership. Berndt had heard of the fracturing amongst the Wehrmacht's senior leadership, most notably between the generalfeldmarschall and the commander of the 938th Training Brigade, Oberst Albrecht. Killing Mueller may well destabilize the High Command as the Americans thought.

I can do this, he decided. That fracturing would be blown wide open with the death of Mueller.

"My name is Oberleutnant Berndt Fischer. My düsen *was* shot down. I was captured, but I escaped and evaded behind American lines for weeks until I was able to steal the düsen I'm in now. I have vital information that the Generalfeldmarschall must hear and I— I think our communications equipment may be compromised. The Americans are more advanced than we thought."

There was a long pause as the soldier manning the radio relayed his message to their superior. Berndt circled the düsenjäger slowly around the Institute of Peace, where the Wehrmacht High Command had taken up residence.

After what felt like ages, the soldier replied. "*Vengeance 519, you are cleared to land at Wehrmacht Headquarters. You will deplane and await the security detail, which will escort you as you relay your message.*"

"Thank you," Berndt replied, easing the aircraft down on the National Mall's grass across the street from the headquarters building.

He powered off the düsenjäger and then stopped before flipping the switch which would turn off the jet's electronics. He figured the extra two minutes not spent warming up the system could save his life. He ran his fingers over the small scrap of wrinkled paper that the doctor handed him before leaving. His preflight instructions that were in his pocket when he was captured.

"One more time, old friend."

He threw the rope ladder toward the ground and he patted the altered German service pistol in the holster on his hip to reassure himself that it remained in place. Upon cursory inspection, the weapon appeared to be a standard pistol, but Doctor Grossman told him that it was much more powerful than a pistol and had instructed him in the weapon's use. It was the key to ensure he accomplished the mission and escaped alive.

He began to climb slowly down the ladder. As his foot touched the ground, a man shouted for him to halt.

Berndt raised his hands slowly. An SS officer came forward and scanned his wrist with a handheld device. He observed the display until it beeped and then looked up from the machine.

"Very well, Oberleutnant. You are who you say you are," the officer remarked. "Follow me; Generalfeldmarschall Mueller is most interested to hear of the technology you say the Americans have developed."

The officer detailed a private to guard the aircraft, ordering him not to let anyone near it until the investigation was complete.

Berndt trailed along behind the SS man, avoiding any stupid moves. Anna promised him she'd be there waiting for him when he returned, and he intended to see her again.

TWENTY-THREE

20 July 2025
Hillcrest Heights, Maryland

Aim. Breathe. Pause. Squeeze the trigger. Breathe.

The mantra repeated itself in Gabe's head as he fought. His father had taught him to shoot; the Army had refined those rudimentary lessons. Now he applied them with deadly accuracy.

"I'm out!" Sergeant Kelley yelled from nearby.

Gabe broke his cheek-to-stock weld and glanced at the snipers. Both men were out of ammunition for their long rifles, all they had left was pistol ammo. The Germans weren't *that* close—yet.

He lowered his cheek and sighted in on a man with some type of tube weapon—likely a panzerfaust, a rocket propelled grenade. Before he could shoot, the man recoiled from the impacts of several rounds.

"That's it. I'm out too."

Gabe looked around at his men. One by one, they were running out of ammunition. They didn't have bayonets like the soldiers of yesteryear, but they could still use their weapons as clubs. It was pathetic. They were members of the most advanced military in the world and they were on the verge of fighting like cavemen.

A massive explosion tore away the perch where Sergeant Kelley and Corporal Hicks were vacating. One second, they were moving off the ledge, the next second they were gone.

Blood smeared the surrounding area, but he couldn't see the two men's bodies.

He turned back, aiming through his ACOG where the man with the panzerfaust had been killed. The weapon was nowhere to be seen. Another German had recovered it. Beyond the nearby scene, the hovertank that Jake Wilcox saw with his drone rumbled into position at the edge of the road.

"Take cover!" Gabe bellowed, knowing a round from that tank was inbound any second.

He scooted backward in the direction of the concrete wall. His foot touched up against it right as another explosion rocked the southern side of the platform.

"*RPG!*" someone, possibly Sergeant Cheng, yelled.

A few soldiers returned fire with single shots, but the men on that side had either rotated from the northern edge and were out of ammo or had passed most of their ammo to the defenders on the opposite side of the platform.

Gabe hooked his foot on the edge of the wall and pulled himself toward it. Below him, on the entrance level, the men fired into the Germans attempting to rush across from the parking lot to the station's entrance. Once they ran out of ammo, there was nothing to stop the Nazis from overrunning them.

Men punched the floor in frustration. They were trapped. If they survived the shelling from the hovertank, the only thing they had to look forward to was being lined up for execution. He could already feel the German barrel against the back of his head.

Once again, he was thrown sideways as a massive explosion ripped a ten-by-ten section of the train platform away. The side of Gabe's helmeted head impacted against the bench where the colonel's body still lay. He wasn't knocked unconscious this time, but he had an oppressive feeling of déjà vu from that day on the beach, making him think he'd been transported back in time.

He found himself staring into the wide, frightened eyes of a blonde woman and he was confused. "Olivia?"

"What?" the woman asked. "No, Gabe. I'm Gloria. We need to get out of here."

"Gloria?" He shook his head to clear away the cobwebs. Everything felt strange, from the incessant ringing in his ears to the odd angle of his leg.

"Shit," Gabe mumbled, drooling blood. "My leg is fucked, ma'am."

"Goddamn it," she said. "*Medic!*"

"He's dead," Sergeant Cheng replied. "Got killed trying to help the LT."

"You sonofabitches!" the woman screamed, pulling Gabe's weapon from his weak grip. She stood on the edge of the platform and fired his last four rounds before cursing and moving back behind the concrete wall.

Her symbolic gesture of frustration was met with a volley from the Germans surrounding them. Chips of concrete splintered off, adding to the shrapnel hazard on the platform.

"I'm sorry, ma'am," Gabe whispered hoarsely. "I'm sorry that we failed to get you out."

"Don't say that, Gabe. This wasn't your fault. This was the Army's fault. You should never have—"

"*Sir!*" Specialist Mendoza shouted as he low-crawled toward the captain.

Gabe rolled his head inside the helmet to see his driver, holding out the radio handset. "Sir, it's Spartan Six. He's inbound with a shitload of helicopters!"

The handset hurt his face as he pressed it to his ear. "This is Berserker Six, over," he groaned.

"Captain Murdock! Spartan Six. We're one minute out from your location. Pop smoke, son."

Gabe chuckled weakly, which turned into a coughing fit. "You'll see smoke from burning shit, sir," he replied when he was able to talk. "Be advised, they have RPGs and at least one hovertank."

A concussion of air buffeted him half a second before the sound of an explosion assaulted his ears, followed by a wave of heat. His men cheered halfheartedly.

"Correction, Berserker Six," the colonel responded. "They *had* a hovertank."

30-millimeter cannons burst to life from the south as Apache gunships sped toward the Metro station, firing at everything beyond the perimeter of the building. The helicopters' guns chewed the Germans to shreds, punching holes through whatever they tried to hide behind.

The fight at the train station was over in three minutes and the Apaches advanced further toward the city, creating a wall of lead between any German reinforcements and the Blackhawk utility helicopters that landed in the parking lot.

Soldiers swarmed from the helicopters like angry hornets, securing the perimeter on the ground and then moving into the station to evacuate the men from Berserker Company. Gabe made sure everyone was accounted for before he let the medics put him on a stretcher and take him toward the helicopters. They'd even been able to find most of the remains of Sergeant Kelley and Corporal Hicks.

Lieutenant Colonel Adams-Branson stood beside a Blackhawk talking with his boss, Lieutenant Colonel Calhoun and Colonel Graves—Spartan Six. Her husband and the children were inside the helicopter and the crew chief was securing their seat harnesses.

Spartan Six held up his hand and stepped quickly to Gabe's stretcher. He leaned down to be heard over the noise of the helicopter's engines. Rotor wash tousled his hair as he took off his helmet to avoid hitting Gabe in the face.

"You did a good job here, Gabriel," Spartan Six shouted. "Your men survived impossible odds because of the position you occupied and the way you arrayed your forces."

He patted Gabe's body armor twice and repeated, "Good job," as he stood up, placing his helmet back on his head.

Then, Gabe's stretcher was loaded into a medevac bird and his stomach fell away as the helicopter lurched skyward.

*****

20 July 2025
United States Institute of Peace, Washington, DC

Berndt was sweating through his uniform. Washington was hot and humid as it was, but now he was nervous as well. His mind reeled at the implications of what he was about to do—and how in the hell he was supposed to get away with it?

The headquarters was in a flurry of activity as aides scurried this way and that. He hadn't been to the High Command's headquarters before, so he assumed it was customary for the staff officers to act in such a manner. The few times he'd been at the Luftwaffe command center, it had seemed just as hectic for him, a simple pilot.

The SS officer led him down a hallway to a small room with a glass wall overlooking a large auditorium. The auditorium had been converted into the command center, the nucleus of the entire Wehrmacht. From this room, Berndt could see the large map of the area, projected upon the movie screen. The Germans, it appeared were completely surrounded.

The American Army and Marine Corps advanced steadily from the landward side, while the ocean was blockaded by a collection of flags, primarily British, French and Russian. Oddly enough, the Russian flag even appeared on the northern front, near the border of Pennsylvania.

What are the Russians doing in America? he wondered.

"Sit here," the SS man ordered. "Generalfeldmarschall Mueller will speak with you when he is able. As you can see, there is a new...*wrinkle*...in our war plans."

The officer left with both of his guards, whom Berndt suspected were positioned immediately outside the door. He puzzled over the map for a moment longer and then the door opened behind him.

Berndt whirled, expecting to see the field marshal. Instead, he stared directly into the eyes of Otto Skorzeny.

"Good afternoon, Standartenführer!" Berndt stated loudly, standing at attention.

"Good afternoon, Oberleutnant Fischer," Skorzeny replied with a rakish smile, made more so by the jagged scarring that ran from the corner of his mouth to his ear. "I hear you have important news for Generalfeldmarschall Mueller."

"Y-yes, Standartenführer," Berndt stuttered as the officer lit a cigarette.

Just as all children in Argus Base were taught to revere the Führer, and Rommel, the Desert Fox, they were taught the exploits and heroics of Otto Skorzeny. His skill as a paramilitary planner and as an undercover operator were legendary.

After the war, he'd been tried for his involvement in the war, found not guilty of war crimes—which Berndt now knew were *not* fabricated by the victors as he'd been taught—and released. He lived in Spain for a period of time and then advised the Egyptian government before traveling to Argentina to work as the head of security for the president and his wife. It was while he was in Argentina that Skorzeny established contact with the remaining Nazi High Command in Argus Base. He took on the role of training indigenous forces worldwide to fight against American, British and Russian expansionism.

The man was, quite literally, a legend.

"Well, are you going to tell *me* what weapons the Americans have developed? It must be very important for you to steal a düsenjäger and land at the Wehrmacht headquarters."

Berndt nodded dumbly. "I overheard them talking about intercepting our radio transmissions—"

Skorzeny slapped the table with the flat of his hand. "I *knew* it! I knew they were listening to us. It's the Enigma Machine all over again." He jabbed two fingers at the projection screen, ash from the cigarette suspended between them falling to the table.

Berndt turned to look at the screen. Their encirclement was almost *too* complete. It was as if they really were intercepting German communications.

"You say you overheard some of the Americans talking about it. Did you see any evidence of it happening or was it only hearsay?"

"I only heard two of the American officers talking about it, Standartenführer. They happened to be walking by my cell, discussing their use of the information to block us in and press from all sides."

"This is not going as expected... No bother," Skorzeny stated. "What of their weapons?"

"They are only weeks away from developing düsenjägers of their own. They have captured aircraft that they have reverse-engineered and have even upgraded the cannons."

Skorzeny didn't seem impressed with this, so Berndt took his lies a step farther. "And, they know we came from the Southern Continent."

The man across from him smiled again, making Berndt uncomfortable, and took a long drag from his cigarette. "Did you tell them this?"

"No, Standartenführer. The only questions they ever asked me about were the avionics of the düsenjägers and their operations. But I heard scientists and engineers discussing such things. They mentioned Antarctica, and… And, they are preparing a nuclear response against the Wehrmacht in Washington!"

Skorzeny's mouth hung open slightly for a moment before he remembered to close it. "You have heard this?"

You've stepped in it now, he chastised himself. In his effort to throw the great Otto Skorzeny off his trail, he'd taken his lies too far. "Yes, Standartenführer. They are evacuating key civilians in preparation for the nuclear attack."

"That goddamned weasel, Albrecht!" Skorzeny roared. "*That's* why they were trying to sneak him out of the city. My men had him at the train station until the Americans showed up in their helicopters and ruined everything. They got him out. Now they know everything… *Everything*."

The SS man stood rapidly. "I must go. There is work to be done."

Berndt stood and shot his arm out, ramrod straight. "*Sieg heil!*"

"Yes, of course," Skorzeny replied, returning the salute quickly. "Sieg heil."

He ducked out through the door, leaving Berndt alone again. The pilot started to relax and began to sit when the door opened once more. He stood at attention as Generalfeldmarschall Mueller walked in, flanked by, Oberst Andreas Wolff, the chief of the Luftwaffe, two light infantry oberschützes—privates—and an oberst that he didn't know.

"Sit, Oberleutnant Fischer," the field marshal ordered.

He sat.

"Oberst Wolff has given me the complete record of your training with the Luftwaffe. You have excellent marks—some of the highest in your entire class. And yet, you allowed yourself to be shot down and captured. How did this happen?"

"The propulsion drive on my düsen was destroyed by a missile, Generalfeldmarschall. I was beginning an attack on an American tank and one of the men with the shoulder-fired missiles emerged from the tree line almost immediately underneath me." He paused, licking his lips. "I was able to control the aircraft enough to crash into a clearing. I must have hit my head because when I woke up, I was a prisoner."

"How long ago was this?" Wolff asked.

"Forgive me, Oberst, but I don't know what today's date is. My mission was on eight July and I was captured immediately on the same day. I remember eight or nine nights in the cell."

"Where were you kept?" asked the colonel who wore the red-orange collar insignia of a military policeman.

"I don't know, Oberst. Somewhere to the west, possibly around one hundred kilometers from here. The computer in the düsenjäger I took should have a point of origin for the flight."

The policeman looked to Oberst Wolff, who nodded his head, confirming Berndt's assertion that the düsenjäger's computers would have all of the required information for determining where his flight had originated.

"So, you say the Americans have secret new weapons," the field marshal stated. "Tell me of them."

"I did not see them for myself, Generalfeldmarschall. Instead, I heard the engineers who worked on replicating our düsenjäger technology speak of them."

"And why were you with the engineers?" the policeman asked, clearly comfortable inserting himself into the conversation.

Berndt glanced at the colonel and then looked back at Mueller. "I was questioned about the avionics, flight controls and tactical employment of the düsenjäger. Men tortured me until I gave them information about how to make the damn things work."

"A traitor!"

"Oberst Henke, stop," Generalfeldmarschall Mueller ordered, triggering Berndt's mind. The oberst was the chief of the Gestapo, the German secret police. "Young

Oberleutnant Fischer escaped to pass along the information of new American treacheries to us."

"But, Generalfeldmarschall, he is clearly trying to cover for his treachery. He gave away Reich secrets of how our düsenjägers operate. Without his—"

"I said to stop!" the field marshal thundered. "When I give an order, you will obey me. Do you understand?"

"Yes, Generalfeldmarschall," the oberst replied.

Fracturing of the High Command, Berndt thought.

All eyes were on the field marshal. He'd provided the distraction that the pilot needed.

It took him less than the blink of an eye to draw the weapon Doctor Grossman gave him. He squeezed the trigger, leaving it depressed as the doctor had instructed. He expected some type of noise or a visible light, but nothing emanated from the pistol.

Across from him, the three German officers and the two privates writhed in pain, their bodies spasmed uncontrollably as the microwave beam boiled the blood inside their veins and cooked their flesh from the inside. The smell of burnt hair, melted plastic and cooked meat filled the small meeting space, and still Berndt held the trigger on the weapon. Flesh split open as the internal heat and pressure escaped the confines of the bodies.

Finally, it was over. The men stopped moving and Berndt released the trigger. He stood tentatively and walked around to the opposite side of the table. All of them were dead.

The pilot glanced furtively out of the room's glass windows to see if anyone witnessed his act. It appeared that no one had. He crammed the weapon carefully into the holster, avoiding the hot metal barrel as best he could.

Before leaving, he took one final look at the generalfeldmarschall and the men whom he'd brought to interrogate him. Berndt felt no remorse at what he'd done. It was a necessity. Now, the High Command would be in disarray as the new Allies descended upon them from all sides. It was a small payback for what the Nazis had done to millions of people during World War Two—and the lies they'd forced upon generations of Nazi children.

Berndt opened the door and peered into the hallway beyond. The same frantic level of activity greeted him and it appeared that the officers in the headquarters were unaware of what had just happened. He reached around and twisted the lock on the doorknob from the inside and pulled the door closed. It would take several hours for anyone to be foolish enough to attempt to interfere with an interrogation headed by Generalfeldmarschall Mueller and the commander of the Gestapo.

When he emerged from the building, he immediately saw that his düsenjäger was gone. "*What?*" he cried and ran down the steps, crossing the street to stand on the grass.

He turned slowly, trying to see if he'd misremembered where he landed, but it was gone.

The soldier who'd been ordered to guard the aircraft stood on the corner and he walked over to him. "You, Oberschütze," he said as he got closer. "There was a düsenjäger sitting here less than an hour ago. What happened to it?"

The private saluted and Berndt returned the salute in annoyance. "The Standartenführer took it."

"The standartenführer? Who—do you mean Skorzeny? *Otto* Skorzeny?" He was the only SS-Standartenführer in the Wehrmacht, of course the private meant him.

"Yes, sir," the soldier replied, looking confused. "He said the generalfeldmarschall had given him a mission and ordered me to move away or risk death from the engine blast."

"*Scheisse! Scheisse! Scheisse!*" Berndt screeched and pounded his fist into his leg.

The private stepped back warily. "Is everything alright, Oberleutnant?"

"No, it's not alright," Berndt fumed. He wanted to shout at the private, to shake the man unconscious for letting Skorzeny take his means of escape. But, the idea of self-preservation stopped him. He'd just murdered the commander of the Wehrmacht. He needed to get away without further incriminating himself than he'd already done.

"I apologize, Oberschütze. I'd hoped to pass a message along to Standartenführer Skorzeny before he departed. I suppose it will just have to wait until he returns."

Berndt didn't wait for the private's response. He spun on his heel and began walking west, toward the bridge.

Somehow, he'd make it back to Anna, the woman who'd promised him the world if he murdered Mueller.

TWENTY-FOUR

07 September 2025
Duke Raleigh Hospital, Raleigh, North Carolina

"Oh, I don't know if I should," Gabe replied when Gloria offered to let him hold the baby.

"Nonsense. Go wash your hands and then sit down so you've got some stability," she said, pointing at his crutches. "It's only right that little Gabriel is held by the man who saved his life."

Gabe did as requested and then sat in the chair that she'd indicated. James lifted the baby from Gloria's arms, wheeling over to him. He handed the baby across to Gabe.

"Watch his neck," Gloria cautioned.

"Here," James said, adjusting the baby slightly. "Yeah, you've gotta support his head and neck."

Gabe looked down at the baby and smiled largely for him to see. The child stared vacantly at him and gripped Gabe's index finger tightly, causing him to laugh. "He's a strong little guy."

"Yeah, eight pounds, ten ounces," Gloria replied.

"Uh… Is that big? I'm sorry, I really don't know much about babies."

"It's on the bigger end of the scale," Gloria answered. "The average baby weighs anywhere from six to eight pounds, so he's just above that."

"Means he's gonna be a football player," James proclaimed.

"No, he's not. He's not allowed to play football, too many injuries."

"I played football in high school," Gabe remarked.

"Yeah, and look at you; you have a broken leg."

Gabe chuckled. She knew the injury wasn't from playing football. She was there the day he lost twenty-four men in close combat against the Germans. That was after eighty-one of his men were killed in a bombing attack by German aircraft.

His thoughts turned dark. So many men and women had died fighting against the Germans. The numbers were still not known, but between the civilian casualties and the military casualties for the New Allies, it was in the millions. The average Nazi soldier was a fanatic who fought to the death rather than surrender as their ancestors had done in Europe. The news said it was something about their being raised in isolation and indoctrinated as zealots toward the Nazi cause.

"I'm kidding, Gabe," Gloria said, shaking him from his melancholy. "I know what happened on that train platform. We were there too."

Gabe frowned. "I'm really glad that you invited me to stop by and see the baby, ma'am," he said. "And I'm beyond flattered that you decided to name him after me, but do you mind taking him back now?"

Gloria nodded and asked James to get the baby. "Gabe, it's okay to have the feelings you do," she said once the baby was safely back in James' arms. "It's called survivors guilt. Soldiers throughout history have experienced it, but you dying on that train platform wouldn't have done anything more than add another name to a list."

"I know… The Army makes me go see a therapist once a week and we talk about survivor's guilt a lot, although she calls it PTSD."

"I'm glad you're talking to someone. If you need to talk to anyone else, James and I are always available too."

"Thank you, ma'am." He clambered to his feet with the assistance of the crutches. "I think I'm gonna go now."

"Of course, Gabe. Don't be a strange—"

She was cut off by a shrill beep from the room's speaker. "*Attention hospital patients and guests,*" an older woman's voice came out of the intercom. "*President Sanchez is addressing the nation to announce the official VN Day. Please tune to channel seventeen on your television to witness this historic event. Thank you.*"

Gabe eased back down in the chair as Gloria turned the television on. "VN Day?" he asked.

"Victory over the Nazis," Gloria remarked. "It's reminiscent of the VE and VJ Days from World War Two for 'Victory in Europe' and 'Victory in Japan'.

"Funny," she continued. "I didn't peg the president as a student of history when I briefed him about the location of the Nazi base in Antarctica last month."

*****

07 September 2025
Ruins of the White House, Washington, DC

Javier Sanchez stood behind the podium that his aides had set up. The sun shone brightly overhead and it was a beautiful day in Washington, if you looked past the horrific destruction of the city's national monuments and buildings.

"My fellow Americans," he began and then stopped, glancing at the teleprompter that displayed the speech that Captain deBoer had helped him craft

He remembered enough of the speech that he decided to go off script. It would be more sincere if he spoke from the heart, he decided. If he got lost, he could always refer to the paper copy in the binder on the podium to point him in the right direction. Besides, he *did* win the California State Speech Championship two years in a row in high school, after all. That was much more stressful since he had had to look at an audience of thousands; today, there were only about forty reporters standing around. *Piece of cake.*

"You know, I don't know why all of us choose to start our speeches that way. It sounds so formal and imposing." Javier grinned. "I have a speech prepared today, and it's been provided to the networks for their own political commentary, but I'm not going to read that speech. I want to talk to our citizens from the heart.

"Our nation is hurting right now. Yes, we're celebrating a major military victory against the greatest threat this nation has ever faced on our own soil, but at the same time, we're grieving the loss of loved ones, friends and family. You'd be hard-pressed to find someone in America who doesn't know someone affected by this tragedy, be it here, in Washington, DC, or in the forty-one sites across the nation where the Nazis attempted to gain control of our nuclear weapons using paratroopers. Our servicemen and women, as well as local law enforcement officials and even the average citizen who took up arms defeated them at every juncture."

He glanced to the side and saw the senior British and Russian military officers smiling politely. "Oh, whoops. Maybe I should have read the script," he said, eliciting laughs from the correspondents in the crowd. "I'd be remiss if I didn't thank our dear friends and allies, the United Kingdom and the Russian Federation. Without their added weight to the fight, America would still be throwing punch-for-punch with the Nazis." He turned and placed a hand over his heart. "Thank you... Thank you."

Javier turned back to the cameras and continued. "Today, we celebrate Victory over the Nazis Day, or VN Day as I like to call it. It is an important distinction that we say it is a victory over the Nazis, *not* the Germans. Let me be clear, the German people have paid their debt to the world. The savages that we fought against here in America were the Nazis, a carryover from the past, war criminals who fled Europe and established a secret base in Antarctica.

"With regards to their base, we received intelligence that it was located near Dome Argus in Antarctica—the coldest and most inaccessible place on the continent, and consequently, on the planet. I have sad news to pass along to the peoples of the world. By the time our forces were able to battle their way through the elements to reach Argus Base, everyone was dead."

He paused for the gasps and the clicking of cameras to stop. "It appears that they had the entire facility rigged with pipes full of cyanide gas. Upon learning of their army's defeat, they triggered the release of the gas, which flooded the base and killed everyone. The first Americans on scene succumbed to the gas as well. The Nazis poisoned a hundred thousand women and children just to keep us from finding them.

"Their labs and engineering facilities were completely destroyed by fires, so the technology that they used to cryogenically freeze their soldiers and the battlefield medical advances that they employed are lost to us, with the exception of any unused samples we found here on our own soil.

"For the losses to our nation, it is still too early to know how many we have lost. The death toll is in the millions, some estimates even going as high as five million Americans who've lost their lives due to the Nazi attempt at retribution.

"We will not let their sacrifices be in vain. We also have intelligence of nations that collaborated with the Nazis against us—some for more than eighty *years*. Rest assured, the governments of those nations will be dealt with."

Javier tried to remember more of the speech's highlights, but decided that he'd hit them all. "Americans are resilient people. We will rebuild and our nation will be stronger than ever. Thank you."

He stepped away from the podium as a cacophony of questions poured from the media section. He gave Becky and the boys a hug and a cheesy thumbs up hand signal for the cameras, and then walked through the curtain that led to a secure area and the giant, armored vehicle he'd traveled to DC in. Bill and Ted nodded respectfully to him, but the blonde woman waiting on the other side did not look happy.

Captain deBoer crossed her arms over her chest, glaring at him. "What's wrong, Ashley? I thought winging it would come off as more sincere."

"Of course, Mr. President. You *did* sound sincere. But, by winging it, as you say, you forgot to mention the losses from all of our other partner nations, who lost thousands of citizens from their embassies when you add them all up, including the French who contributed troops to help us. You also forgot to talk about the heroes of the war. We'd put that part in the written speech to give our citizens something to cling to as a beacon of hope during these dark days."

Javier waved her off. Indeed, he'd forgotten to mention the German defector who killed the Nazi commander or the rescue mission to save that Army officer with the information on the Nazi base. In reality, he *should* have discussed the church deacon who organized a resistance movement to fight a guerilla war in

Grudge | 363

DC. His constituents would have loved that story, but he'd let the excitement of the moment blank his mind.

"You've taken your own speech to heart, Ashley. Never do that, or you'll end up getting upset every time," he counseled. "I hit all the highlights of the speech we had prepared. We can spotlight on those heroes over the coming days to keep the people distracted and hopeful."

Her lower lip trembled slightly. "Hey, you did a great job of seeing me through all of this. There's a long, hard road ahead of us all, so you're gonna need to toughen up a little bit if you're gonna be playing ball in the big leagues."

"*Big Leagues*, sir? We're talking about the death of millions and the destruction of our capitol city."

He placed a hand lightly on her upper arm. "True, it's terrible, but isn't it exciting as well? We'll be able to shape this country as it was truly meant to be."

Javier let his hand drop as he walked past her to the RV. He had so much to plan. From an emergency election to a budget, there were months and months of federal government requirements that he would personally oversee. His fingerprints would be on everything for the next century.

He smiled at that thought, secure in the knowledge that his twenty-one years in politics at every level of government had prepared him for this moment. The sweeping reform of the New Deal Coalition's programs and policies would pale in comparison to those of Javier Sanchez. *This is America's moment*, he thought.

"Correction, this is *my* moment," the president muttered as he took a seat at the desk in the RV. He pulled out his journal and jotted a few notes. Maybe one day, they'd be worth something.

EPILOGUE

10 September 2025
Aokigahara, Mount Fuji, Japan

Timbak's hand trailed along the tops of the grass growing beside the trail. He knew what must happen; the Council would demand an all-out war now that the conflict between the Nazis and the Americans had played out. The time for observing and acting as a passive observer were over.

As he walked toward the clearing, he found himself dreading reintegration with his people. He'd lived amongst the Terrans for almost a century; of course he felt attached to them in some way. He was just as human as they were. Their shared ancestry bonded him to them in ways he never thought possible—until it was time to sever those bonds.

He'd been saddened to learn of the cyanide gases in Argus Base. The Nazis were a cruel people, but even he hadn't foreseen the poisoning of their own kind. Maybe the admiral he'd met with earlier this year was correct; the Terrans' time on this planet was at an end. That level of barbarism had no place amongst civilized humans.

Timbak entered the clearing into a whole host of fleet officers. The sheer number of them surprised him. A familiar face appeared among the crowd and he bowed his head in deference.

"Ah, Science Officer Timbak," the admiral said. "I'm so glad you could join us. The men and women before you represent the fleet's planners. We are in position to attack and require the latest intelligence on our enemy."

Timbak smiled sadly, knowing that any details he gave his people would result in millions—possibly billions—of deaths. The Terrans were inferior creatures, little more than beasts in the fields, but they were human, so were the Aryans at one time.

Timbak no longer believed that to be the case.

THE END

If you liked this book, please leave a review on Amazon:
www.amazon.com/dp/B06Y5QS6J6

ABOUT THE AUTHOR

A veteran of the wars in Iraq and Afghanistan, Brian Parker was born and raised as an Army brat. He's currently an Active Duty Army soldier who enjoys spending time with his family in Texas, hiking, obstacle course racing, writing and Texas Longhorns football. He's an unashamed Star Wars fan, but prefers to disregard the entire Episode I and II debacle.

Brian is both a traditionally- and self-published author with an ever-growing collection of works across multiple genres, including sci-fi, post-apocalyptic, horror, paranormal thriller, military fiction, self-publishing how-to and even a children's picture book, *Zombie in the Basement*, which he wrote to help children overcome the perceived stigma of being different from others.

He is also the founder of Muddy Boots Press, an independent publishing company that focuses on quality genre fiction over mass-produced books.

FOLLOW BRIAN ON SOCIAL MEDIA!

Facebook: www.facebook.com/BrianParkerAuthor
Twitter: www.twitter.com/BParker_Author
Web: www.BrianParkerAuthor.com

LINK TO ALL OF BRIAN'S BOOKS

www.amazon.com/Brian-Parker/e/B00DFD98YI

OTHER AUTHORS UNDER THE SHIELD OF

SIXTH CYCLE

Nuclear war has destroyed human civilization. Captain Jake Phillips wakes into a dangerous new world, where he finds the remaining fragments of the population living in a series of strongholds, connected across the country. Uneasy alliances have maintained their safety, but things are about to change. -- Discovery leads to danger. -- Skye Reed, a tracker from the Omega stronghold, uncovers a threat that could spell the end for their fragile society. With friends and enemies revealing truths about the past, she will need to decide who to trust. -- **Sixth Cycle** is a gritty post-apocalyptic story of survival and adventure.

Darren Wearmouth ~ Carl Sinclair

DEAD ISLAND: Operation Zulu

Ten years after the world was nearly brought to its knees by a zombie Armageddon, there is a race for the antidote! On a remote Caribbean island, surrounded by a horde of hungry living dead, a team of American and Australian commandos must rescue the Antidotes' scientist. Filled with zombies, guns, Russian bad guys, shady government types, serial killers and elevator muzak. Dead Island is an action packed blood soaked horror adventure.

Allen Gamboa

INVASION OF THE DEAD SERIES

This is the first book in a series of nine, about an ordinary bunch of friends, and their plight to survive an apocalypse in Australia. -- Deep beneath defense headquarters in the Australian Capital Territory, the last ranking Army chief and a brilliant scientist struggle with answers to the collapse of the world, and the aftermath of an unprecedented virus. Is it a natural mutation, or does the infection contain -- more sinister roots? -- One hundred and fifty miles away, five friends returning from a month-long camping trip slowly discover that death has swept through the country. What greets them in a gradual revelation is an enemy beyond compare. -- Armed with dwindling ammunition, the friends must overcome their disagreements, utilize their individual skills, and face unimaginable horrors as they battle to reach their hometown...

Owen Ballie

Whiskey Tango Foxtrot

Alone in a foreign land. The radio goes quiet while on convoy in Afghanistan, a lost patrol alone in the desert. With his unit and his home base destroyed, Staff Sergeant Brad Thompson suddenly finds himself isolated and in command of a small group of men trying to survive in the Afghan wasteland. Every turn leads to danger.

The local population has been afflicted with an illness that turns them into rabid animals. They pursue him and his men at every corner and stop. Struggling to hold his team together and unite survivors, he must fight and evade his way to safety. A fast paced zombie war story like no other.

W.J. Lundy

ZOMBIE RUSH

New to the Hot Springs PD Lisa Reynolds was not all that welcomed by her coworkers especially those who were passed over for the position. It didn't matter, her thirty days probation ended on the same day of the Z-poc's arrival. Overnight the world goes from bad to worse as thousands die in the initial onslaught. National Guard and regular military unit deployed the day before to the north leaves the city in mayhem. All directions lead to death until one unlikely candidate steps forward with a plan. A plan that became an avalanche raging down the mountain culminating in the salvation or destruction of them all.

Joseph Hansen

THE ALPHA PLAGUE

Rhys is an average guy who works an average job in Summit City—a purpose built government complex on the outskirts of London. The Alpha Tower stands in the centre of the city. An enigma, nobody knows what happens behind its dark glass. Rhys is about to find out. At ground zero and with chaos spilling out into the street, Rhys has the slightest of head starts. If he can remain ahead of the pandemonium, then maybe he can get to his loved ones before the plague does. The Alpha Plague is a post-apocalyptic survival thriller.

Michael Robertson

THE GATHERING HORDE

The most ambitious terrorist plot ever undertaken is about to be put into motion, releasing an unstoppable force against humanity. Ordinary people – A group of students celebrating the end of the semester, suburban and rural families – are about to themselves in the center of something that threatens the survival of the human species. As they battle the dead – and the living – it's going to take every bit of skill, knowledge and luck for them to survive in Zed's World.

Rich Baker

THE RECKONING
Australia has been invaded.

While the outnumbered Australian Defence Force fights on the ground, in the air and at sea, this quickly becomes a war involving ordinary people. Ben, an IT consultant has never fought a day in his life. Will he survive? Grant, a security guard at Sydney's International Airport, finds himself captured and living in the filth and squalor of one of the concentration camps dotted around Australia. Knowing death awaits him if he stays, he plans a daring escape. This is a dark day in Australia's history. This is terror, loneliness, starvation and adrenaline all mixed together in a sour cocktail. This is the day Australia fell.

Keith McArdle

Printed in Great Britain
by Amazon